1976

RANDOM HOUSE NEW YORK

RHINE

RANDOM HOUSE · NEW YORK

REPLICA

MARTHA ALBRAND

All the persons and events in this book are entirely imaginary. Nothing in it derives from anything that ever happened.

First Printing Copyright © 1969, by Martha Albrand
All rights reserved under International and Pan American Copyright Conventions. Published in the United States by Random House, Inc., New York, and simultaneously in Canada, by Random House of Canada Limited, Toronto. Library of Congress Catalog Card Number: 70-85597. Manufactured in the United States of America by Kingsport Press, Inc., Kingsport, Tenn. Designed by Joan Bastone.

TO CATHERINE HUTTER
WITH GRATITUDE

RHINE REPLICA

Reception" was crowded, but then that was to be expected. I was accustomed to people queuing up in front of desks behind which harassed clerks were trying to accommodate weary and impatient tourists. Resignedly I took my place in the long line to the left of the hotel entrance, directly opposite the shiny mahogany desk where keys were left or handed out, mail sorted and distributed, theater, opera, train tickets ordered, messages received, passed on or forgotten. The man looking up at me when I finally got to him reminded me of a groundhog, popping out of his hole every time he had to face a new guest and popping back again, alert, cautious, always anticipating trouble. He sported old-fashioned whiskers, graying at the ends where the rinse had rubbed off. His beady eyes were shaded by rimless glasses and his breath whistled slightly as he leafed through an

3

oblong folder. "Sorry, sir, but we don't seem to have . . ."

"Waldron," I repeated, almost soothingly. "Andrew L. Waldron. I made the reservation two weeks ago. From Rome." I spelled my name. "Would you please look again?"

The man wetted his thumb, turned pages, went down a line of w's with the rubber end of a pencil, shook his head. "I'm sorry, sir."

"But I have your confirmation." I pulled out the telegram. "Here. February twenty-third to twenty-eighth, a single with bath."

The piece of paper lay between us like a challenge, but the man chose not to fight. He picked up the telegram, read it and handed it back to me. "Undoubtedly there has been a mistake. If you will give me a little time to find out . . . perhaps you would be more comfortable waiting in the lobby."

In spite of its dimensions, which were immense, the lobby, like a railway station at rush hour, was filled to capacity. I couldn't find an empty table nor a seat at the bar. I was tired and not feeling nearly so serene as I'd just pretended to be. I'd been looking forward to these five days in Cologne, to seeing the old treasures that had been spared, some of the famous restorations that had been undertaken in this city which had been almost completely destroyed by war, and to at least three nights of dancing madly, eating well and carousing generally during this last week of Cologne's famous carnival. For reasons not quite clear to myself I had never visited Germany before, and possibly wouldn't have come now if, one night in Rome, an odd little man hadn't convinced me that I was missing something unique in Europe. It had been a mistake. Most impulses are foolishly motivated.

"A Jack Daniel's," I told one of the barmen. He didn't

hear me. That annoyed me too. I clapped my hands, some-thing you could do in Germany—so I'd been told—without being insulting, just as you could whistle for a waiter in France. Nobody paid any attention.

I turned to go back to "Reception"—perhaps in the meantime my reservation had been found—when there he was, the little man with the wrinkled face of a monkey who was responsible for my being here. He was sitting at a small table, alone, with a beer in front of him. "Hello," I said. "I guess I should have expected to meet you here." But like the waiter at the bar, he didn't seem to hear me. I leaned closer. "Rome. Emilio's Bar. The drink of the gods, to which you invited me. The famous basso who had lost his voice—you had him sing while you drew me." He looked up then, his dark, sad little eyes stared at me, closed, opened, he shook his head.

I grabbed the empty chair next to him, sat down and tried my German, which my grandparents had insisted I learn and keep up. "Don't you remember me?"

Again he shook his head. What was the matter with the fellow? I couldn't be mistaken. Not with that face. Then, suddenly, he spoke. "I can't recall that we ever met."

The voice was the same too, an old voice, a little too high, too emphatic. It made me settle back in my chair. "But you . . ."

"Professor Florian." A girl I hadn't seen approaching was standing at his side. She was quite tall, almost my height, and so slender, I felt tempted to put my hands around her waist to measure it. She was wearing a dark green outfit, pants and jacket, which clung to her body like skin. There was a smell of cinnamon about her. It made me feel hungry. The way she stood, I couldn't see her face clearly, only a few strands of hair which had escaped at the nape of her neck from under a tight fur cap. They were the color of wheat. I watched them. Somehow they seemed to be trembling from an inner excitement rather than from the current of air drifting in from the lobby.

Professor Florian? Had he introduced himself that night in Rome? I wasn't sure. But I was surprised when he jumped to his feet to greet the girl, then sat down frowning. "What brings you here, Bettina?"

"Can't you guess?" She pulled over a chair from the next table and sat down.

"I would think you could find better experts in Florence."

"I finished there two weeks ago. This has nothing to do with the Uffizi. It's Savaire again, with a piece from . . ."

He interrupted her rudely. "I'm very busy. The next few days . . ."

"I'll wait," she said, smiling. "It's carnival time and I haven't had any fun lately."

Her voice was soft, melodious, deep. It should have belonged to a dark-haired, dark-eyed type. She turned to look at me. Her face was a perfect oval, but the structure of her forehead remained secret, her fur cap having been pulled down to her eyebrows which ran straight, in an almost uninterrupted line. Her eyes had an oriental slant which I took at first for a clever make-up job, but at second glance recognized to be genuine. I couldn't determine their color. Just then they seemed to be green, but I knew they were reflecting the deep green of her jacket, so it was hard to tell. I guess I could describe her nose as aristocratic. It was finely chiseled, with a very slight indentation at the tip. Her mouth was surprisingly large and one right tooth was a bit crooked, just the sort of imperfection that puts one at ease.

6

And it was obvious that I wasn't going to be introduced. I rose. "Waldron," I said, "Andrew Waldron."

She acknowledged the introduction with a nod but without giving her name; instead, looking from me to the professor, she asked, "Where did you two meet?"

"We haven't met," the old man answered. "He just sat down without even asking permission."

He was making me feel like a fool. Irritated, I replied, "I can't imagine why you suddenly don't want to know me." Turning to the girl I said, "A few nights ago, in Rome, he asked me if I'd mind if he sketched me in profile, and he did —I had nothing against it—on the back of a wine list."

The professor's face reddened, then turned a sickish gray-white. "I don't remember," he murmured. "I don't remember."

"And we talked. I wouldn't be here now if it hadn't been for you. You made this city sound like something that shouldn't be missed, and when you topped it all with the carnival . . ."

"There are more important mosaics in Ravenna," the professor said, wearily now, "than the Dionysos Mosaic in Cologne. And Le Corbusier's work is more original and important than Mataré's. Or Böhm's. Visit Ronchamps. You haven't lived until you have seen Corbusier's chapel. And when you are young you can create fun for yourself without a carnival. Young men should never listen to an old man reminiscing." Quite unexpectedly he looked me full in the face. "Go back to the station. There are many trains at this hour. Take the next one. To France. To Italy." He stood up abruptly, bowed to the girl, "See you later," and left.

I watched him wind his way between the tables, tottering

slightly, probably he had been drinking too much for a man his age. "What a queer old bird," I said. "There he was, going on and on, his enthusiasm for Cologne finally catching my imagination . . ."

She had been watching him too. "It's a shame," she said. "He can't stay away from alcohol. I've known him for years. He's a very fine sculptor. I studied under him."

"Oh. You're a sculptress."

"Well . . . yes. But not as creative as I'd like to be. But I'm good enough to copy museum pieces and do repair work. Sometimes I'm called in to help assemble fragments that have been dug up. That's what I was talking about just now." Her English was perfect and colored slightly by an Oxford accent. "Did you really come here because of him?"

"Partly. My grandparents came from the Rhineland, and the professor aroused a sudden curiosity in me for an almost forgotten section of my origins."

"You spoke German with him."

"I had to learn it as a child and kept it up in school. It made for an easy course." Again I tried to attract a waiter's attention. In vain.

"What do you want?"

"I'm dying for a drink. A Jack Daniel's."

She clapped her hands softly. As if by magic, a *piccolo* appeared, a small boy in a uniform he still had to grow into. A few minutes later a waiter came with our orders. Hers looked like pink lemonade. "What on earth's that?"

"Lemon, some raspberry juice and soda. Alcohol makes me dizzy."

"I wonder," I said. "Right now I feel like taking the professor's advice and leaving."

"Why?"

"They couldn't find my reservation. Apparently they haven't found it yet. Just like the professor, they never heard of me."

"Try a place nearby."

"But I want to be in Cologne."

"Everybody does, during the last week of the carnival."

"But where could I go? I'm a stranger here and haven't the slightest idea. Would you know . . ."

"Reception" wove his way to our table. Since I had seen him last, he seemed to have aged. *"Gnädiges Fräulein,"* he addressed Bettina, "the car will be here in ten minutes. I'm sorry I couldn't get it for you before."

She said, "Thank you, Feldman."

"And what about me?"

"What about you, sir?"

"I showed you the telegram with your confirmation. A single with bath. I've been waiting for quite a while."

"I'd appreciate it if you'd accommodate Mr. Waldron as soon as possible," said the girl, and Feldman, or whatever his name was, looked at me with sudden respect, then back at the girl. "If I may make a suggestion . . . I hate to admit it, but someone must have slipped up about the gentleman's reservation. We don't have a room for him. I wonder if at the Lindwurm . . ."

"Is that where you're going?" I asked.

"Yes," she said pleasantly, not as if she found my question indiscreet. "It's a hotel in the Siebengebirge, less than an hour's drive away. Lovely country."

I wouldn't have cared if it had been a desert; all I wanted was to go where she was going. I turned to Feldman, "Do you think they could give me a room? Would you be good enough to call?"

When he came back, she didn't look up to ask if he had been successful or not; in fact, she paid no attention to him

9

and I had to repeat the good news that I had a room at the Lindwurm before she turned to me. "Oh, really?"

She sounded bored. Perhaps she was annoyed by the prospect of yet another young man on her trail, but she did offer me a lift. "Well then, let's go," she said, with sudden impatience. "The car should be here by now."

We were stopped from entering the lobby by a gaily costumed and partially masked crowd. Shouting and laughing, they had beleaguered the elevators. Watching them, she began to smile, and an extraordinarily tall man did exactly what I had wanted to do—put both hands around her waist and lifted her off the floor. "Come along, beautiful." When he put her down again, her eyes were sparkling. "You've got your tickets, I hope," she said to me.

"Tickets?"

"Well yes. For tribune or window seats for the parades, and for the dances."

"Do you have to get them ahead of time?"

"You certainly do, during these last few days. Never mind. I'll talk to Feldman about it while you get your luggage."

Finding my bag caused another delay. Baggage that had not yet been sent up to the rooms was mixed up with that of tourists still waiting to be assigned one, or those frantically trying to phone other hotels for accommodations; there were simply too many stacks of blue airplane satchels and standard luggage to point with any assurance to the one that belonged to you. Except for some easily spotted leather suitcases and a wardrobe trunk or two, nothing was distinguishable. It was no great help to the bellboy to learn that mine was black fiberglass. There were dozens that could qualify.

I couldn't blame her for looking surprised and probably

thinking I was slow and incompetent when I finally turned up with just one piece. "Is that all?"

"I travel light. Where are yours?"

"In the car."

Outside it was snowing. She sniffed the air. "Damn it."

"Why? Don't you like snow?"

"It'll spoil the parade on Sunday."

A short distance away, a car stood waiting for us. A young man sprang forward. "Careful," he said. "It's slippery."

He put a broad hand under the girl's elbow and led her to the car, then came back for me. It wasn't often that I ran into such luxury, and I enjoyed it. I let him take my undistinguished bag and watched him store it deftly next to her things in the trunk. I even stepped closer and pretended to care about the way he was placing it.

Traffic was heavy. We had to stop again and again for cars letting people out in front of hotels, restaurants, private houses. Men were in white tie or dinner jackets, women in *grande toilette,* going to private balls, the theater, the opera. Near the bridge we had to cross to get to the Autobahn; on the other side of the Rhine, we ran into such a jam, we didn't move for more than ten minutes. I didn't care. As a matter of fact, I wouldn't have minded walking for a while, to get a whiff of the strange city, to be one for a moment with the young people dressed up for a night of fun, boarding buses, cycling with cool audacity wherever they could slip through between the traffic. But the girl seemed concerned. "I wonder, Rudi, if we shouldn't go back and buy something to eat on the road. It's going to take some time to get there in traffic like this. I skipped lunch today and I'm hungry. But the restaurants will be crowded. Maybe we could try . . ."

"Don't worry," Rudi told her, "Feldman took care of it."

The moment we were across the bridge and out of the city proper, he turned on the inside light. Driving with one hand, he reached for a picnic basket beside him on the floor and handed it back to us. The car veered a little and the girl said sharply, "Do be careful."

"Sorry."

"And pull up, please. I don't want you to drive with the light on inside, and I don't enjoy eating in the dark." Then her voice changed; almost apologetically she added, "I didn't mean to offend you. I know you're a wonderful driver, but wet roads scare me. What about you? Have you had anything?"

"I had dinner just before Feldman called. Thanks."

The contents of the basket proved to be surprising because they were hot. A casserole dish of a *Halver Hahn,* Cologne's famous chicken, noodles, rolls in tin foil, coffee in a thermos, but the beer was cold. "I like a head," said the girl. "About two fingers."

"I thought you didn't care for alcohol."

"Hard liquor, no, but beer, wine, champagne—yes. What about some coffee, Rudi?"

Rudi, who had been reading the evening paper, turned, a broad grin making his round face even wider. "I don't need any coffee," he said. "I'm wide awake, if that's what you're concerned about. But I'd like an apple, if you don't mind."

"When I was a child," said the girl, "I ate an apple after every meal to get out of having to clean my teeth. Why do children hate to brush their teeth?"

I'd hated it too, but I hadn't known that apples could be substituted for brush, toothpaste and water. I decided we had something in common. She put plates, glasses, cutlery and cups back into the basket and put it on the floor, rested her feet on it, then turned down her window, scooped up the snow that had gathered on the sill and washed her hands. "Why does it have to snow right now? It hardly ever does."

"It'll stop," said Rudi. "The weather forecast is for clear skies tomorrow. It'll be gone before you know it."

I couldn't make out his relationship to the girl. On the one hand he seemed on equal terms with her, on the other he was servile in a way I didn't like. Was he a chauffeur? But the moment he turned out the light and started the motor, I stopped wondering about it. It was warm in the back of the car, a pleasant warmth that didn't give you a headache, just made you feel comfortable and drowsy. Again there was that scent of cinnamon which had somehow got lost in the crowds around us. It was then that I kissed her. First her hair, then her forehead, and very gently, her ears. They were small and thin, and if I hadn't controlled myself I would have bitten her right lobe. She didn't stir. She seemed to be asleep. I placed the thumb of my left hand against her lips. They were trembling. I thought of the strands of hair at the nape of her neck, and moved her head so that it came to rest on my shoulder and kissed those little hairs; but I didn't open the zipper of her suit. I kept touching her neck with my tongue, lightly, casually. She didn't make a sound. I glanced up to find Rudi's eyes watching us in the mirror over the dashboard. Yawning loudly, I sat up straight. "I must have dozed off," I said, and I said it in German. She didn't answer and I knew she was pretending to be asleep, but her leg, touching mine, was trembling. "Rudi," I said, authoritatively, loudly, "isn't there a lap robe somewhere? I'd like to cover her up."

"Behind you on the ledge," Rudi answered in English.

I found the robe and held it up high as I unfolded it

clumsily, on purpose. It gave her time to collect herself. She stirred, sat up, said, "I'm not cold. Oh . . . did I fall asleep on your shoulder? I'm sorry."

"Why don't you stretch out?" I said. "I can sit with Rudi and you can really nap."

Rudi stopped at the next clearly marked spot where cars were allowed to park in emergencies, and I got out. I almost slipped in a puddle of sleet at the edge of the shoulder and after I had got in beside Rudi, I took off my shoes and shook the water off them.

"There are some socks in there," he said, pointing to the glove compartment. "I never drive without an extra pair."

I took mine off and put on his heavy hand-knitted ones. "My grandmother used to knit socks for me," I told him. "She came from Bingen."

He seemed to take my words as an unwelcome attempt at intimacy and didn't say anything. I turned the knob of the radio. "I'd like to hear the news."

"Who wants to hear the news these days?" he said. "Besides, the radio would wake her up."

I decided to sound him out. "Who is she?"

My question stumped him. I could tell, because he turned to stare at me instead of keeping his eyes on the road, and had to brake sharply to avoid hitting a car just ahead of us. "Don't you know?"

"No. We just met. Something went wrong with my reservation at the Dom and she told me she was booked at the Lindwurm, and the hotel got me a room."

He grunted softly but that was all.

"Have you known her long?"

"Bettina von Alten? She was fourteen when she came to Cologne. My mother was housekeeper at the finishing school she attended, a swanky private affair. We lived in the

14

gatehouse. She had quite a time with me, what with all the young girls around and I the only boy. But she was smart enough not to oppose me when I developed a crush on Bettina. She let me have her down to the house whenever I liked and she could get away. 'But don't fool around with her,' she said, 'or I'll wring your neck.' And she meant it."

"And did you?"

He grinned. "Not at fourteen."

I offered him a cigarette. He accepted it, pushed in the lighter, handed it to me, and I lit mine before passing it back to him. He coughed, inhaling the first draft. In sympathy I coughed too. I couldn't explain to myself what made us friends suddenly. "And you?"

"I own my own business, a sort of German equivalent of Hertz. I drive her because she's so deadly afraid of cars, though she drives like the devil herself. She was in a bad accident when she was nineteen, almost died. Head-on collision. No, she wasn't driving, somebody else was. She was in a hospital for months."

"Bettina von Alten," I said, tasting her name as if it had been a morsel of strange food. "Bettina von Alten."

"The whole business . . . I mean, her car accident has always been a bit of a mystery. She never would talk about it. Maybe you could get something out of her."

"I don't think so."

"Why?"

"There isn't time. I'm only staying a few days. Till Ash Wednesday."

"I thought," he said, "the way you looked at her, that you were interested."

I couldn't help laughing. "I'm interested in any pretty girl, to a degree. Aren't you?"

And Rudi, as if we'd been pals from way back, "For a

piece of tail there are others. I can put you on to a lot of nice girls, no whores, understand? Just good clean sex."

"Thanks, but I prefer to find my own."

"Naturally. But I'll give you my private number just in case." He reached into the pocket of his jacket and handed me a small white card. "Whenever you need me . . ."

A few minutes later we left the Autobahn. "Ash Wednesday, that's when you're off?"

"Correct."

"I'll drive you to the airport."

I couldn't make out whether his offer was motivated by kindness or if he wanted to make sure I was really leaving. We passed through the main street of a small town. For a second the headlights illuminated the ornate outlines of a small Baroque church. "What's this place called?"

"Watch it, Rudi," Bettina called from the back. "I hate that curve." After that, for about ten minutes, the road was winding and rose sharply.

Nothing had prepared me for the sight that now loomed up before us. I had expected a country inn like those that have a shingle hanging from a pole over the entrance, depicting the animal they are named after—a golden lamb or a shaggy bear or a silly-looking lion. I saw I had been fooled by the name. The Lindwurm. It wasn't just another small country hotel; it was a castle.

Like most Rhine castles, it stood on a hilltop, its ground plan limited by nature, and whatever spaciousness it lacked in breadth was made up for in height. Story upon story culminated in four towers with a parapet running between, all this rising above a sea of trees, snow-covered at the moment, which hid the sheer rock of its foundations. There was even a drawbridge. And it was in front of the drawbridge that Rudi stopped. About forty feet long and eight

feet wide, it was held by powerful steel cables and spanned
—not a moat as I had thought first—but a crevasse. "A
good five hundred feet to the bottom," said Rudi. "A landslide created it centuries ago." He started the motor again.

"Don't drive across it." There was fear in Bettina's voice.

"But the cables are new."

"I'd rather walk. Honk your horn, please."

She got out of the car. I didn't know what to do—follow
her or stay with Rudi. "About three years ago," he said,
"the bridge gave way and a car with three people in it . . .
friends of hers . . ." He sounded his klaxon. It echoed back
a hundredfold and lights sprang up all over the courtyard
which before had been lit dimly by a couple of lanterns.
Suddenly I wondered if I could afford to stay in such pala-
tial surroundings. "What kind of a place is this anyway?"

"Half swank hotel, half sanatorium."

"Owned by whom? The state or privately?"

"It used to be private property, but its owner wouldn't
maintain it. Right after the war it was used as a rehabilita-
tion center, but there was no running water or electricity.
Then a crazy American bought it and had it restored. It
took years, and a small fortune, to modernize it. The people
in the neighborhood made good money, and still do, as
employees. I think the man's name was Smith, anyway, it
was one of those common names you forget. He lived here
for a few summers and through some of the winter seasons.
He was crazy about the wines. And it's so central. Maybe he
ran out of money, or his wife got sick of it; whatever the
case, he turned it into a moneymaking proposition all right.
A sanatorium at first, for convalescents, and when there
weren't enough of them and the prices got too steep, the
right wing was remodeled to accommodate guests."

"You seem to know a lot about it."

"I was interested at the time in the hotel end of it, but it didn't work out."

Bettina hadn't crossed the bridge yet. She was standing at the iron railing which ran along both sides of the drawbridge, staring down into the abyss. I told Rudi I'd join her, that he should drive on ahead. I nearly slipped on an icy spot which must have formed before it began to snow. Regaining my equilibrium, I went to stand beside her. She had picked up some small stones and was throwing them, one by one, into the crevasse. You couldn't hear them land. I put my hand under her arm. "Why do you come back to a place of unhappy memories?"

"Because of Professor Florian."

"Oh. Is he staying here?"

"He does . . . off and on."

I was going to ask her what exactly she needed his help for when there was a sound like thunder, like a hundred horses's hooves on wood. It was only our car, its width equal almost to that of the bridge, rumbling across it and into the courtyard. We walked in behind it. The bright red tail lights painted the snow a watery red, the color of blood. Two porters came running from the entrance to help unload our luggage. I stopped to say good night to Rudi. He was sitting behind the wheel, his arms crossed, quite the haughty private chauffeur who considers it beneath him to lend a helping hand. I leaned into the car through the open window but he only pushed his cap deeper down his forehead. "Don't lose my number," he murmured, and raised the window so fast, I was almost trapped. Bettina, to my surprise, had walked on without as much as a wave of the hand to her childhood friend.

The entrance hall was long and surprisingly narrow. As

in a gallery, life-sized figures, armored from head to toe, were placed statuesquely at regular intervals. Some wore the flat-topped tilting helmets that were so easily dislocated, others the light sallet with visor, which hadn't been much of an improvement; only three of the knights had on the helmet with beaver that could be opened and closed at will. The walls were hung profusely with bows, swords, maces, axes, spears, lances, halberds and pikes, muskets and finely inlaid pistols, some of them arranged around even earlier forms of protective dress—vests made of leather or clumsily quilted fabrics, several of them interlaced with chain mail. A display that made any future visit to an armory unnecessary.

There were several doors, all of them labeled in Gothic lettering—dining room, billiard room, tearoom, writing room, and as I stepped closer to one, it opened by itself, like the door of an American supermarket, and remained open until I went away.

At the far end a young man dressed in casual gray flannel pants and a brown jacket was talking to Bettina across a large, oblong table, its top painted with flowers and animals. She turned when I came up to her and introduced me. "Welcome, Mr. Waldron." The young man bowed slightly. "I hope you had a pleasant trip. We have a room in the south tower for you. It's the only one left, and it's at the top. You'll have a beautiful view."

I thought of the height of the towers, and he laughed as if he could read my mind. "We have elevators, naturally, to all four towers. Now, if you care to eat something—light dinners are being served in the Stübl on the second floor."

"Thanks, I'm not hungry, just tired."

"Are the saunas still open, Richter?" Bettina asked.

Richter shook back his right sleeve to look at his watch, a thin one with a small inset showing the day of the month. "You'll just make it."

"Then that's what I'm going to do," said Bettina. "A sauna, an hour or two of sleep, then back to Cologne to dance all night."

"You can dance all night here if you want to," said Richter.

"Here?"

"Until Shrove Tuesday we have private parties booked, and guests of the Lindwurm are welcome. Tonight is fancy dress."

"Compulsory?" I asked.

Richter's smile was thin. "Not very. Anything will do, really."

"Fine," said Bettina. "Will you meet me in about two hours? Shall we say at the bar?"

"I certainly will."

The elevator was a small but quite complicated affair, a cage with three doors. It reminded me of a ski lift I'd been on once, from which different doors led to various stations. Astounding, the way they'd arranged an elevator system in a building erected before even the architectural use of steel. We both got off on the same top floor, but I had to go up ten steps to get to my tower room. Bettina's was at the foot of the stairs.

My room was small and round. There were no radiators, just electric heaters on two sides, but they seemed to be adequate. The bathroom was as miniature as the one on a Danish ship I'd taken last year from Harwich to Denmark, yet it contained everything one could possibly require. I looked for my luggage, but couldn't find it until I opened the closet. My suitcase had been unpacked, and nobody had sneaked a drink from my bottle of Scotch which I always took along in case I felt like having a drink after everything was closed. It stood on a small table near my bed, on a tray, with a container of ice, a carafe of cold water and two glasses. Again I began to worry about what all this was going to cost and cursed myself for not having asked. I walked over to the door, expecting to find a price list fastened to it, but there was none. I could only hope that I wouldn't be overcharged because I was an American. After all, we had pretty well outlived the myth of our unlimited means.

From somewhere below came a sudden noise. I went to one of the windows and drew back the curtain. An ornate wrought-iron grillwork made a geometric crisscross pattern through which I could see across the Rhine. A haze of lights. A city. For a moment I was puzzled, then decided that it must be Bonn. I had forgotten how close the West German capital was to Cologne. I drew back another curtain from another window—the same grillwork—and could see the courtyard. A carriage had just arrived. Plumed horses and people in costume. Like a window display at Schwarz's toy shop on Fifth Avenue. I watched it disappear after unloading its guests. Faintly I could hear the plaintive tune of a hurdy-gurdy. I've always liked the sound, and have thrown down numerous little packets of change wrapped in paper from rooms in Rome, Paris, London. But there was no one in sight. Still, that thin little tune drifting up to me through the damp air changed my mind. A sauna and an hour's sleep might not be a bad idea. There was a bathrobe of thick toweling hanging next to the shower. I undressed and put it on, went down the ten steps, rang for the elevator and once in it, pressed the button that said "Sauna." I landed in what I thought was the cellar but was actually one floor above the caves in which the wine and firewood and frozen foods were housed—a busy place. Girls in white uniforms and men dressed like hospital aides were hurrying around, and I was told I would have to wait at least ten minutes. I was asked if I wanted "the treatment." I said no. One winter, skiing in Norway, I had happily submitted to being beaten with birch rods and awakened stiff in every muscle and unable to walk for two days.

On the way up again, feeling relaxed and looking forward to a Scotch and a nap, I pushed open the elevator door at my floor—or so I thought—but instead of facing the ten steps that led to my room, I found myself emerging into the strangest surroundings I had ever seen. Obviously I had taken the wrong elevator. I was standing on a ledge about five feet above something that in the obscure light looked more like a huge nest than a room. I stepped back hastily, but too late—somebody must have rung for the elevator. The door closed before I could reach it.

The ledge was a narrow ramp. No railing. Since there was no way back, all I could do was jump down. The ground I touched was soft, and, as I soon realized, was carpeted with straw, in the center of which lay about twenty dead hares. I looked up, and I think I would have begun to shout for help if I hadn't realized suddenly that it was carnival time, when people dressed up according to the craziest whims of their imagination. On second thought, though, I wasn't at all sure that the creatures I was looking at were human.

I was surrounded by twelve man-sized eagles. I told myself that I couldn't possibly have been transported by elevator to an eyrie of giant birds, that they were definitely *not* birds but men dressed up as eagles. Each of the twelve wore an eagle head for a mask. Their arms were hidden under black shiny wings, sleeves evidently, because they worked like arms and their span was enormous. Their bodies were clad in some sort of black stretch material; their legs, like divers's legs, were encased in black rubber, which also covered their feet, upon which claws had been painted with white luminous paint. In my bathrobe, with my legs sticking out, I felt helplessly embarrassed. "I'm sorry," I said. "I didn't mean to break in on a private gathering."

My words were greeted with loud guffaws of laughter, very human laughter, and it occurred to me that finding myself in these weird surroundings might not be an accident but a practical joke, played on unsuspecting guests at carnival time. The dead hares, which I had tried to avoid touching, turned out to be stuffed. Then a voice, a gutteral voice, spoke. "Since you are here, tell us who you are."

"Must I?" I said. Of course I could have pretended not to understand German, but I was intrigued and ready to enter into the spirit of their crazy game. "Do I have to?"

23

"We're very selective," the same voice said. "If you want to join us, we must know your name."

"Andrew Waldron."

"American?"

"Yes."

"Where from?"

"New Jersey." How silly it sounded!

"Born?"

"Forty-one."

Questions I had filled out God knows how often when applying for college, to get a passport, crossing borders, registering in hotels.

"Married?"

"No."

"Parents?"

"Dead."

"Next of kin?"

Really! "No kin."

"Profession?"

"Author."

Another voice asked, "What kind of things do you write?"

This question I didn't like. I hadn't made my mark yet, and it seemed brash, suddenly, that I should have called myself an author when all I had written were some articles, a short play, produced unsuccessfully Off Broadway, a few reviews, essays, and what you call "Letters from . . ." Paris, London, Rome, for unimportant papers in the sticks. "All sorts of stuff."

I could detect genuine interest in the voice that now addressed me. "And beside that?"

"Take your choice," I replied. "Whatever comes into your mind."

"Such as?"

It amused me to give them my career in a nutshell, the more or less typical story of young men like me, ambitious in a way, yet drifters. I don't know why, since their faces were hidden and their movements obscured by their wings, I should have thought of them as old men, but I did.

"Washing dishes at a Miami hotel." How did one say "bouncer" in German? "Throwing unwelcome guests out of gambling houses in Las Vegas. Skiing in Utah. Walking dogs in Chicago. Selling books in New York City from five to one A.M. Parking cars, working as a clerk at Kennedy Airport, as a janitor in San Francisco."

"All to gather material?"

"No. To keep myself fed."

"Religion?"

"Presbyterian."

"Do you believe in God?"

I hadn't been asked that since high school. I shook my head.

"Then in what do you believe?"

I wasn't really prepared for an interrogation of my private reasoning. There had been too many moments in which I had zigzagged between extremes, sometimes considering it a sign of strength to be an atheist and a cynic, above using any crutches human frailty might require, unable to attach myself to any faith or ideal, or, in times of depression reverting to passionate belief. Yet I found myself answering, quite against my will, "I believe in life."

"You mean action?"

Suddenly I had had enough. A joke can never become serious without losing what made it fun in the first place. "Yes. My own," I said crossly, and looked up at the direction from which I had jumped. But it was too high to shinny

25

up, with nothing at the top to get a grip on but the smooth ledge. There were steps. But those damn birds stood between me and them.

"And in what else?"

"I don't know what you mean." Hell, who wanted to join a group of zanies who didn't know when a game was over?

"In the power of your country?"

The eagle who said it leaned slightly toward me, and I realized that they were not going to let me off until I had somehow satisfied their curiosity. "Any country can be powerful at a given time and impotent at others. History tells us that."

"Then you're not a patriot."

"Not in that sense."

"Ask him," another eagle whispered, but I couldn't hear what he was proposing until the eagle whom he was addressing turned to me and said, "Mr. Waldron, could you tell us to what idea or point of view—political or personal —you feel most strongly committed?"

Now commitment was a word I had erased from my personal credo long ago, even from my ambitions as a writer. For if ever I were to find out that I could, let us say, paint better than I could write, I didn't want to feel that because I had spent years doing one thing, I was committed to go on doing it for the rest of my life. Since nobody had invested in me, I felt perfectly free to invest myself however and whenever it pleased me.

"I'm committed to nothing."

"Not even to yourself?"

"Least of all to myself."

Silence fell. It lasted quite a while during which time I looked up once more at the ledge, trying to gauge how much of a leap it would take to reach it. Suddenly there was a flapping of wings. "We regard your point of view as a sin."

At another time I might have felt like asking each of them what their point of view was and to what they were committed, but I was irritated and tired, and I was longing for a drink.

"You stand convicted," said a hoarse eagle.

"Guilty, guilty, guilty," the others chimed in.

I couldn't have cared less about their verdict, nor apparently did they take themselves seriously, for suddenly everybody laughed. Two eagles bent over me. For a moment I felt stifled as their wings enfolded me, held me, lifted me. Then I was in the elevator and, a few minutes later, back in my room.

I lay down on my bed and drew the light eiderdown in its white linen case over me. I had a drink, then another, but as happens so often when one is overtired, I was suddenly wide awake. Inhaling deeply, I propelled myself out of bed and under a cold shower. When I looked at my watch, a small traveling alarm clock, I was surprised to see that it was already a few minutes past ten. I began to dress, then realized that it had to be "fancy," but I didn't have anything with me that could serve as a costume. At least that's what I thought until I remembered the shabby black corduroy jacket I had intended to throw out long ago. With a wide beret I had bought in Portugal, and a silk scarf knotted around my neck, I might pass for a nineteenth-century painter, or even a more up-to-date artist. I looked for my hat, which sported a chamois brush, pulled it out of the ribbon, fastened it with some tape to a pencil and stuck it behind my left ear, wondering all the time if I was being driven by a specific childishness or by the deeper, more general desire of man to pretend to be somebody else. I

27

couldn't resist glancing into the mirror. I still looked pretty much like myself. The men who had been wearing eagle's heads had certainly done a lot better as far as disguise was concerned. I took off my beret again and recombed my hair until it fell in bangs across my forehead. It made me look like an idiot, but then, that was what I felt like.

Contrary to the lobby, with its green marbleized floor, the third floor corridor was covered with thick wall-to-wall carpeting and furnished with small sofas and chairs. I couldn't tell if they were genuine Louis XVI or imitation. They stood along its tapestried walls, but as in the lobby, there was a table opposite the elevator. A woman dressed like a hobo, her face painted white, a battered top hat on her head, her suit a wild mixture of primary colors, asked me, "Would you like a mask?"

"Yes," I told her.

There were half-masks in every color and a pile of others that covered your whole face. I tried on both kinds, but found that the full mask made breathing difficult and chose a half one. She helped me fasten the ribbon under my beret. "By the way, who's giving this party? Don't you think I should know?"

"The Eagles," she said. "It's a yearly affair. The bar is on your left, second door."

It had the longest counter I'd ever seen, at least sixty feet. The men tending bar wore frog's heads, light green, with bulging plastic eyes that caught the light. Like their heads, their uniforms were the green of swamp creatures. I was struck by the fact that they all seemed to be the same height, then, after glancing around me, I began to wonder if the party had a theme, in this case animals, for I could see a lion with a bushy mane, a monkey, a couple of white poodles—women, judging by the way they moved—and a rabbit with exaggeratedly long pink-lined ears. And of course there were the eagles.

Why did men like to discard their human shape and pretend to be animals? Did frog and rabbit signify a secret desire for the ability to propagate rapidly? Did the lion betray the ambition to be as strong and powerful as the king of beasts who made his wife provide the food? Did those dressed up as dogs evidence a subconscious urge to obey a master, and the monkey an allegiance to facile wisdom? And the eagles . . . what did they signify? Freedom. The sky the limit. Proud loneliness. The rest were dressed as gypsies, pierrettes, apaches, peasant girls. I could see a Napoleon with his Josephine, a walking clock, an Indian princess with a maharajah, an odalisque, Chinese coolies, cowboys, cowgirls, and a lot of clowns. Their choice of costumes probably also betrayed the characters they preferred to their own, or at least admiration for the life the others had led. There was a sprinkling of black ties and evening gowns with wild *décolletés,* diaphanous pant suits over sequined bikinis, and I felt like a fool because I had never owned a dinner jacket. Most of those present wore masks. All in all, about sixty people. How many of them were hotel guests, I couldn't say.

Bettina was leaning against the far end of the bar, between a tall eagle and a man who was evidently the joke of the gathering. He was in full armor, like the knights downstairs, and having made his way thus far, could now hardly hold himself up. "At least take off your neck-guard or you won't be able to move your head tomorrow," she was advising him as I came up to her. "And there's really no need for the lance rest, since you're not carrying one."

She looked stunning. Her long blond hair—I should have guessed it was long from the little strands I'd kissed earlier

29

—fell to her shoulders. I've always liked long hair. It makes the girl more feminine and me seem more of a man. But I didn't care for the wreath of seaweed she was wearing like a crown, with streamers floating down to the hips. Smooth green silk, as tight-fitting as stretch material, showed off the perfect lines of her body except for her long legs, which were hidden in a clever arrangement of folds that ended in the long tail of a fish.

"Water sprite," I said, "I believe we have a date."

She looked at me as if she didn't know me, Oh, not again! "We do have a date," I said, in my broadest Americanese.

"She can't dance," said the knight, breathing heavily.

"The tail is detachable," said Bettina, ripping it off.

"That's better," said the eagle, throwing the discarded tail into the air. It landed behind the bar. Bettina made no effort to retrieve it.

A fanfare of music and the wall at our end of the bar fell away, disappearing apparently into nowhere, and we were facing a ballroom, two stories high, all white, green and silver, with graceful rococo stoves in two corners, a mirrored ceiling and balconies running along three sides, the orchestra housed in one of them. The eagle bowed ceremoniously and stepped aside to let Bettina pass. With her tail detached, her dress fell in long wide pleats to the floor. Her feet, in green silk, high-heeled sandals were all I could see; the rest of her was hidden by the eagle's wings.

"Have a glass of champagne," the knight said, "and reach me mine, if you don't mind."

"For God's sake, why don't you take the thing off?"

"I can't. I haven't got a stitch on underneath. Stark naked and perspiring like hell."

"Whatever made you get into it in the first place?"

"It was a bet. I was drunk. I didn't know what I was letting myself in for." He opened the ventail to take a sip from the glass I handed him. By this time the bar was almost empty, nearly everyone had gone into the ballroom to dance, and some of the frog-waiters had turned around discreetly to take a puff from a cigarette or a nip from a bottle. Before he tipped down the beaver again, he brought his face as close as he could to mine and said softly, "I'm a friend of Rudi's."

A clown was headed our way. "Here comes the doctor," said my armored friend, straightening up, and in a normal voice he introduced me. The clown gripped his wide pants at both sides and spread them apart as if he were about to curtsy. He was a very tall man, and by the way the suit fluttered on him, also very thin. Under a black skullcap, from which dangled a red tulip, his face was painted chalk white, even his lips were white and when he parted them it came as a surprise to see the sudden pink of his gums. He seemed strangely familiar, but it took a moment before I knew where I had seen him before—not him, of course, but the greatest mime of all. He was a splendid imitation, at least as far as his costume was concerned, of Jean-Louis Barrault.

He introduced himself. "Klausen. I'm the doctor here. I hope you won't need me," and his wide grin split the white mask of his face.

"You're not supposed to reveal your identity," said the knight.

"In a moment everybody's going to unmask anyway," said the doctor, and turning to me, "I just want to pick up a bite. They have only heavy food downstairs—sausages and beer. Come along, Rembrandt, you look starved."

It took me a moment to realize he meant me; I had

31

completely forgotten the outfit I was wearing.

"You might bring back a little something for me," said Rudi's friend. "I'd never make it to the buffet in this get-up." We passed Bettina. She was dancing with the jeweled maharajah. Klausen tried to break in but she shook her head. "I don't like clowns. They make me feel sad, and I don't want to be sad tonight."

Klausen pulled an invisible string. It made the tulip stand up straight, dithering, and Bettina laughed. But he stepped away without saying anything more.

Beyond the ballroom lay what Richter had called the Green Dining Room, and justly so. A barrier of evergreens, with little gates in between as in a park, formed small niches with tables set for four or six. The cloth of the buffet was green, so were the dishes. Here, too, the waiters were dressed like frogs.

"What a spread!" said Klausen.

I had seen lavish displays like this in ship advertisements, First Class of course, which I had always considered the height of extravagance since one could travel to the same destination at half the price. Cold venison, hare and deer with Cumberland Sauce, whole piglets with candied apples rammed into their snouts, all varieties of fowl, roasts, hot and cold, all kinds of salads, breads, cheese, fruit and trays and trays of French pastry. Girls in white dirndl skirts, black velvet vests, white blouses and aprons helped you to load up your plate.

A while back I had felt hungry, but this display of rich food killed my appetite. I helped myself to fruit and a cup of coffee, then picked out some smoked salmon, several slices of goose, a triangle of ripe brie and a piece of mocha-hazelnut torte for Rudi's friend. But when I got back to the bar, he was gone. "I'd appreciate it if you'd send a bottle up to my room," I told a waiter. "Scotch. South tower. Number Forty-seven." I felt angry and let down, and I left the bar without making any effort to find Bettina.

I took the elevator to the entrance hall. It was deserted. I started to count how many steps it would take to reach the door, wondering if my first estimate of its length had been correct, but forgot my count when I saw a pile of black metal pieces lying on the floor—breastplate, backpiece, vambrace, cuisses . . . I had guessed correctly. Rudi's friend had borrowed one of the displays. Why had he wanted me to know he was Rudi's friend?

The door was locked, but there was a bell-pull at the right. I pulled it. Almost at once a man appeared. "May I be of any help, sir?"

"I'd like to get out."

"The drawbridge is up."

"I just want a breath of fresh air."

"I see. Of course." He disappeared, and a moment later the door opened by electrical device.

It had stopped snowing, just as Rudi had prophesied. Two boys with long brooms were sweeping a path, a third was scattering ash onto the cleared cobblestones from a sack tied around his hips. Here too a railing ran along the width of the chasm on either side of the bridge which now, pulled up, formed a barricade. Somebody was leaning against the guard-rail—heavy metal bars, wired below and above, man high, with spikes on top. I had hoped it was Bettina, but coming closer I saw it was a man, a boy, rather, dressed like a twelfth-century German minnesinger, the false nose of his mask protruding like a misshapen carrot. I was reminded of a German fairy tale which had for its hero a dwarf, Dwarf Longnose, something like that. I recognized him only when he spoke. Professor Florian. I wasn't surprised. Bettina had said he was staying here.

He was staring across the Rhine at the haze of lights I had seen from my window. "Bonn?" I asked.

"No. Bad Godesberg. Although today they run together." And I recalled that Bad Godesberg, once just a spa, was now the seat of all foreign embassies and consulates. And Bonn, in former years simply a university town, but today the capital of the German Federal Republic, and so close to Cologne that it wouldn't take a man moving more than four hours, briskly, to walk the eighteen miles that separated the two cities. I said as much to the professor. He smiled. "You may have something there. Your man on foot might do better than in a car in today's traffic. Why didn't you take my advice?"

The change of subject matter was so abrupt, I didn't know at first what he was talking about. Then it came to me. "But I did. I came to Cologne for the carnival."

"I didn't advise anything of the sort. All I did was speak about the city's beauty and the fun I had when I was your age. Why didn't you leave as I told you?"

"You also told me that young men should never listen to old men."

"Did I say that?"

"And why should I leave? Can you give me one good reason?"

His breath made little white clouds in the damp air. "No," he said finally, "no reason whatsoever." I didn't like the tone of his voice. It sounded resigned suddenly, too resigned.

"I thought you loved Cologne."

"I do. But that's not the reason."

"Then what are you doing here?"

"I have a commission," he said, "and I'm not rich enough to turn down a sum of money that will allow me to continue the work I love to do. There aren't many people around nowadays who want to see themselves immortalized in stone."

The expression "immortalized" made me smile. So he wasn't as modest as he looked. I felt a sharp pang of envy for such self-confidence.

"The girl," he said, and stopped.

"Bettina von Alten?"

"How long have you known her?"

"Since this afternoon."

"She's a tease. Not that I don't like her, but you don't have a chance. Why did she have to turn up right now, anyway?"

I glanced at him, surprised. "She spoke very highly of you."

"Glad to hear it." His voice betrayed that he couldn't have cared less.

"She said she studied with you."

"So she did. Just steer clear of her, if you want my advice."

Other people were coming out for some air—a man who was very drunk and promptly proceeded to vomit over the railing, a woman walking her dog, and a couple who started to chase each other coyly. Their laughter drew others. Then Richter appeared. "Ladies, gentlemen, please. You are disturbing the guests who have gone to bed. Dancing continues, but inside, please." He gestured toward the door. I went inside with the others, and straight to my room.

The bottle I had ordered had been placed next to my bed, with a container of fresh ice. You couldn't complain about

35

the service at the Lindwurm. I took one swallow from the bottle, then thought how stupid it was to drink by myself. Certainly I could find a girl. Richter had said dancing was still going on, and I hadn't danced once tonight. But I had never been one for substitutes, they left me depressed, and I wasn't frustrated enough to make love to one woman while dreaming of another. I didn't bother to put on my pajamas, partly because I didn't want to put on a clean pair, partly because I liked sleeping nude. I left them where the maid had arranged them, over the back of a chair. In bed, my feet touched something hot—an old-fashioned metal hot water bottle in a crocheted coverlet. It sent a comforting warmth through my body. Bettina. I should have accepted Rudi's offer before giving her the chance to spoil my evening. Inviting me to meet her and then dancing off with someone else. "A tease," Professor Florian had said. But the way her leg had trembled against mine in the car . . . or had she just simulated an excitement I had taken to be real? I reached for some brochures, put out by tourist bureaus. Cologne, Bonn, Bad Godesberg, the Siebengebirge . . . the Seven Mountains—hills really—picturesque and famous for the Drachenfels with its ruined castle, according to the brochure. Germany's most popular excursion trip. Byron had once sung its praises and three million people toured it yearly to see the stone dragon, in commemoration of Siegfried's dragon, presumably once housed there, the Nibelung Hall with Wagner memorabilia, or to visit the restaurant at the top and drink the famous Dragonblood wine. I wondered if you could see the Drachenfels from the Lindwurm. More brochures—Rhine excursions, heavily curtailed at this time of the year, and the carnival schedule, in German, English and "köl'sch". . .

"I was afraid you might be asleep."

I hadn't heard her steps outside the door, nor seen the knob turn. I sat up. She was still wearing the green dress that was so tight around the upper part of her body, I could see her nipples pressing against the silk. I was too glad she had come to say anything snide about the way she had let me down, and too proud to show surprise. "May I offer you a drink?"

"I'll stick to champagne. I don't want to have a hangover." She produced a bottle of Veuve Cliquot. The cork popped like a shot when I opened it. "It's warm."

"I like it over ice."

She walked to the door and locked it. "It says here to lock your door at night."

"I never lock anything—luggage, closets, doors."

"You look it."

"Look what?"

"As if you didn't care."

"I don't. I have nothing to lose."

She lifted a hand to the nape of her neck. I thought she was going to scratch the back of her head, instead she must have undone a hook or whatever held her dress up. Suddenly she was naked. The green silk simply fell away from her body like a snake shedding its old skin in spring. She stepped out of the material, which had gathered like a small wave on the floor, and lifting it with one foot, pushed it out of the way. Her neck was long, her shoulders broader than I had suspected, her breasts set high and full, her stomach like a board, all muscle. I had never had any girl with legs as long as hers, two sturdy pillars rising out of her knees, elongated toward her feet which were narrow, like her hands, with long, slender toes. She stood quite still for a moment and let me look at her as if she were a piece of merchandise a buyer might consider.

"You look nice."

"I am nice," she said, and drew back the covers from my feet. "Throw me a pillow, will you?"

So we sat opposite each other in bed, she balancing a glass of champagne on her knees, I with my legs pulled up sideways, sipping my Scotch. "Do you mind if I smoke?" I couldn't remember ever having been so polite and feeling quite so stupid.

"No. Should I?"

"It's up to you."

She smiled, but said nothing for a while, then she asked, "What do your friends call you?"

"Drew. And you?"

"You'll have to find your own name for me."

"Why didn't you keep our date? I thought you were looking forward to dancing with me."

"I was," she said, "but let's not go into that. I'll tell you sometime. Anyway, this is better, isn't it?"

"How old are you?"

"About to be twenty-three."

"Mind if I ask you a couple of questions?"

"Don't." She shook her head. "I hate questions. They make me feel as if I were on trial. That's when I lie."

"I was on trial today, in a way. Maybe I should have lied. But I didn't."

"On trial?"

"The eagles got me, or rather I invaded their eyrie by mistake."

"Oh, that stupid bunch." She frowned sharply.

"Yes. Pretty childish," I agreed. "They asked me what I believed in. What do you believe in, Bettina?"

"What is there to believe in but luck?"

"Do you think I'll bring you luck?"

"I'm willing to give it a try."

I crushed my cigarette, finished my drink, took the unfinished glass of champagne from her, pulled her into my arms, then I turned off the light. "Don't," she said. "I'm afraid of the dark."

"You seem to be afraid of a lot of things."

"I wasn't always." She left me to switch on the light in the bathroom, and leaving the door ajar, came back to me.

"But you aren't afraid of me."

"No."

"I'm glad," I said, and took her in my arms.

Her skin was smooth and taut, like that of not yet fully ripened fruit. Again I wanted to bite into it, to taste what it covered with so much promise, but I didn't want to frighten her because, as in the car, she held herself motionless, and if it hadn't been for the trembling that made her body quiver like water rippled by a gentle wind, I would scarcely have felt her presence. Yet it was her silence and the slight trembling of her tense muscles that excited me more than if she had responded with greed. The less she moved, the more I wanted her to react wildly, and I kissed her, all there was of her—the inside of her legs, the tiny cold buds of her breasts, her feet. The rhythm of her breathing never changed, and its singular steadiness made me think suddenly of the professor's warning, "She's a tease." At that moment I wouldn't have been surprised if she had suddenly sat up, smiled, and left me. I looked at her and saw her eyes, wide open, watching me as if she and her body were unrelated to each other. I think it was then, in the anticipation of her leaving me coldly, that I wanted nothing more than to see those slanting eyes show some emotion. I made my hands into fists, pushing them into the small of her back, and entered her cruelly. But the expression in her eyes didn't change, nor did they close in satisfaction, only her hands touched me for the first time, lightly at first, then digging with welcome pain into my shoulder blades. There was a little sigh, the next moment she was crying, just a few tears, rolling from her still wide open eyes, across her cheeks, toward her mouth. She opened her lips and caught them, shaking her head and still crying, silently, slowly. An immense satisfaction filled me with a tenderness that was quite new. "Hush, darling, hush." And I began to kiss her tears away.

"Salty as a Dutch herring."

"I'm sorry."

"Don't be silly."

For a while we just lay without changing positions. When she finally stopped shivering, I lifted myself away from her. "I'm afraid I'm too heavy. I didn't mean to crush you."

She didn't answer, and I went into the bathroom. Closing the door I prepared myself for the talk I felt was inevitable and something I loathed when my body, relieved of all tension, took command over my mind and I longed for sleep. But I needn't have worried about being kept awake, because when I came back she was asleep. Lying just the way I had left her. Unreasonably, instead of being thankful, I felt disappointed, more than that—angry. There were so many questions I had wanted to ask her, questions that could be asked only in the intimacy of bed, in that certain atmosphere created after the sharing of physical pleasure. I sat down on the one big comfortable armchair. It had a footrest which could be pulled out by leaning heavily on the elbows. Crossing my legs, I poured myself a drink and watched her sleeping with all the lights on. She must have turned them on while I was in the bathroom. I remembered that she was afraid of the dark. I went over to the bed and sat down on the edge. I picked up her hand. It was heavy with relaxation. "What are you afraid of, Bettina? Life is too short for fear—of cars, of chasms, of accidents, of people. We all have to die some day."

But she didn't hear me. It made me feel deserted, and all of a sudden I could understand those tedious women who were forever complaining about their husbands falling asleep directly after the act. I poured myself another drink, watched her for a while, then went over to the bed again and this time crawled into it. After all, I wasn't just a sleeping draught. "Bettina . . ."

Without opening her eyes she said, "Don't worry, I won't snore."

"You just did," I lied.

She rolled away from me to the far side of the bed, and since there was no protective wall there, she might have fallen out if I hadn't caught her. I rolled her back to me. Her skin was warm, and I couldn't resist the temptation of feeling it quiver again. At my touch she turned, still saying nothing, and put her head on my shoulder and let me lead her hand. Again I was with her, and that was the way we fell asleep.

When I woke, the space beside me was empty. She was gone, and for a moment I lay there, in my tower room Number Forty-seven, about ten steps up from the elevator, in unaccustomed isolation. A woman had expended herself with me—for we had awakened, made love and gone to sleep again—how often I couldn't remember, but now there was no trace of her, not a note, not even the aroma of her body. She must have opened the window before leaving, for the air was cool, cold actually. Her bottle of champagne had disappeared, so had the green silk dress she had kicked out of the way. The ashtrays had been emptied and the glasses been carried into the bathroom.

I looked at my watch and started with surprise. It was almost three o'clock. Not only had I missed breakfast but possibly luncheon as well, and although I didn't particularly care what I ate, for no better reason than that I couldn't afford to be a gourmet, still, food was pretty essential to me. A cold shower, and I tore into my pants like a pupil afraid of being reprimanded by a stern headmaster. Outside my door I found the sign turned to "Please Do Not Disturb." I turned it around to make it read "Please Make Up My Room As Soon As Possible," and rang for the elevator. There was a button which read "Stübl," and I recalled that the desk clerk had mentioned, when Bettina and I had arrived, that dinner was still being served in the Stübl. Perhaps it was open now too.

It was on the second floor, almost directly opposite the elevator, a small room, comfortably furnished, like those you see in ads praising a small-restaurant atmosphere. It was empty. I chose a table next to the white rococo stove and tapped the bell which stood on the bare brown wooden table like a baby turtle with a pimple on its back. A girl appeared, and I asked her if there was still a chance of getting some orange juice, bacon and eggs, toast and coffee, and she smiled pleasantly. "Naturally, *mein Herr.*"

The orange juice was ice cold and not out of a can, but

freshly squeezed; the eggs were done just the way I liked, sunny side up, their white edges curled to a soft tan; the coffee was strong and aromatic. I drank several cups, and just as I was getting up, the waitress came in with assorted cold cuts and a cheese platter. But I didn't want any more. When I questioned her as to where everybody was, she shrugged. "Asleep, I guess. Most of our guests went to bed late last night. Some may be in the solarium."

I felt less guilty about getting up so late, and followed the green arrow that read "Solarium," to another elevator. But I didn't take it. Instead I took the stairs beside the elevator shaft and walked all the way up to the top floor of the hotel. For exercise.

The view from the solarium was spectacular. All traces of snow were gone. Rudi's forecast had been correct and Bettina need not have worried. Below me, in exquisite clarity, the land sloped down to the Rhine, studded with trees, bare now except for the evergreens, and ran out into dun-colored meadowland and vineyards. To right and left, two towns, villages probably, neatly embedded in the landscape at the edge of the river, cedars pointing upward, dark green, out of parks and gardens; on the river—traffic, white cruising boats, barges; on the opposite bank, Bad Godesberg, flanked along the river's edge by small docks, a wide boulevard, shade trees which would be a show when leafed, beyond it all a busy highway and above me a pale blue sky, the whole thing as if sketched in tempera. But what was perhaps most impressive—to my right and across the Rhine, which at that distance ran out silver into a haze— the Cologne Cathedral, a Gothic giant. It *couldn't* be that big! And I was reminded of the Empire State Building, vast out of all proportion, pointing fat and square into the sky as

43

one approached New York City from the Long Island parkways. Distance and atmosphere did strange things to such mammoth edifices.

On the solarium, however, everyone seemed accustomed to the view. Quite a few people were stretched out on long chairs, reading newspapers or books, a few women were knitting, one was doing petit point. Others were sitting close to the windows in comfortable wicker chairs, playing bridge, canasta or gin rummy. Again I was reminded of First Class passage on an ocean liner. But if I had expected to find Bettina here—and no doubt about it, I was subconsciously looking for her—I was disappointed.

There was a door leading to a walk with a crenelated parapet. Here it was cold, with a strong wind blowing. I had no coat on and soon felt chilled, still I couldn't resist watching the skaters for a few moments, cutting figures on a small, artificially iced pond below me, to the left of the courtyard. I hadn't noticed it before. Beyond it the landscape swooped gently downhill, and I could detect a dirt road winding through the woods, quite different from the approach we had used, with no chasms, no wildness, no signs of hazard, but it may have been less broad than the road by which we had come, and too narrow for a car. I couldn't judge. I was too high up to tell. Nor could I distinguish Bettina among the skaters that were weaving to and fro like brightly colored ants.

As I walked along the parapet, which I soon realized connected all four towers, the landscape immediately below me changed abruptly, the gentle tree-studded slope fell away, or rather became bare rock once more, and it was evident that the Lindwurm could be approached from only two sides—across the drawbridge, the way we had come, or

44

via the road through the woods which I had just seen, the only way to reach the castle if the drawbridge was up. The other two sides were sheer, formidable rock.

Suddenly a heavy iron gate barred my way. It seemed to lead to one of the towers, but, gazing through the grillwork I could see steps hewn roughly into the wall of the tower, rising above me and descending below me to another iron gate. The whole thing reminded me of a fire escape, except that these steps had no railing, and for a moment, staring down what seemed at least a thousand feet to the river level below, I felt dizzy. If I missed a step . . . On the second gate there was a sign that said "Private." Above it, on a cord, hung a primitive metal bell.

Cows in Switzerland, grazing on summer pastureland, wear such bells attached to their collars to warn their owners of strays. Each has a different sound, so that you can tell which animal has wandered off. This one had an ordinary sound, just a bell. Behind the gate was a small platform, like a balcony. As I rang, the face of a man appeared at the French window beyond it—Professor Florian. He was shaking his head violently, and his left hand, pointing to the sign, seemed helpless with surprise. "Hey!" I yelled, "Professor! Let me in."

Instead of answering, he went away from the window, and I had almost given up hope of being admitted, when he reappeared and opened the gate. "It's you again," he said, in that resigned voice which was somehow depressing. "What now?"

"I hadn't planned on finding you here," I said, "but the steps ended and I didn't feel like climbing back up them if there was any other way of getting inside."

"The upper gate is always locked."

"Well it wasn't."

"And you didn't see the sign that says 'Danger. Do not use this gate?' "

I couldn't remember seeing any such sign. I shook my head.

"Strange," he said. "I'll have to report it. Come in."

Like mine, his was a round tower room, but unlike mine its walls were covered with sketches and blown-up photographs of what looked like ancient stone carvings. I realized now that the parapet I had just walked connected the southeast and southwest towers. "I'm sorry if I'm disturbing you."

"Sit down," he said. "I wasn't doing anything anyhow." Yet he must have been working, for even as he spoke, he was picking at some crumbs of clay clinging to his right hand, and the clay spread out on a sheet on the floor was still damp and manageable. Now he covered it, dunked his hand in a pail of water, sprinkled some on the cloth, then wiped his hands on a rather dirty towel without bothering to take it off the holder.

"But you were working." I stepped closer to the turntable. It too was covered with a freshly watered sheet. "May I look?"

"No!" he cried. "Certainly not. I don't like anyone to see my work before it has reached a certain stage, satisfactory to me. Anyway, I was only preparing the clay."

He was contradicting himself. I sat down in the deep armchair he offered me, and watched him being almost swallowed up as he sank into the depths of its companion piece. The ashtray on the table between us was full of white powdery ash, cigar ash, and he said almost defiantly, "I hope the smell doesn't bother you. I hate cigarettes. They make me cough." But at Emilio's Bar in Rome, he had

46

smoked cigarettes. Somebody else then had quite evidently been smoking cigars in his room just now, someone he didn't want me to meet or know about.

"What happened to the sketch you made of me?"

"I tore it up."

But last night at the Dom, he had pretended to know nothing about it. "What a pity."

"It wasn't good."

"I'd like to own something by a man as famous as you."

"Fame." He spat out the word. "When you're young you think it's all that matters, but what a trap it turned out to be."

"A trap?"

"One pays too dearly for vanity."

"As for instance?"

"Never mind, though right now I wish *you* were famous."

He didn't make sense. Suddenly he fixed his gaze on me. There was something eerie about the way he looked me up and down, sizing me up as if indeed he had never seen me before. I began to feel uncomfortable. Then, just as if we had been discussing the neighborhood, he said, "I suppose you know you're in the heart of the German legend district. This is Nibelung territory. It was over there that Siegfried killed the dragon," and he pointed vaguely in what I supposed was the direction of the Drachenfels which, as I had meanwhile discovered from my walk along the parapet, was not visible from the Lindwurm.

He got up and walked over to the wall. Using his finger to point at some of the enlarged photos, he said, "Isn't it fantastic how the legend turns up in so many parts of the world? Teutonic, yet first recorded in Scandinavia, in song and on stone. Here—in Sweden—the Ramsunberget stone, and in Ockelbo. On the stone cross of Kirk Andreas—that's on the Isle of Man. And as far afield as Russia, on this axe found in Vladimir-Susdal." He moved to another wall. "Andvari with the ring, on a piece of jewelry found in the Latvian fortress of Daugmale Pilskans. Primitive carvings, the subject sometimes scarcely recognizable—yet always, wherever we have the Dragon, we have Sigurd," and he pointed again, "ramming the sword into its vulnerable flank."

I got up. I couldn't see any figures until he pointed them out to me—sometimes only a fragment, crouching, sword-hilt in hand, under a winding band. The Lindwurm.

Wagner, I thought. This was where he had found his inspiration. And Heine. I mentioned the Lorelei. He nodded. "But before Heine—Brentano. In his tale *Godwi* we already meet the Lorelei, luring the unsuspecting Rhine fisherman to his death. But you know our legends. How extraordinary! I wouldn't have thought an American . . ."

"My grandparents came from around here," I told him, as we settled down again. "Bingen. They fed me on German fairy tales and folklore."

"So you're part German."

"They were German to the core, but I think of myself as an American."

Again he gave me a searching look. "Regin," he said. "Did your grandparents tell you about him?"

"Wasn't he the smith who told Siegfried how to kill the dragon?"

"Sigurd," he corrected me. "In the Volsunga Saga it is Sigurd and Regin, later, in the Nibelung Lied we have Siegfried and Mime, but in either case, the dwarf and the hero." He nodded, almost happily. "Strange, how history can be interpreted individualistically, according to one's own point of view or behavior. Right now I feel like a twentieth-century version of Regin. Not that I look upon you as Sigurd, you innocent little American without a goal. But to kill the dragon you have to know where he is vulnerable," and he began to quote, " 'Make thee a hole and sit thee down therein and smite him in the heart.' "

He stepped closer to me. I could feel his breath. Though there was no liquor on it, I was sure he was drunk. Who the hell was he expecting me to smite? Unexpectedly he began to sing, " 'Don't trust Regin,' the birds in the woods sang, 'for now that you have the treasure he will think of ways to eliminate you.' So you'd better not trust me. After all, he was a treacherous coward." His face darkened, all his élan was suddenly gone. "Just like me."

I looked up, but quickly lowered my eyes again, and the words I had been going to say—something to the effect that one could carry historical identification too far—died on my lips, for he was crying. Big tears, the kind of tears children cry, were rolling down his wrinkled cheeks. I lit a cigarette and had smoked half of it before he said, "Who am I to talk? I who never dared to stand up for anything. If you want to meet a coward, here you have him," and he thumped his chest.

For a moment I wished I could think of some way to calm the poor fellow, but I couldn't. To ask him why he considered himself such a coward would probably only have upset him more, and to ignore his statement might make it seem a fact with which I agreed. For a moment I thought of reminding him of something he had told me, after quite a few drinks, in Emilio's Bar—that rather than live and work under the Nazis, he had chosen emigration, a step which to my way of thinking took courage. Perhaps not to his. So being a coward myself, I took the easiest way out

—I changed the subject. Looking at my watch I said, "In about an hour I'll be off to Cologne."

He sat up in his chair. "You're going where?"

"To Cologne. With Bettina von Alten. She wasn't able to get tickets for the tribunes, but she got window seats for the rest of the carnival, the Torch Parade and the parades on Rose Monday and Shrove Tuesday. Tonight we're going to the Guërzenich."

He said nothing about Bettina but repeated, "The Guërzenich. Dear God, when I was young . . ." then he interrupted himself to glance at me. "You're sure you're going?"

"Positive."

I watched his Adam's apple rise and fall in his thin throat. And Bettina is not a tease, I wanted to say. If ever there was a girl less a tease . . . but he was still looking at me out of narrowed eyes, his brows knit, his mouth working. "Would you mind if I joined you?"

"Of course not." He wouldn't be much bother, I thought, and we would eventually get rid of him if the crowds were as thick as he had told me in Rome.

"I couldn't be more grateful," he said, rising.

"Grateful?"

"Well . . . you see, I don't want to lose track of you."

"So suddenly you don't mind my staying on?"

"Not at all." He sounded almost gay. "But now go. In about an hour, you said? I'll meet you in the courtyard."

He opened a door almost directly opposite the French window through which I had entered his room, and I found myself in a narrow passage with no elevator in sight, until by instinct I turned left and came upon some steps which led down to it. I stopped at the ground floor and walked to the reception desk where Richter, who had received us the night before, told me, "No, I don't have a message for you."

I refrained from asking him to put me through to Bettina's room, but crossed the long entrance hall, with all the armored knights in position again, and went up to my tower. In spite of the fact that we had a date for the evening, I couldn't get over my initial disappointment, on awakening to find her gone, that there was no sign of life from her, no acknowledgment whatsoever of my existence. There wasn't now, either. No note had been slipped under the door. I walked down the steps again and knocked at Number Forty-five. No answer. I tried the handle of the door. It was locked. It couldn't be possible, I told myself again, that a night spent together could mean so little to a girl. I could still see her sitting opposite me in my bed, her legs pulled up, juggling her glass of champagne. Narcissa? But narcissistic girls didn't let you embrace them; they escaped after whetting your appetite.

"She's feeding the deer," a voice behind me said.

I swung around. A waiter was standing there, balancing a heavily loaded tray, grinning at me. "She loves animals. Always has. You'll find her in the park, on the north side, at the third haystack."

The voice was vaguely familiar, the face was not. The face belonged to a young man, about my age and height but more heavily built than I. Dark-haired and brown-eyed, with Roman features, an aquiline nose, a heavy-set chin.

"Who are you?"

"My name is Hugo."

"Have we met before?"

"I don't think so, sir."

A chambermaid came along the passage, black dress, white apron, a lacy ribbon perched like a tiara on top of her black hair, and her hands were gloved. A Mary Petty maid straight out of the *New Yorker*. "Forty-one," she said to the man called Hugo, "has rung the kitchen three times, complaining because her order hasn't been filled. I know it's your first day, but if you want to keep your job here, you'd better be sharp." She turned to me. "Can I do anything for you, sir? If you've forgotten your key, I'll be glad to open up for you."

I watched Hugo walk away briskly and told the maid, yes, I had forgotten the key to my room, and would she be good enough . . . I didn't like her; I didn't like the way she never asked me what my room number was but walked on ahead, up the stairs and inserted her passkey in the lock. As soon as she had gone, I locked the door and hung a handkerchief over the handle. I'd learned that trick in prep school and found throughout life that it sometimes paid off to have the view through the keyhole obstructed.

Although I usually traveled light, there were a few things I found essential to have with me—my typewriter, a camera, a Japanese version of a Bell and Howell, a small transistor radio, a pair of binoculars and a memorizer, an oblong little gadget, not much bigger than a man's hand, into which you could talk and listen back to whatever you had said, just like an ordinary tape recorder, only a bit more shrill. I first took out my binoculars and walked along the windows until I found the one that faced north, then I focused it on the gentle slope I had seen from the parapet. After a moment or two I caught Bettina in its powerful lenses. She was walking between fir trees in the direction of the castle. Again she was dressed in the green tight-fitting pants and jacket, and it looked to me as if she was moving along as fast as she could, as if she didn't want to talk to the man who was following her. I thought of leaving my room and running down to meet her, but figured that by the time

I'd reached the courtyard, the man in obvious pursuit of her would have caught up with her, and we wouldn't have a chance for privacy.

Next I took my camera. Even from such a distance it was possible to catch the movements of the body. But the light was fading, and I put the camera away. Then I took out the memorizer. Last night, when I had told her I frequently made notes on it, she had wanted to hear her voice and had talked into it. Now it was I who wanted to hear her voice, and there it was, a husky little cough, but then came words she hadn't spoken last night, at least not while I'd been listening. "I'll keep our appointment. Six o'clock sharp. But I may not be alone. Don't fret. Erase, please."

For quite a while I stood in the middle of the room, caught in a state of surprise that acted like a vise, holding me immobile. Why hadn't she left me a note, in my room or at reception, but instead resorted to my recorder when she couldn't have been sure I would use it? But in the end I relaxed and played the innocuous little sentence over a few times, just to get the feeling of her presence. Then I erased it. The only thing bothering me now was the possibility that we might not have the evening to ourselves. Yet what right did I have to expect her to turn down people she may have known for years, at carnival time, of all times? She would find an opportunity, I felt sure, as she had done last night, for us to be alone.

A gong sounded. According to the booklet on my desk, afternoon tea. Breakfast all morning, luncheon in the Stübl until four, tea between five and six, bar open from five o'clock, dinner from six to midnight, supper after twelve, etcetera, etcetera, "We recommend the following *köl'sch* dishes," and a whole page of them, "but if you prefer French cuisine . . ." As I read on it occurred to me that I had forgotten to call one of those places that rented dinner jackets. I would have to wear my makeshift "Rembrandt" outfit again.

"It doesn't matter," said Professor Florian, as we stood in the courtyard, waiting for Bettina. "Nobody'll pay any attention to what you're wearing."

We were interrupted by the sudden appearance of a chocolate-brown Volkswagen bus. Somehow I had expected a limousine to drive Bettina and me, and any friends she might have with her, to the Guërzenich, but apparently other guests were also driving to Cologne, and the bus had been provided by the Lindwurm. I heard a gong being rung inside the hotel, and a moment later the people who must have been waiting for this sign of departure, came out into the courtyard. Ten altogether, among them Bettina, walking beside a tall, muscular young man who wore a perfectly cut dinner jacket. He hadn't stooped to fancy dress, but he did have on a rather garish jockey cap, front to back, which on him looked ridiculous. He simply didn't look cut out for fun.

If the way she walked hadn't been so unmistakable— shoulders squared, long strides—I would have had trouble recognizing Bettina. She was wearing a long, black curly wig, and what one might have called the outfit of a Latin Quarter apache's girlfriend. Contrary to last night at the bar, she came straight up to me. "Good evening, Mr. Waldron," she said. "Let me introduce an old friend of mine, Günther Gevern."

Gevern extended a long strong hand and pumped my arm almost out of its socket. "Delighted," he murmured, and helped Bettina into the bus. I was going to follow him and try to find a seat next to Bettina, when I heard the professor cry out furiously. I turned around. Dr. Klausen, in his clown costume again, was trying to stop the professor from boarding the bus. There was something almost comical about their appearance, like an act by mimes whose physical incongruities alone provided an element of humor. A midget fighting a giant whom he didn't have a chance of defeating, yet with a mind that could outwit the greater physical strength of his opponent. For the professor suddenly brought his right knee up and kicked it swiftly and precisely into the doctor's groin. Klausen fell to the ground, gave a painful moan, but was on his feet again in seconds and knocked the professor down. A guest, a woman, was screaming; another, a man, was berating Klausen for fighting someone so much smaller, when I reached the spot where the professor had fallen.

"He's crazy," Klausen said. "An out-and-out nut. Has been for years. Harmless, of course, or we wouldn't allow him on the premises. And he's obviously drunk. I can't give him permission to join the party."

I helped the professor get up and now he shook his fist at the doctor. "You're the one who's mad," he yelled. "No sane man would have lent himself to the things you . . ." and he flung himself at Klausen, but this time was stopped by a male nurse who must have witnessed the scene from a window, a huge fellow who, pinning the professor's hands behind his back, picked him up as if he had been weightless, and carried him off, Florian shouting, "You can't stop me. Nobody can stop me. Let me go. You have no right . . ."

Across his shoulder I could see Bettina. She had slipped down in her seat and was sitting motionless, her eyes closed. If she had heard anything or seen the fight, she had chosen to dissociate herself from it. The expression on her face said quite clearly that she wanted no part of it. If she had looked at me anxiously or questioningly, the spark of responsibility flickering inside me might have gone out—I don't think I would have wanted her involved—but her attitude, real or simulated, challenged me. I shook my head and said to the driver, "If you don't want to wait, go ahead, but I've got to . . ."

"Oh, don't get mixed up in it," said Gevern. "They're probably putting him in a strait jacket right now."

Of all people, Dr. Klausen suddenly spoke up for me. "Very well, let's have a look. I'm sure Schlau will have done the right thing, but young people can be harsh." Perhaps he was ashamed that he had hit the professor with all the odds on his side.

Together we walked quickly back to the entrance door and through the corridor, but this time in the opposite direction from the reception desk, into the east wing of the castle, the hospital wing. Here the arrows leading to the elevators were painted red instead of green. "But his room is in the west tower."

"They should have taken him here. I'll be right back."

He stopped in front of a door on which was a sign that read "Hospital," and "Quiet Please," on both sides. "Isn't there a room I could wait in?" I asked, determined to be on the spot and see for myself what they had done to the professor.

Klausen closed the door on me but was back in less than a minute. "He managed to escape the orderly. Let's go up to his room."

We had to retrace our steps and take another elevator which shot us up without stopping once; then came the narrow corridor I had passed earlier in the day. The door to the professor's room stood open, the room itself was empty and in complete disarray, a room in which quite obviously a

56

vicious struggle had just taken place. The turntable on which he had been preparing his new work was lying on the floor, the work itself—it must have been a bust—had been bashed in by some tool or other and made unrecognizable, a mass of gray, wet clay with surprising patches of color, as though someone had drawn on it with yellow, red and blue markers. There was a small rectangular piece of clay which clearly showed a network of purple veins. Several papers, torn to shreds, fluttered in the draft as if still suffering from the violence with which they had been rendered illegible.

"What the devil!" said Dr. Klausen, rushing over to the French windows through which the professor had let me in only a few hours ago. They stood wide open, almost flush with the wall. I followed him out onto the balcony. The gate, with its artless cowbell, was open too. As if I were still standing on the steps leading down to the professor's lodgings, I shivered. "He couldn't have tried to escape that way," I said.

"He must have. But why, when the gate is always locked?"

It wasn't this afternoon, I started to say. And I had been the one who had told Florian about it. I could hear his voice again, high, furious, determined. "You can't stop me. Nobody can stop me."

I forced myself to look down the steep, almost vertical rock. At the bottom, a few lights cast the outlines of barred windows into the darkness—undoubtedly the windows of the cellars which lay below the saunas. And there were flashlights, like fireflies on a hot summer night, two, three, four of them, and voices, unintelligible from where we stood, like the rubbing of wings, a gentle burr.

"I'd better call the police," said Klausen, and stepped

back into Florian's room. The tulip on top of his skullcap was shaking as if its string were being pulled by nervous hands, and I thought how absurd the two of us looked, costumed, in the tragedy of the moment. Dr. Klausen's hands were still. The long narrow forefinger of his right hand looked like an inanimate object, an ivory pencil, as it manipulated the letters on the dial, and his voice when he gave his name was the cold, impersonal voice of the professional man used to dealing with death. He put the receiver back almost immediately. "Police have already been called," he said. "I'd better get down."

He seemed annoyed when I followed him. "There's no reason for you to come along."

"For me there is."

He looked at me questioningly, sharply. "Curiosity," I said.

No elevators led from the floor where the saunas were housed to the cellar, only a paternoster, an open freight elevator, which was in steady perpetual motion and much too slow for our purpose. So we took the steps, endless steps, lit by naked bulbs which cast only small areas of light. Between the lights, the steps were dark and slippery from the damp. As we approached the bottom, they narrowed considerably. From here no door opened to the outside; the spaces between the bars of the window were too small to permit anyone to slip through. Through them we could see a doctor in a white, hip-length coat, the male nurse who had taken Florian away, and two policemen. Someone must have lowered a stretcher, or maybe the police had come from outside and brought the stretcher with them. On it lay a crumpled heap.

"Leise!" called Klausen.

The man in the white coat looked up. He shrugged. "Schlau!"

The male nurse came running to a stand below the window.

"What happened?"

The man seemed shaken and had trouble speaking coherently. "He escaped. I had him securely, suddenly he was gone. Just dropped from me, fast as lightning. He reached the elevator before I could. I took the one to the solarium, but as you know, it stops on the floor below. I ran as fast as I could, but he was already in his room when I got there. A madman. He was using the axe from the fire equipment in the hall, destroying what was on his turntable. He held me at bay with it while he tore up some papers with his teeth. I couldn't get near him. Suddenly he had to stop for breath. It gave me a chance. But he was like an eel. I couldn't hold onto him. He made for the gate to the parapet. I ran after him. Then it happened. He lost his footing. I think the force he had to use to handle the gate threw him back. He almost took me with him as he hurtled past."

After a brief pause during which no one said anything, one of the police officers asked, "Where do you want us to take the body? To the hospital or directly to the morgue?" He pointed to the ambulance parked on the road below.

"To the morgue," said Klausen. "Or what do you think, Leise?"

"He's dead all right," said the man called Leise. "There was nothing we could do. Nothing."

He bent to help the male nurse lift the stretcher, and carry it the short distance to the ambulance which had not been able to drive to the spot where the professor had fallen to his death. Not a word was exchanged while Klausen and I went up the steps and back to the sauna floor, but in the elevator he turned to me. "You'd better stay outside, Waldron. Inquests aren't exactly entertaining."

I had no desire to be part of one nor to get involved as witness to what had led up to Professor Florian's attempt to escape; still, I couldn't control my sudden fury over such an unnecessary death, and his tone. "Are you going to tell them about the fight you and he . . ."

"Of course."

When we got back to the courtyard, the brown Volkswagen bus had left. Where it had been waiting there now stood a police car, its red light flashing. Police inspectors all over the world have always looked the same to me; this one, though, was an exception. Horizontal red and white stripes showed under the sleeves and pants of a hastily put on uniform, and above his shirt. "I was just going off duty," he said, "when your call came in."

"I appreciate your coming, Ginster." Klausen shook the inspector's hand. "A most unfortunate accident. Where do you want to talk?"

"I don't see any need for it now." Ginster blew a cloud of cigar smoke into the air. "I've been in his room and my men have sealed it. And what could you possibly tell me when you weren't there when it happened? Leise said he was already dead when he reached him, and I've questioned Schlau. He's the key witness. I talked to him as soon as I got here. But how come you went after them? Did you anticipate trouble?"

"I just wanted to make sure Schlau had told Leise to look in on Florian and give him a sedative, instead of trying to handle it by himself. No, there wasn't a reason in the world to expect trouble."

"Conscientious as usual. Well, I've done my duty for tonight, and so, I think, have you. Let's forget it until tomorrow. After all, since we can't change anything, let's at least have some fun. Want me to give you a ride in? I understand you were going to Cologne with some friends."

"Did you mention anything to them about this?"

"The people in the bus? No. They'd already left when I got here. Tired of waiting. Richter told me."

For a second I couldn't remember who Richter was, then I recalled the young man in gray and brown flannels at the reception desk.

"I'd be grateful if you could keep it quiet, maybe prevent it from getting into the papers. The bridge that collapsed a few years ago, and now a gate wasn't locked that should have been. It doesn't exactly help the reputation of the Lindwurm."

"I quite understand," said Ginster, shook hands again, got into his car and drove off.

We watched the car out of sight. Klausen hadn't introduced me nor had the inspector paid any attention to me. Perhaps he hadn't wanted to embarrass a guest. "Well," said Klausen, "I'm going to join them. Feel like coming along?"

I no longer felt any inclination whatsoever to mingle with a riotous crowd, but I did want to get away. I nodded.

Klausen drove a Porsche. He drove fast, going into the curves full speed, and once we had reached the Autobahn, weaving in and out of line, determined apparently to overtake every car ahead of us. "Do you always drive this fast?"

"Yes," he said. "It relaxes me to have to concentrate on it."

"How long did you know him?"

"Florian? Oh, about thirty years. I used to admire his early work. It was great."

"The Nazis didn't seem to think so?"

"What?"

"Didn't he have to leave Germany when they came to power? That's what he told me in Rome."

"The same old lie."

"Lie?"

"He didn't leave Germany until it was all over, and then he left because he was afraid the Allies wouldn't think very highly of a man who had achieved fame and fortune while his colleagues were being hounded, imprisoned or killed, and their work branded as *entartete Kunst*. Cultural Bolshevism, I think, is what you call it."

I couldn't recall the exact words Florian had used when he had said something about fame being a trap and had berated himself as a coward, but now they began to make sense.

"He did them all." Klausen took both hands from the wheel to describe a circle. "In stone, bronze, terra cotta—the whole gang. Officially exhibited and rewarded with the highest honors. He practically ruled the Academy, but not once did he lift a finger to help a colleague maintain his position, or contribute money when a faked passport was a matter of life or death, or even when the bare necessities of life were all that was needed. But, of course, thirty years later people have forgotten, or they don't want to remember, or they're just plain dead. Nobody around here is anxious to uncover *that* phase of our past. So he could get away with his story of emigration, and arouse admiration. And pity. In the end he may have believed it himself."

"I think he regretted it."

"I know. It was driving him out of his mind. That's why he came to the Lindwurm. For help."

"I don't understand."

I didn't. I lit a cigarette and waited for him to go on. I had found out long ago that silence can sometimes act as the strongest stimulant to make the other person talk.

"The man who owns the castle took a fancy to him and asked some of his friends to commission Florian to do statues for their gardens, or a piece they could donate, tax free, to a museum. It was Leise's idea, to keep the poor old fellow happy, a sort of therapy."

"I haven't met Dr. Leise."

"He's our resident psychiatrist, a very good man."

"You've got a resident psychiatrist at the Lindwurm?"

For the first time since I had met him, Klausen laughed. He sounded like a goat.

"Haven't you noticed? We have quite a few sick people at the Lindwurm, mostly cases of depression in varying degrees. We're very successful with them. The hotel facilities are a help. There's no forcing the patient to meet other people or take part in a normal social life if he isn't equal to it. But whenever he feels like it, all he has to do is open a door—on a healthy impulse—and an active life, with all the comforts anyone could possibly want, is at his disposal."

"But he hated you, didn't he?"

"Florian? Yes. I knew him too well."

"What was he accusing you of?"

"Oh." Klausen sighed. "He was referring to my experiments with animals. Transplants. He loved dogs and could never reconcile himself to the fact that research made such things necessary. Damn all sentimental fools anyway. And they're the first ones to yell for help when some baffling disease hits them."

"And you?" I asked. "What did you do under the Nazis?"

"I was lucky. I was able to exercise my profession. I applied my knowledge to those who needed it—the wounded, the dying. Mostly at the front. I didn't leave Germany, if that's what you mean. I didn't belong to any

63

underground organization either. I stayed because I loved Germany, always have, always will."

"Your country right or wrong."

"Yes." No passion colored his voice; he said it dryly, almost resignedly, like a man shrugging off an accusation. I had to respect his attitude.

Cologne, as every tourist knows, is a city of bridges, bridges of all architectural styles and designed for every kind of traffic—passenger trains, freight, cars, cyclists and pedestrians—all crossing the Rhine. Since I had no idea how many had been destroyed by us or blown up by the Germans to delay our approach, how many had been reconstructed or newly built, I couldn't really appreciate the effort and planning that had gone into the task of raising, literally from the ashes of war, this two thousand year old city. All I could do was look with enchantment across the broad stream with its countless docks, steamers, ferries, tugs, barges and boats, all of which we had seen behind us yesterday. Besides, on that ride, there had been other things on my mind.

Klausen glanced at his watch. "I usually make it to the bridge in half an hour." He seemed annoyed that our conversation had made him drive more slowly. I thought of yesterday evening again, when the short distance of thirty kilometers had seemed to take twice as long. Perhaps because Bettina had fallen asleep in the back of the car? Anyone asleep in my presence somehow makes time pass slowly.

We had to make several detours since some streets were closed to traffic because of the parades. To find a parking place turned out to be impossible. "Well, let's give up," said Klausen, and drove straight to the old city hall where he handed an attendant the key to his car and asked him to take care of it. By the reluctant way he peeled off a few notes from a wad, I realized with amusement that what he had "given up" was the hope of being able to save a large tip. To part with money seemed to hurt.

The crowd was staggering. A sea of people with masked, painted or bare faces. They broke around you like waves, they filled the lobby, they sat on the steps of the two staircases that swung up to the Festsaal, they barred your way everywhere. As far as I could see, the Guërzenich was a schizoid colossus. Gutted by our bombs in 1943, the fifteenth-century walls of this medieval festival building had been given a new interior, as modern as and not dissimilar in style from our own Lincoln Center—cold, functional, glittering with plexiglass lighting. The crowd outside had been too great for me to admire the bronze plated doors by Mataré, but I had seen enough of them to want to come back for a quieter look. In the foyer, though, I stopped Klausen and insisted on going over to peer through the metal openwork screen that separated the foyer from the ruin of the Church of St. Alban which, he explained, had been cleverly and most curiously incorporated in the rebuilt Guërzenich. In gray stone, Käthe Kollwitz's grieving parents, the grim inconsolable father, kneeling, arms crossed tensely in adamant implacability, opposite him the mother, arms crossed gently as a madonna, head bowed in a humbler grief, the austere old stones of the demolished church as background—the damnedest thing, I thought, to include in a building dedicated to revelry. I said as much to Klausen. "Yet somehow fitting, don't you think?" he said, "for those who should never become too gay."

A clown rubbed shoulders with me. He was wearing a little round white hat and something that reminded me of those dreadful bathing suits that were fashionable at the beginning of the century, white, with horizontal red stripes all around in a peppermint candy effect. For a moment I thought he was Inspector Ginster, enjoying himself at last, incognito under the heavy white paint smeared on his face instead of a mask, and like most of the clowns present, sporting a big red nose over his own.

"Did you lose my telephone number?"

It was Rudi.

"I didn't have any reason to call you."

"How did you get here?"

"I came with Dr. Klausen."

"I don't like to see anyone drive with him. He's a reckless driver."

"We got separated." Klausen stepped between me and the clown. "Not a good idea, with thousands of people milling around. Follow me. They're in the Isabellensaal."

It took us almost half an hour to get through to it. The noise, the smoke, the smell of perspiration, of wine, beer and liquor were suffocating. Last night at the Lindwurm I had enjoyed the whole thing, but that had been a small affair. The Isabellensaal was better. Only a few hundred guests filled it. Klausen evidently felt he had to continue to function as guide for he explained that the hall was named after the bride of the thirteenth-century emperor Friedrich II, an English princess who had given an unforgettably brilliant reception in Cologne. He then pointed to the windows, glazed in several shades of stain with modern plant motifs, designed by a man whose name I promptly forgot. But they were impressive, however remote in style from thirteenth-century receptions.

Klausen steered me to a table at the far end of the room. Bettina and the others had dined in the Cellar Restaurant in the basement, now they were drinking champagne. "We were just talking about you," said Gevern.

When we had been introduced in the courtyard, I hadn't been able to see his face clearly. It had been too dark. Now I was almost shocked to see that he was extraordinarily handsome, in a Teutonic way. Very blond, with thick, flaxen-white hair; blue eyes with an overcast of violet; a short strong nose and a broad, stubborn chin. But I had been right—except for a dimple in his left cheek, his face—or perhaps it was only the expression in his eyes—betrayed a total lack of humor. As he got up at our approach, I noticed how well he was built—tall yet sturdy—and he moved with assurance. Showing the whitest, most even row of teeth I had ever seen on a man who still possessed his own—and these quite obviously were—he went on, "We were wondering why you hadn't been drafted for combat in Vietnam." He sounded tipsy. "Anything wrong with you that was useful enough to keep you out of it?"

"There's nothing wrong with me," I told him. "I did my bit at the beginning."

"Volunteered?"

"Are you out of your mind?"

He caught on all right. "Wars have their own good purpose," he said. "They squash rebellions, take care of over-population, clear the air . . ."

"If you had been here in May, forty-three," said Klausen, setting down his glass which the waiter had just filled, "you wouldn't talk such rot. Because you wouldn't be here. Except for some outside walls, nothing was left standing. Clear the air . . . I'll say."

"Cologne should have been declared an open city."

"So should . . ." but Bettina interrupted Klausen. Quite

67

clearly she was anxious to prevent any trouble between the two men. "How is Florian?" she asked. "Did he calm down?"

Klausen gave me a quick look over the rim of his glass, then started to drink. I had the feeling that he didn't want to tell her, not yet at any rate. "He's dead," I said.

"Dead?"

Everything about her was suddenly in motion. She shifted in her seat, she reached for a cigarette, she shook her head, hunched her shoulders, only the pupils of her eyes remained strangely immobile. They didn't move, she didn't blink, not for quite some time; then they lost their stare, she threw back her head and addressed Klausen. "Please tell me."

"Well," Klausen reached into the pocket of his wide clown pants for a shiny leather case made for just three cigars. He held one to his right ear, rolling it a little between his fingers, then smelled it and lighted it slowly, deliberately. "He broke loose from the male nurse and climbed up the steps outside his window, the ones that lead to the parapet, and lost his footing."

Gevern's thin mouth curved into a smile. "What an enviable death. No fear, no premonition, no pain."

Then why don't you take those steps? I felt like saying. I didn't know why, but I loathed the fellow. I had always prided myself on not reacting with unreasonable emotion, so now I resented resenting him.

"You wouldn't ask me for a dance, would you, Mr. Waldron?" said Bettina. Obviously she wanted to get away from the conversation.

I had expected that as soon as we were away from the table, she would suggest going somewhere where we could be alone; but she really wanted to dance, so we did. She had a beautiful sense of rhythm and let herself be led easily, and when we separated and came together again, she invented motions and gestures the like of which I'd never seen before. She was a born dancer. During one of the moments when I was holding her close, I saw that her eyes were filled with tears.

"He meant a lot to you."

"Of course he did, and quite apart from what he did for me. He was a remarkable man."

Her reaction surprised me. I had taken her first response as the natural shock that comes with death, any death, in this case with the added horror of Florian's tragic fall. "Remarkable?" I repeated. "In what way?"

"I think anyone is remarkable who has the strength to admit he was wrong."

"Did he?"

"Yes."

"And you didn't mind that he was a collaborator?"

"How could I? How do I know what I'd do in a similar situation if I were that ambitious? He was a man in hell. Like so many of us."

"Not me."

Either she didn't hear me or didn't like my remark, anyway she said nothing.

"And he was crazy."

She shook her head. "He merely betrayed sometimes the fact that he couldn't live with himself. I always felt that one day he would commit suicide. But that he should do it in the place where he felt safest," she murmured, almost as if to herself.

"Why do you suppose he tried to make me leave?" I asked her. "You were there when he said, take the next train and all that."

"Perhaps because of me. He thinks—thought," she corrected herself, "that I'm poison."

"Are you?"

"To some men."

"Well he wasn't trying to save me from you because today, when I told him I had a date with you to go to the Guërzenich, he brightened up and wanted to come along."

Gevern suddenly clapped his hands against my ear. "Time to change partners." Without the slightest objection Bettina glided into his arms. I didn't return to our table. I walked out of the Isabellensaal, looked into some of the conference rooms on the same floor, which had been thrown open for private parties, and tried to find Rudi among the many clowns. A girl dressed from top to crotch in a plastic bottle—how the hell had they ever got her into it?—was passing for the world-famous Johannes Maria Farina Eau de Cologne and was a show stopper. Like one of those ships inside a bottle, which sailors work on for years, she was totally inaccessible except for her legs which were free and permitted her to walk around. Finally, unable to go upstairs to the Festsaal, which held over a thousand people, or downstairs, where I might have found something to eat, I went back to the Isabellensaal and found Bettina still dancing with Gevern. His rather obscene motions offended me. I decided it was my turn to clap hands, but he led Bettina away from me, and I could hear her arguing with him. Then she pushed him away and came over to me.

"He's jealous," I said, putting my arm around her.

"Most men are."

"Have you slept with him?"

"Yes."

"When?"

"Years ago."

First her honesty struck me as primitive, then as calculated. "What did you tell him?"

She was quick. "How we met? The truth. It turned out to have been a mistake. Stupid. But sometimes it bores me to have to think things up." She danced away from me. "It was suicide, wasn't it?"

I hadn't expected her to bring up Florian's death again. "I guess you can say so. He must have known that with the male nurse in pursuit he didn't have a chance."

"Then it couldn't have been an accident. It had to be suicide."

"Why is it so important to you, one way or another?"

"It just is."

"The suicidal person often creates the accident that leads to his death." I could feel her trembling violently. "What's the matter? What is it?"

"There have been too many accidents." Her voice was almost inaudible. "And it's always the people that I'm fond of who get killed."

It certainly was a macabre conversation for a carnival night and not at all like the "fun" the professor had led me to expect. "Who has been killed?"

She answered like someone thinking out loud. "Three of my friends, when the bridge collapsed. All the other guests had been warned that the bridge was unsafe and told to use the footpath to the road to pick up a bus."

"How do you know your friends weren't told?"

"I don't."

"Then why do you assume they weren't? Maybe they were reckless enough to take a chance."

She shook her head.

"Wasn't there a sign or something?"

"There was. Posted to the left of the bridge. But there

71

also was a child, a little boy who took it down and made a kite of it, just a little while before they crossed over."

"That's quite a coincidence, yet things like that happen."

"And Lisa, one of the few close friends I had—we studied photography together—she died of an appendectomy. It's true, she complained of not feeling well when I invited her to spend a week with me at the Lindwurm, and she was running a fever next day. I asked Klausen to have a look at her, and he took her straight down to the hospital wing. He's an excellent surgeon. He said later that the appendix was perforated and she couldn't be saved."

Suddenly the foul mood I had been in ever since Klausen had so brutally tried to stop Florian from joining us turned into a fit of real temper. "Bettina," I said, "the best doctor in the world is powerless when it's too late. Your friend should probably have seen a doctor before she went on a holiday."

She didn't answer. Her face tense, she nevertheless tried to force a smile which made her look so pathetic, I felt sorry for her. My mood worsened. "Are you aware of what you are insinuating?"

Her lips parted with a sudden breathlessness. "Don't," she whispered, "Don't say it."

I said it. "Murder."

The stare that had fixed her pupils momentarily on hearing of the professor's death came back to her eyes. She turned her head away. "But that's exactly what you're hinting," I went on mercilessly, "that all the events you've mentioned weren't accidents but only made to look like accidents. Is that what fills you with such anxiety?"

She swallowed several times, hard and as if painfully, but she remained silent. I danced her to the door of the Isabellensaal, hoping that now the foyer might be less crowded and we could get out for a little fresh air. But it was just as crowded out there, so, leaning closer to her in order to make myself heard above the din of music and voices and the blowing of whistles, I spoke firmly.

"First of all, you have no proof, and without it you can't make me believe that just because a young girl didn't survive an appendectomy, someone was trying to murder her. At best you can accuse Klausen of having slipped up in one way or another. And the drawbridge collapsing. Other bridges have collapsed with hundreds of cars on them. Here the guests were warned, a sign was posted. A little boy came along with nothing on his mind but to make a kite, and he used the sign. How can you classify anything like that as murder? Just because friends of yours happened to be in the car? It could have been any other car with people in it who meant nothing to you. And Florian. You yourself said he couldn't live with himself. A man can reach a point when he is so filled with contempt for himself that he'll do anything to escape it. And there is only one escape from oneself—death. The professor had his heart set on going to the Guërzenich with us, I have no idea why, but suddenly it seemed all-important to him. And he was stopped. It may have been the last straw."

"You're right," she said. "Quite possibly I'm not sane either. The way I always imagine . . ."

A circle of dancers surrounded us, drawing closer and closer until Bettina and I were pressed so tightly together, we could hardly breathe. It seemed to afford everyone but us great amusement. They promised to set us free if we would join hands with them. We did, and a moment later I heard Bettina laugh gaily, as if she didn't have a worry in the world. A neurotic, I thought, possibly even a nympho, occupied solely with herself, associating everything that happens with herself.

I left the circle and again went in search of Rudi. At last I managed to work my way up the stairs to the Festsaal, which was crowded to capacity. Again there were innumerable clowns, many costumed in tight-fitting red and white striped suits, some in elaborately sewn, multicolored rags and patches, with all sorts of different colored hats and painted faces. The clown seemed to be the symbol of Cologne's carnival. I had always loved clowns until I had run into one who was desperately sick with TB and worrying what would happen to his wife and children when he couldn't make a living any more. But I had never been able to stop wondering what kind of a man was hiding behind the ridiculous costume and the zany pretense of idiocy with which they entertained their audiences. By now, most of the people had removed their masks and many had wiped off the paint from their faces to let the skin breathe in the exhausting heat issuing from so many bodies worn out with frenetic dancing and hot with alcohol. But I couldn't see Rudi anywhere.

I would never have made it back to the lower foyer if a group dressed as Red Sparks, in memory of the former town regiment, hadn't noticed my predicament. They lifted me up and yelled at the top of their lungs to their comrades standing below, to pass me on; that was how I was catapulted down the next flight of stairs, passed like a football from hand to hand amid laughter and loud applause from the onlookers. But there was no Rudi in the crowded Cellar Restaurant either, nor the remotest chance of finding a seat or getting something to eat. Every chair was taken.

I had been told that I would find buffets on every floor,

but seen none, possibly because of the crowds beleaguering them, and I was much too worn out at this point to stand in line if I found one. Everything was getting on my nerves. I made for the exit. I didn't even glance at the handles of the doors which the professor had said were works of art I shouldn't miss. That they occurred to me at all annoyed me, because I wasn't really thinking of them but of the professor, and I didn't want to think about him. Yet I couldn't control my mind. I kept seeing him at the morgue, in one of those drawers that are kept under refrigeration. He had been so grateful when I had said he could come along, and had said he didn't want to lose track of me. Well, he'd lost track of me all right, poor devil.

Quite a few people were leaving, some were still arriving. It took me five minutes to find an empty spot to lean against, a wall of some house or other, or perhaps it was still a wall of the huge Guërzenich building. My shoulders against it felt good. I lit a cigarette. The air was damp, just as it had been last night when I had talked to him in the courtyard. The hell with it!

"There you are." It was Gevern. "I've been looking for you everywhere."

"Why?" Of all persons I could think of, I could have done best without him.

"To apologize."

"Whatever for?"

"Bettina said I was rude."

"Forget it."

I saw a taxi pull up and drop some people. I was tired of it all; in fact, I couldn't fathom why I'd ever thought it would be fun to mill around with a lot of people who considered it their duty to dress up and be wildly gay, just to preserve a century-old tradition of revelry. Suddenly it all seemed terribly forced, with an effect quite opposite from the one intended. There were plenty of trains and planes out of Cologne. After all, its very central location in the heart of Europe was what had made it so important to the Romans. It was in many respects the hub of Europe.

I hailed the taxi. If I called the Lindwurm from the station, they would certainly send my things down to me, and the bill. A hotel of such magnificence was surely prepared to cater to that sort of whim, even be used to such capricious behavior on the part of its guests. But when I felt automatically for my passport, it wasn't there, nor was my cash. I must have made some sort of noise, for Gevern asked, concern in his voice, "Anything wrong?"

I told him, "My passport, my cash . . . they're gone." But he wasn't surprised that I'd been robbed. "I take it pickpockets don't exist in America," he said, irony in his voice again, but he cut it out immediately. "Your passport will probably turn up. The cash . . ." He shrugged. "I hope it wasn't much."

"For me quite enough."

"Well, we'd better report it."

"Sorry," I told the taxi driver. "I've changed my mind." Contrary to Klausen, Gevern turned out to be generous, unnecessarily so in my opinion, for the driver could pick up as many fares as he wanted. I hadn't done him out of a thing, still Gevern tipped him for holding the cab.

I went back into the Guërzenich with him. We told some tired guy in a little office what had happened, then, paradoxically, since I was no longer master of my fate until I had my passport back, I relaxed and started to enjoy myself, actually for the first time that evening. I still couldn't find Bettina anywhere, so I danced with whoever looked danceable and kissed quite a few girls, all of them pretty and none of them refusing. Even if you were married or going steady, kissing was *de rigeur*. The only one miserable was the girl in the Eau de Cologne bottle. She didn't want to break it open until the prize for the best costume had been voted for, and she was missing all the fun of dancing close and could talk audibly only when somebody uncorked her. Then her voice was startling, like the voice of someone trapped at the bottom of a well.

"It seemed such a good idea," she mourned. "My husband's. And maybe it was—for him. The sadist! Getting me into this outfit so's he wouldn't have to worry about anybody making a pass at me, while he . . ." But long before the end she had had enough of her imprisonment; the first prize for the most original costume no longer seemed important. "Get me out of this," she yelled, and it sounded like a foghorn. "I don't care how much it cost to have this damn thing soldered around me. I've slept in it, I've eaten in it, I can't stand it another minute! Get me out!" And we had a hell of a good time cracking her open with anything that came in handy.

It was she who finally got me some food. Having been starved herself for hours on end, she had the uncanny sense of a woman and found a way to one of the buffets. Her name was Elinor. I forgot her the moment I had eaten. At some time or other after that, Gevern came along and dragged me off to a restaurant that was famous for a special fish soup, very hot and spicy. Beer was served but no coffee. I must have been as drunk as the others when we finally climbed into a car, Dr. Klausen, Gevern, Bettina—where had she come from suddenly?—and some little runt who had attached himself to us. I didn't recall when. It was only when the car stopped in the courtyard of the Lindwurm that

I recognized the driver—Rudi, in a brown uniform this time, and a visored cap. As I stumbled out of the car he put a hand under my arm. "First everyone wants me to leave, now they seem determined to keep me here," I mumbled. "What are you doing in that outfit?"

"I'm driving for the Lindwurm tonight. I do when they're short of drivers." He let me go. "I want to see you tomorrow," he said. "Meet me at the third clearing, where they feed the deer. Around three o'clock." In the condition I was in, I found nothing odd in his request.

I went up to my room and straight into the bathroom. I was drunk and I knew it. I put a finger in my mouth, tickled my throat and was at once violently relieved of champagne, beer, cognac, a famous Rhine wine and more of the same. I brushed my teeth, I took a cold shower. When I made for bed, my teeth were chattering. The bed was occupied. Bettina was sitting in it, drinking coffee. "Instant," she said.

"Where did you find it?"

She pointed to a little gadget you had to stick into water to make it boil, and a small jar of instant coffee. "I always carry it along."

"You're adorable."

The curtains had been drawn, but I pulled one back and opened the window to let in some fresh air. No moon. The night was black. It made the coffee taste hotter and better than it actually was. We drank it in silence, she in my bed, I in the comfortable chair with the footrest. Again she seemed irresistible. When I kissed her she didn't draw away.

"You like making love, don't you?"

"Yes. It makes me feel quiet and alive at the same time."

"With any man?"

"Don't be stupid."

"What about Gevern?"

A moment's hesitation, then she said, "He threatened to kill me if I didn't."

"Oh come on!"

"It's true."

"Nonsense. You chose to believe it because you wanted . . ."

"No," she said quietly, "I didn't believe it. I thought he was crazy. But then he veered the car from our lane and straight into the truck."

Rudi had said, "That whole business . . . her car accident . . . she never would talk about it." But here she was, talking about it simply, easily.

"He was thrown clear," she said, in the same quiet voice. "The driver of the truck died of his injuries and I was badly hurt."

With all my imagination I simply couldn't conceive of a man wanting one particular woman so fanatically that he would risk not only her death but his own as well. It happened of course, among those ruled insane by the courts. Criminally insane. "He must have been mad."

"It was when I was up and about again that I slept with him," Bettina said, and after a moment's silence, "don't ask me why, but certainly not because I wanted to." She was lying on her right side, her eyes were closed. She didn't open them as she went on talking. "He's always been insanely jealous."

"Who is he jealous of?"

Her blond hair, free of its ribbon, fell loose around her shoulders. It reminded me of Gevern's hair, and I could see them lying together. I pushed my coffee aside and reached for the bottle of Scotch which, as on the night before, had been set out with ice and glasses on a tray near my bed. Suddenly she sighed, a deep sigh, more like a moan. "He's jealous of my uncle."

"Your uncle? I don't get it."

"He isn't actually my uncle. It's a hangover from childhood that I call him uncle. He's a second cousin of my father's, and he's much older than I."

"How old?"

She smiled, almost tenderly. "He's cagey about his age. I think he's in his early sixties."

"And you're twenty-three?"

"Will be, next month." She opened her eyes. "The difference in age wouldn't bother me. Europeans don't pay as much attention to age as Americans. It wouldn't bother me at all, if I loved him." She sat up in bed. "If I really loved him."

"If I'm to make head or tail of this," I told her, "you're simply going to have to do some explaining."

"But he loves me. He always has. Since I was a child. He wants to marry me as soon as . . ."

"Now wait a minute. Nobody can force you to marry anyone you don't love or want to marry."

"He's been so good to me," she said. "I know that sounds feeble, but I can't describe how good." She spread her hands, palms outward. "You see, my father and mother died in a plane crash when I was six. My grandmother would have liked to take care of me, but she was ailing. There were an aunt and uncle who had never wanted children. I can remember quite clearly how relieved I was when Hannes stepped in. He was my favorite."

A few hours ago I had berated her when she had complained that everybody she loved got killed; now, suddenly,

I felt sympathy for her. No wonder she had developed a complex about the death of people she was fond of.

"From then on he took care of me. And in a bachelor household it couldn't have been easy to have a lively six-year-old tearing around the place, but he had endless patience, and understanding that went far beyond the usual sympathy for a lonely child."

"Bachelor?"

"I should have said widower. His wife died very soon after they were married. Anyway, I was a pest." Memory made her laugh. "I rebelled against all the traditions. And believe me, Brazil has some ridiculous ones."

She certainly had a gift for making you stay awake when you had theoretically retired for the night. "Brazil? Did you live in Brazil?"

"I was born there. The first von Altens settled in Pôrto Alegre around 1825. My father was German, my mother English. They were what's called today "the beautiful people." But they weren't really interested in cattle raising. Mama was a great sport. She went up the Amazon as far as it was possible for a woman to go, with just some Maku Indians. She wasn't afraid of anything, not even snakes. Father was more interested in art. They traveled a lot. But I loved Santa Clara. I think I knew the hacienda better than either of them. I much preferred to stay there than be dragged through museums or live in hotels. Odd, isn't it, that later I developed Papa's passion for art, but at the time an outdoor life meant everything to me. And then there was Domenico, a gaucho. He let me ride in front of him. He taught me everything I know about horses, cattle, pasture land."

The delicious naked woman in my bed disappeared and became a sentimental little girl reveling in the past. I had few memories of my father and mother. By the time I was three they were divorced, and for convenience sake had stored me away with my grandparents.

Bettina went on talking. " 'Never marry a German,' my mother used to say when she was exasperated. 'They're respectable, they can be noble, but they're unrealistic dreamers. And sometimes they're as exaggerated as their vision of themselves.' That's in her diary. And there I was at ten or eleven, refusing to go to church because I couldn't believe anything that was being preached. It seemed so unreal. I didn't realize that so many people went simply as a gesture."

At that age I had been more obedient. For my grandparents' sake I had done what they asked of me. I had hurt them only much later, by dropping out of college, by going against so much of what they had expected of me. "Go on."

Bettina rubbed her nose. "Where was I?"

"Rebelling against the way you were being raised."

"Oh yes. Well, I never owned a dress until I was ten. Then things began to change. Uncle Hannes sent me to a convent school, near Pôrto Alegre, but living with nuns just didn't work out. Not for me. Imagine, I couldn't get into a bathtub naked. I had to keep on my panties and bring a shirt along to cover the upper part of my body. I think I decided then that when I was grown up I wouldn't wear clothes but run around nude."

"You're doing all right," I told her. "I'd say they succeeded fairly well in killing your inhibitions."

"Well, it didn't last long. Next we moved into our townhouse and I had a German governess and went to day school. That was all right. But oh, the house! It was so dreary, and so big. So many empty rooms, and just a little garden. It stood in what was called "the German quarter." Strange, how they stick together, the Germans I mean, and take practically no part in Brazilian life, except of course when it comes to business, or on official occasions. I might just as well have been brought up in Germany. The worst thing was that even on holidays I wasn't allowed to go back to Santa Clara. I went just once, but then it was no good. Domenico had died, most of the old hands were gone, those who were left treated me with a formal respect, and their children and I had lost everything we'd had in common. Then Hannes fell from his horse, a stallion, a huge beast—I forget how many hands it stood. He broke his neck and Hannes almost did. He was terribly sick for a long time. His nose was never quite the same after his operation. Soon after that, he sent me away. To a *pensionat*. Here in Cologne. Sooner or later all girls in Brazil are entered in European schools, but I was younger than most. I didn't want to go at first. Later I didn't want to go back. I had made friends here and I knew hardly anyone in Pôrto Alegre. But he insisted that I come back for all my vacations. Not to lose touch, was how he put it."

She left the bed and started to walk up and down the room, apparently completely unaware that she was naked. For a while she said nothing, then, with a gesture that I had begun to recognize as typical of her when she had made up her mind about something, she threw back her head and said, "And then there came the day—I was fourteen—when he asked me to come and sit on his lap. I had often sat on his lap and always felt comfortable and sheltered in his arms. I can't remember what we were talking about, but I think it was when I told him that he really should marry again that he said, when the time for that came, he was going to marry me. And suddenly he kissed me. I mean, really kissed me. Then he apologized and went back to whatever he'd been doing at his desk."

I realized with surprise that I was more of a square than I had thought. The vision of a father, or a man with the responsibilities of a father, making love to his young daughter went against the grain. "Did it frighten you?"

Bettina shook her head. "I was startled. On the one hand I found it rather silly that a grown man should behave that way; on the other I was flattered to be taken seriously as a woman. At that age! And that he wanted to marry me." She laughed. "After all, it was my first proposal. No, I guess I was intrigued. Anyway, it stuck in my mind, a puzzling thing, but I can't say that it bothered me too much. When I came home for my next vacation he was outraged because somebody had written to him that I was fooling around with a boy—but to be scolded for something like that seemed quite normal. All my friends were in the same boat."

"So he let you go to Europe but kept you under the same strict surveillance as in Brazil, is that it?"

"Quite. And when I found out, I began to think up tricks. Like in a game."

"Did he ever try to make love to you again?"

"No. But when I think back, of his letters, they were rather like love letters. He wrote regularly, once a week, and always told me how much I had meant to him during the past years and that I was going to grow up to be a beautiful woman; that sort of thing, the way a father might write to his daughter—at least that's what I thought—full of loving advice, asking me to please tell him everything because he was interested in everything I thought or did."

"Did you?"

"Not always the truth. Sometimes I made up things I thought he would enjoy. One should never write letters at night, when one is lonely. But that was usually when I wrote to him. And when I thought of that old house with him all alone in it. You see, Hannes didn't come to Brazil until after the war, and he never made any close friends, certainly not among the Brazilians. Just a few old men. Germans. They play chess a lot. Sometimes they make music, pretty poor music, or just sit around talking."

"Didn't you say he was in his sixties? I would think that's an age where you can begin to take it easy." She had made so many things come clear, but this "uncle" I just couldn't see. "What does he look like?" I asked.

She cocked her head to one side a little. "Johannes Bolte?" And after the briefest pause, "Come to think of it—you're a bit like him. You've got the same narrow face and high forehead, and your nose is rather like his was before he broke it. And neither of you seem to have any real goal in life. His is so idle, with no real purpose. He says he's writing his memoirs. I always thought that was something people did when they considered their lives finished. Well anyway, to get back to us—I guess I must have sounded more loving than I felt, and he misunderstood. The last time I saw him, at Christmas, he asked me officially to marry him. He looked so crestfallen when I said no, that I had to assure him over and over again there was nobody else, and that I would think it over."

"What is there to think over? You don't love him, you don't want to be the wife of an old man, you want to choose your own husband."

"It's not as simple as that." Her expression betrayed her distress over the situation. "If only I didn't feel so indebted to him. I respect him for the man he is—proud, gallant, in spite of the fact that he was bitterly hurt by everything that has happened to Germany."

"So were millions of others."

"I know. But his country meant everything to him. The division of Germany nearly killed him."

"What did he expect?"

"I don't know. I only know he identifies with Germany, all true German patriots do, and suffer accordingly. And that it remains divided is something he simply can't adjust to."

"And you think you can alleviate his unhappiness by marrying him?"

"Things might be less painful for him. I mean, I think I could prove to him that there are other things in life than nursing a wound. I could distract him from politics, and that's something he needs. The world isn't very pretty right now, but it's all the world we have, and I think with me at his side he could learn to enjoy himself again. We could travel. He hasn't been out of Brazil for over twenty years. Just sitting there and brooding, and for company usually people who, like him, foresaw the disaster and therefore resent Germany's fate even more."

"Well, if you want to sacrifice yourself, go ahead."

"I don't want to sacrifice myself. I'm not the sacrificial type." She paused.

"You have a very chronological mind," I said dryly, "which is rare in a woman. But what about Gevern? Haven't we lost track of him?"

"Günther Gevern," she said, and for a moment closed her eyes as if looking into herself for preciser memory. "He was simply there one day when I came back from Europe for summer vacation. I couldn't remember that Hannes had ever mentioned him but he said he had, and that I must have forgotten about the nephew he'd been worrying about for years."

"Worrying about? Why?"

"It came back to me then that he had told me about a little boy—his sister's son—who had been lost when the Russians entered Berlin. Apparently for years no one knew where he was until some old friend of Hannes's traced him and notified Hannes, and Hannes arranged for Günther to come to Brazil, and there he was, behaving as if the house were his. At first I was terribly jealous and afraid Hannes would lose all interest in me, and for a while I think he did. He's a man who should have had a son, someone he could bring up in the old traditions of Fatherland, and all that. Anyway, later . . ."

She paused. "Later?" I asked, when she turned her head away, apparently unwilling to say more. But I was wrong. She answered without hesitation, "It was fun to have an older brother who took me places I couldn't have gone to alone. And he had such an air about him. Everybody admired him. He always managed to get the best place, the best table, the quickest service, you know, that sort of fellow. And then he fell in love with me."

"Was this before or after your uncle told you he wanted to marry you?"

"After. I was sixteen when Günther came to Brazil, and I told him that if I ever married anybody, it would be Hannes. And he was furious. Funny, he adores Hannes, worships him, but that didn't seem to prevent him from wanting me."

I could see her, a young girl growing into a woman, naïvely, subconsciously or perhaps with the innate bitchiness of puberty, enjoying being desired by two men, one old and impressive, the other young and impressed by her, two men who were also bound to each other. "But Hannes didn't seem to mind at all that Günther was flirting with me." She shook her head. "I've never understood it. Once in a while he'd turn up in Cologne because Hannes had asked him to look me up. And then it happened."

"What happened?"

"The accident."

She was far away again. "Forget it," I told her, "and come here."

She came into my arms like a child looking for warmth and understanding. Warmth I could give her, but understanding? Not really. I made love to her and gradually aroused her response. When I finally reached for a cigarette, she struck a match for me, oddly polite, but then kept it between her fingers, staring at the flame, until I said, "You'll burn yourself." Then she dropped it in the ashtray. I took her hand and kissed it. It was the first tender gesture on my part. I shouldn't have made it, for suddenly she said, "Would you marry me?"

I swallowed some smoke, coughed, and stupidly echoed her words, "Marry you?"

"We could run off together. I know my way around here. Rudi would meet us and drive us anywhere we want."

I stared at her. It was the third proposal I'd received, and like the others it gave me gooseflesh. "Marriage is not on my calendar. Sorry."

"I didn't think it was."

"Then why ask? You don't want to mess up your life just because you enjoy sleeping with a man."

"You misunderstood," she said. "You wouldn't have to live with me."

I finally caught on. "Christ, I don't understand you. For over half an hour you go on and on about your uncle, how indebted you are to him, how you don't want to hurt him,

88

and then . . . you don't think it would hurt him if you ran off with a perfect stranger."

"He might understand an impulse better. After all, a girl can fall in love suddenly and decide to elope. It might be easier than going back to Brazil and saying no again."

"Then don't go back."

"I don't want to." She got up, reached for her robe, put it on. A gloriously wild design. It didn't quite reach her knees. "I was planning to go back to Paris. I have a studio there, and I have work to do, but all that's changed now. Hannes has to have an operation that can't be postponed. I think I should be there."

"Did he ask you to come?"

She shook her head. "No. He's always been very considerate not to spoil any plans I have. He didn't even want me to know."

"Then how do you know?"

"Gevern told me. He came over with some papers for me to sign, and finally came out with it. Of course he's in a hurry to get back, particularly since we can't get a direct flight from here."

"I can't understand how you can bear to be with him after what you told me."

"Unless I explain to Hannes what I have against Günther, he wouldn't understand. And how can I tell him? They adore each other. Good night, Drew. Sleep well."

She gathered up her things and was gone before I could kiss her good-by.

When I awoke, I felt drowsy. This rarely happened. Normally all sleepiness left me even before I opened my eyes. I've never been one to turn around again for an extra couple of minutes. Usually I obey the first reaction of my body by getting out of bed at once and taking a cold shower, even if it's too early to start the day. I react in the same way to fatigue. Once my bones tell me they want to relax, I give in to them. But right then I didn't feel the slightest desire to rise and go through the customary ritual of a cold shower and, if possible, a brisk walk or some setting-up exercises, followed by a hearty breakfast. My lids felt as if a couple of twin weights were resting on them, and I had the disagreeable sensation of being hot one moment, cold the next. I also felt slightly nauseated, and there was a nasty stabbing pain in my chest, on the right side. Breathing hurt. Gingerly I probed the sore spot but could feel nothing. Still the pain persisted.

I touched my forehead to feel if I had a fever, but what I touched wasn't my skin but some kind of material, and the second my fingers began to probe it, a voice said, "Don't." I had never heard the voice before. A female voice. In spite of its gentleness, it had an authoritative ring. I opened my eyes and looked in the direction from which the voice had come. A woman, dressed in white. A big woman with heavy breasts but surprisingly thin legs. I watched her approach my bed, strangely satisfied that she should walk as I had expected her to, lightfootedly and gracefully. Just the same,

I decided she wasn't real but part of a dream I was remembering. The room wasn't real either, about twelve-by-twelve, with two heavily curtained windows. It was furnished in ultra-modern style, somewhat like the rooms you see on exhibition to show the latest trends in furniture—a wide, white, blown-up couch with a glass table in front of it and a couple of black leather chairs on chrome legs. There was a lot of chrome or stainless steel, around lamps, door handles, a rather high table next to my bed, everything was utterly unexpected and utterly strange.

"Where am I?"

She took no cognizance of my question. "You mustn't touch the bandages," she said. "Under no circumstances must you touch the bandages."

Her words had the opposite effect on me. They made me feel my forehead again. The material I had touched before turned out magically to be gauze. The last time I had felt the ominous texture was years ago. My patrol had been ambushed and the medic bending over me had assured me it was nothing; the bullet had just grazed me. It's nothing, I thought now as I had thought then, and started to smile. It hurt. It hurt to smile. The woman in white moved toward me. She took my pulse. "Is your throat dry? Would you like something to drink?" She picked up a glass of what looked like water, with a bent straw in it.

I leaned back. "Where am I? What happened? Why is my face bandaged?"

"You're at the Lindwurm."

At the Lindwurm, of course. That was where I had finally got a room after they had lost my reservation at the Dom in Cologne. Feldman, the reception clerk, had suggested to Bettina that he'd call what I had thought would be a modest country inn.

"Then why am I not in my room? I had a room in the South Tower. I . . ."

"Don't get excited, please. This is one of the best rooms we have in the hospital. It faces south, which at this time of the year . . ."

To hell with her! As if at this point I could be interested in what direction the room faced. And to hell with me for having forgotten that the Lindwurm was hospital and hotel combined.

"Why am I here? For Christ's sake, woman, can't you understand plain German? *What happened?*"

"My name is Elly," she said. "Sister Elly. I do not like to be called 'woman.' I am accustomed to being treated with respect. I am a registered nurse."

"Then behave like one and don't aggravate the patient. Tell me why I'm here and not in my room."

"I do not know," she replied, stressing every word, probably to make it sound more convincing.

I sat up. I moved my head. When I moved it there was pain. The pain increased, became sharper, like a knife inserted into the nape of my neck. I lay back, momentarily defeated. "Why don't you know?"

"Nurses aren't told everything. All I know is that you were in a car accident."

A car accident? When had I been in a car? In what car? Whose car? Who had been driving?

She was taking a pill out of a small bottle. "Please swallow this. It will help you to sleep."

I didn't want to sleep. I shook my head. And regretted it. It hurt to smile. It was only logical that a rather violent neck movement would be worse. Still, I managed to say, "I don't want a pill. Give me a shot of Scotch."

"Sorry. I'll have to ask Dr. Klausen's permission first."

Dr. Klausen? He too had escaped my memory. I had seen him last in the car in which Rudi had driven us from the fish restaurant in Cologne back to the Lindwurm. Or had I? "Well, call him."

"Call Dr. Klausen?"

The surprise in her voice surprised me. "He's the doctor here, isn't he?"

"Yes, and he'll be coming in, but not at this time."

"I have no idea what time it is." Cautiously I lifted my left arm to look at my watch. To lift my arm didn't hurt, but my watch was gone. Suddenly I remembered that my passport and cash were gone too. For a moment I didn't care what time it was, but she told me anyhow. "Almost five o'clock. A.M. Unless his presence is absolutely necessary, he can't be disturbed. He'll be doing his rounds at seven."

There was indignation in the way she let me know that a doctor's attention wasn't necessary, a fact that should have reassured me rather than added to my nervousness, as it did. Anyhow, I had no intention of waiting two more hours to find out what was wrong with me. "If you don't call him, I will."

I swung my legs out of bed, in total disregard of the stabbing pains in my rib cage, but she was there, quickly, pushing me back. "You must be quiet."

"Only if you call Dr. Klausen."

She shook her head, the little scene was played over, I swinging my legs out and onto the floor, she trying to make me lie back. "Look," I said, "I'm stronger than you are, and I don't want to hurt you."

"Will you please do as I say?" Her voice rose with excitement, mine with frustration. Together they were apparently heard, for the door to my room opened; Schlau, the male nurse, came in. "Need any help, Sister Elly?"

He seemed even more of a giant than when I had seen him first in the courtyard. Actually, though, he wasn't taller than I. What made him appear so oversized was the shape of his body—a solid piece of flesh with no waistline or curves to interrupt the mass; and the way he held himself, arms close to his sides. His heavy legs, their combined width the same as that of his trunk, added to the impression of his being a block of wood rather than human. In comparison, his head was small, too small, and was perched on his broad shoulders like the dot on an *i*. And it all didn't go with his name, Schlau, which means "sly," smart-sly, in German, and which would lead you to expect a frail torso and little physical strength. Seeing him standing there I recalled the brute force with which he had picked up the professor and carried him into the Lindwurm. All ambition to see Klausen and find out what had put me in the hospital wing of the Lindwurm left me, fast, and I lay back meekly.

"Thank you, Schlau," said Sister Elly, and smiling at me with false joviality, she added, "We promise to be quiet now and go back to sleep, don't we?"

"We do," I said furiously, and closed my eyes.

So there I lay, pretending to have fallen asleep again, longing for sleep which simply wouldn't come. For some time I was able to think of nothing but what the nurse had said, that I had been in a car accident. I forced myself to repeat the words over and over again, "Car accident . . . car accident . . ." hoping they would somehow crystallize into a definite picture, but after a while they became absolutely meaningless. I might just as well have murmured eenie, meenie, minie mo to myself. All the while the nurse sat there, half slumped in her chair, watching me, although she was pretending to be concentrating on her knitting. For a long time the soft rapid clatter of her needles was the only sound to be heard. At some time or other it must have lulled me to sleep, for I didn't notice her getting up and coming over to my bed. "Six o'clock," she told me, with the horrid gaiety people simulate when they want to disturb you. "Time to wash and get ourselves ready. I'll help you if you want me to."

"This not being Japan," I said, "I'd rather do it myself."

She was much too obtuse to get my insinuation that if she had been a lovely Japanese girl in a bathhouse, I'd have leapt at the offer, but she smiled and started to run my tub. When it was half full, she turned off the faucet, nodded and closed the door.

As soon as she had gone I went to the washbasin and stared at myself in the mirror. I looked like a man wearing a ski mask made of white bandages and open at the top, leaving the hair free. Creepy. I hadn't braced myself for the shock, and a shock it certainly was. I took off the coarse hospital gown and saw that my right side was badly bruised. Having discovered the cause of the pain there, I tried to forget it. I washed, taking my time. When I opened the door, Sister Elly was waiting for me and offered me her arm. I took it only when I was halfway across the room, surprised to find I needed it.

My bed had been made and cranked up high so that I had to use the footstool in front of it. That it felt good to be back in bed came as another shock. Like everybody else, I hated the idea of being laid up, even for a short time. I tried to assure myself that nothing could be seriously wrong with me, or, as the nurse had said, Dr. Klausen would have been in to see me before this. Breakfast came, the same breakfast I had ordered on my first day at the Lindwurm, cold fresh orange juice, strong coffee, eggs sunny side up. They must take notes, I decided, of what their guests order. Soon after

I had finished, another nurse stuck her head in the door. A pleasant voice asked if I felt all right. Sister Elly answered for me, rather sharply, "We do."

"Who is she?" I asked.

"The Floater. Now there's someone nosy . . ."

Muted noises in the corridor, trays being put away, the swishing of some electric gadget or other, a chair being pushed, and then steps. I listened to their soft tread. Since childhood I had usually been able to tell who was coming by the sound of their steps. Klausen, like a dancer, put his full weight on his toes first, then let the foot slide forward onto his heels. He was coming closer. At my door he stopped. I could hear him give an order to someone in the passage, then he came in.

I don't know what I had expected him to look like. I had never given a thought to what kind of face might have been hiding under the stark white paint of his clown mask. But I saw that he was a much older man than I had assumed, though why I had thought of him as young, I couldn't tell. Perhaps because of his voice. It was a strange, very narrow face that reminded me of a portrait Bosch might have drawn, but his strong hooked nose and receding chin also brought a bird's face to mind, an eagle's. It must have taken a lot of time and effort and layers of make-up to camouflage those strong features. He was completely bald, the skin of his pate shiny, as if it had been waxed. His eyes were heavily lidded, with such deep shadows underneath them, that I suspected him of suffering from a kidney ailment.

"Well," I said, "at last. You're lucky I didn't go mad during the last two hours."

"Why should you have gone mad?"

"Put yourself in my place. I wake up. I find myself in a hospital room. I'm told I've been in an accident and then

I'm not allowed to talk to the one person who might give me an explanation. Christ, I've never wanted to talk to anyone so badly."

"Why didn't you have me called?"

"Why didn't I have you called? Jesus! You don't seem to know the regulations here. I gave up struggling with Sister Elly only because I didn't want to be knocked out by Schlau."

"Schlau?" Klausen frowned. "Schlau had no business in your room. Why did he come in, Sister?"

I took a childish pleasure in watching her face grow pink, then red. "The patient became so violent, Schlau must have heard the noise and . . ."

"Why wasn't I called?"

She began to stutter. "But Herr Professor, perhaps Herr Professor remembers that he gave strict orders not to be disturbed."

"I also gave orders to wake me at once should Mr. Waldron unexpectedly come to."

Suddenly I had had enough of reprimands and justifications. "She told me I was in a car accident."

"You were," said Klausen. He motioned to the nurse to leave us alone and she went out, shaking her head over the insults she had had to suffer.

"How could I have been in an accident when I can't even remember having been in a car?"

"You can't?"

"No," I said uneasily. "Although for two hours now I've been trying to recall what I did after I watched Miss von Alten and Mr. Gevern leave the Lindwurm together."

"Sometimes after a complete anesthesia, the patient suffers a lack of memory. That happens. It will come back to you, all of it. Don't worry."

"What do you know about it?"

"Not very much. Just what the clerk told me. According to him you wanted to go to Cologne to see if your passport had been turned in. You asked him to call a taxi. He explained that this wasn't necessary, that there were always two or three drive-yourself cars on the premises."

His words awoke a dim recollection of me standing at some window or other, watching Bettina, assisted by Gevern, climbing into the brown Volkswagen bus. Then, quite unexpectedly, I could remember the feeling of rage that had swept through me, rage directed at Gevern, but also at Bettina and the infantile attitude with which she faced her problems. Yes, I had been worried about the disappearance of my passport and the loss of almost three hundred dollars in cash. I had gone downstairs and talked to Richter. But had I asked for a cab?

"I remember asking Richter to put through a call for me," I said, "but not that I wanted a car."

"Well, it's a fact that you drove off in one of the Lindwurm cars. Several people saw you trying it out in the courtyard to get the hang of the gear shift."

All right then, I *had* taken a car to drive to Cologne. "What time did I leave here?"

"In the early afternoon, after lunch, around two, I believe."

There was no further penetrating the blank surrounding my actions, no memory of passport inquiries. And the accident itself. "What sort of accident did I have? I didn't kill or hurt anybody, did I?"

"No. Nothing of the kind, fortunately. Your car overturned. Apparently the steering wheel came off. Nobody knows what caused it. Our mechanic here has always mistrusted those collapsible steering wheels. This model has been known to do that. Of course the car you used had been carefully overhauled for any defects, but," he shrugged, "mechanics aren't what they used to be, let's face it. Nobody takes pride any more in his profession. Anyway, the car caught fire."

"Where did it happen?"

"On your way back, just before the last curve. Luckily for you some of our guests had gone for a walk before dinner. They pulled you out just before the whole thing went up in flames, and got you up here."

The last curve? It was a badly constructed curve, banked all wrong, and I had taken it slowly because there had been someone at the side of the road trying to hitch a ride, standing too far into the road, the way they always did, so that you had to stop or run them down. It tired me to think of it. But one word Klausen had said stirred me to look at him. "Anesthesia. You mentioned complete anesthesia. Why did I have to have it? For this?" I pointed to the bandages that swathed my face and neck, which, in my efforts to remember preceding events, I had forgotten.

"We don't usually give a complete anesthesia for facial operations, but in your case, I thought it better to put you out of your misery."

Klausen probably thought it strange that I hadn't inquired first about what kind of injuries my face had suffered but had worried primarily about my mental condition, but this almost impregnable blackout worried me more than any wounds I might have suffered. After all, wounds mended, but a loss of memory might never be recovered. I'd heard of cases . . . Now, though, my interest turned suddenly to my injuries. "You performed a facial operation?"

"Under the circumstances . . . it seemed the thing to do."

"Was I burned?"

Once we had pulled a pilot out of a crashed helicopter. I had never been able to forget the sight of his face nor the self-control it had taken to look at him. Third degree burns . . .

Dr. Klausen shook his head. "No. I told you you were lucky. If those people hadn't been there . . ."

"But you operated on my face."

"You suffered quite a few deep cuts that required stitching. But don't let it upset you. I'm an old hand at plastic surgery. During the war I took care of many faces, in far worse shape than yours. Your face is going to be perfectly all right."

"When?"

"In about six to eight weeks, depending on how your skin heals. And of course, since the accident happened in one of the Lindwurm cars, the management will be happy to have you stay as their guest as long as you choose."

So a sense of responsibility hadn't totally vanished from our planet, I thought. Or the Lindwurm was well insured.

"We shall remove the bandages in about six days, and the stitches probably ten days from now."

Ten more days at the Lindwurm with all expenses paid. That would solve a problem. The small apartment I had rented outside Rome would be available only on the fifteenth of March. Meanwhile I could start to write my *European Guide Book for Bachelors* right here at the Lindwurm, sans cost or loss of time.

"Do I have to stay in bed?"

"No. Though I want you to rest as much as possible. Too much motion won't do. The tissues have to settle, and for that they need to be still."

I bet they did, I thought, the way they ached even when I

100

talked, and this in spite of sedation which I could tell, by the drowsiness I couldn't shake off, must have been plenty.

"We'll give you some pills for pain. What about your rib cage? The right side's taken quite a beating."

"Hurts like hell."

"And will, for several weeks. We'll take care of it too. No taping though. We prefer . . ." He pulled out his stethoscope and went all over me with it. His face, as he listened to heart, lungs and stomach, became even narrower, even more like that of a bird. His shiny pate lay on my chest like an ivory billiard ball; from it came a strong sweet odor. I had smelled it before. When? Where? On a girl. Chanel No. 5. I'd bought some for her. A woman's perfume. And he had smelled of it the first time I had met him, when he had led me to the buffet in the Lindwurm's ballroom. The effeminate gesture with which he had held his wide pants out full width and now the almost tender gentleness of his slim fingers, touching, probing. Dr. Klausen was a homosexual. And good for me, I thought. They're usually artists at whatever they undertake. He'll have done a good job on my face.

"What about moving back to my room? I loathe a hospital atmosphere, and since you're allowing me to move around . . ."

"Look," said Klausen, "you're not exactly a cheerful sight. Let's say that for the sake of the guests you remain here until Wednesday. After Ash Wednesday the place will be empty. The Lindwurm's season begins in May and reaches full capacity during June and August. And again in October, when the first new wines act as a lure. This being Sunday, that's only three days." He sounded almost pleading, but the smell of whatever they used to disinfect the air irritated me; the strictly imposed quietude would drive me nuts, and the idea of Sister Elly's attentions, with Schlau in the background, was nothing to look forward to either.

"I'd rather turn down the management's offer and pay than be cooped up here."

"Very well. But remember, you must be only moderately active."

"I promise, only get me back to my room."

Sister Elly appeared half an hour later. She handed me my clothes, not the ones I had worn the day before but the only other suit I had brought along, a blue one I'd had custom made in Madrid, at a ridiculously low price. "I give you my word of honor," she said. "You must believe me. If I had known Dr. Klausen wouldn't mind being called . . ." She couldn't stop justifying herself. In the end I started dressing in front of her; I don't think she noticed it. When I was ready and making for the door, she waved me back and peered out into the passage, to right and left. Then she took my arm and led me through the long corridor to the entrance of the hospital wing where I had waited for Klausen to find out how the professor was faring. The lobby was deserted, and she walked me quickly to the elevator. Klausen needn't have worried about my being too active. Any quick motion hurt.

When I tried to stop Sister Elly from entering the elevator with me, the former rigid authority returned to her voice and manner. "My orders are to see you to your room."

Once we had reached it, I told her enough was enough and gave her a gentle shove when she didn't leave promptly enough to suit me. I locked the door behind her and, filled with a glorious sense of achievement, fell into the chair that by now looked as familiar as if I had grown up with it. I was rid of Sister Elly and Schlau. A moment later, all satisfaction vanished and I fell into a deep depression. Reaction was setting in. I hadn't realized what an effort it had been not to panic when I had awakened in that stinkingly quiet room with its muted light and a nurse who was unwilling to explain what had put me there.

A car accident.

Why couldn't I remember it when there must have been that split second of terror that lingers in mind and body, sometimes for years afterwards? I tried to recall what it had been like, going into the too flat curve and suddenly holding a steering wheel in my hands, but I couldn't. I glanced at the tray with Scotch and ice that had been set out next to my bed as if I had never left the room. Maybe a shot would help. Then, remembering that sedatives and alcohol didn't always mix, I decided against it. My head had to be clear. I reached for the small oblong memorizer, not bothering to take it out of its black leather case. I moved the red lever to "Talk," and spoke into it, reporting to myself step by step what had taken place since I had come out of the anesthesia. Then I played it back, listening to my own voice, impatient to reach the word *accident,* hoping it might arouse hidden recollections. It didn't. I turned on the radio. A local station was describing a parade winding through the streets of Cologne. Every now and then applause and laughter interrupted the announcer's voice. But I wanted music. I finally found a tune which brought back an evening at Arthur, and as I visualized the frenetic motions of the dancers and heard the beat of the drums, the sharp high brass filling my ears almost to the point of hurting, I longed suddenly to be back in New York where I knew the people. All sorts of people. Cops and reporters, bums, taxi drivers, curators of museums, drug addicts, writers, teachers, and a lot of girls. In with the stationery in my desk drawer there was an assortment of postcards, some depicting the Lindwurm but most of them showing the famous tourist spots along the Rhine. I looked at them all before I took out my pen. But pen in hand it struck me that not one of them would really be interested in where I was or what sort of a time I was having. They weren't friends, merely acquaintances.

The fact that I hadn't a close friend in the world hit me suddenly with an impact I hadn't foreseen. I turned off the radio and sat for a while, maudlin and passive, until there was a knock at the door. A waiter came in with a tray. Hot broth, some crackers and fruit. It was Hugo.

"Something light," he said. "And my sincere congratulations for still being alive with nothing worse than a few cuts and bruises."

This time I was sure he was the silly man dressed up as a medieval knight who had told me he was Rudi's friend. How could he be both—guest and employee? An embarrassing question. I didn't ask it. "So you know about it."

"I do. That curve should have been reconstructed years ago. You have to slow down to at least twenty miles to make it safely."

However slowly I'd been going, it wouldn't have helped me when the wheel came off. Again I searched my memory for the moment when I must have sat there, stupefied, holding in my hands an object which I had believed stationary.

"Those drive-yourself cars . . . I've often wondered what shape they're in. You could have been killed."

For the first time since I'd come to, the possibility that I might have been killed entered my mind. When Klausen had smilingly told me that indeed, I had been lucky, it hadn't occurred to me that I might have died of my injuries. Perhaps I was still young enough to dismiss death as a chance in a thousand. It can happen to the next fellow but not to you. Without the blind faith that it's the other man who is going to be murdered, die in a fire, drown, step on a mine or have some fatal illness, no one could enjoy life. Somehow I couldn't picture myself no longer actively with it, although in my passport it reminded me bluntly . . . in case of death, next of kin. Next of kin? I had no kin. An old aunt somewhere, an uncle I'd never seen. Notified, he or she would have to puzzle out who I was. "Now let's see. Did Rose? No, Rose had girls. Five. Whatever happened to the third one?" What had happened to my passport? Had it been found? I should go down and ask the clerk. Go down? There was a telephone on my bedside table. I picked up the receiver. A voice smooth as flannel answered. Richter. "Sorry, sir. As yet we haven't received any message that your passport has been turned in. But don't worry, during the carnival people lose all sense of responsibility. Wait until after Ash Wednesday. Then everyone sobers up and life becomes normal again."

Right or wrong, I was worried. I found myself wishing I'd stayed in Rome. Hugo picked up the empty tray, and juggling it over his head on the palm of one hand, grinned at me, apparently trying to convey again how glad he was to find me still among the living. "The footpaths through the woods are delightful, if you like to walk. And they're rather empty after lunch when most of the guests are napping."

I watched him cross the room and open and close the door before it hit me that he had been trying to tell me something. Why otherwise should a waiter suggest to a guest, who obviously should be resting after lunch, that he go walking in the woods? I got up quickly to call him back, but the passage was empty. I looked at my watch, on my wrist again where Sister Elly had restored it after bringing me my only suit. It was one thirty. Then life was suddenly complicated by the fact that the suit I wore was all I had with me, except for the corduroy jacket I'd used as a costume. I never carried a coat. Now the suit seemed too good for a footpath where branches might tear it, and the corduroy jacket somehow inappropriate. And too thin. After five minutes of fussing about what to wear, I suddenly realized how unlike me this was. I'd never given a damn about clothes or what I looked like. That I could waste my thinking powers on such trifles yet have forgotten much more important facts frightened me momentarily. But, no doubt about it, to concentrate was an effort. Klausen had warned me against too much physical exercise but had failed to tell me that mental strain would tire me even more. And it tired me especially to think back, to recall the person who, before Hugo, had mentioned something about the woods. Something about deer. Deer feeding in the third clearing. When it finally came to me, it was like taking a new lease on my old self. Rudi. After the night at the Guërzenich, when I'd tumbled out of the car he was chauffeuring, he had told me under his breath to meet him at three o'clock at the third clearing. I hadn't met him. I had forgotten our appointment. After watching Bettina leave with Gevern I had ordered a car to drive to Cologne. Now I couldn't get it out of my head that Hugo's casual suggestion had been made because Rudi would be at the third clearing today.

The hotel wing was deserted. No one was using the elevator and none of the many buttons were lit to show it was being needed on any other floor. The lobby was empty. Reception was unattended. The large entrance door stood half open. Except for two men sweeping the courtyard, no one was in sight. From what I'd seen of it, it was a neat quadrangle with only one source of entry, the drawbridge.

But from my window—or had it been from the parapet I had walked along, which led to the professor's quarters?—I had noticed a skating rink and a narrow path through the woods. Now I didn't know how to reach them. One of the sweepers, whom I asked for directions, told me that to go skating—he must have been surprised that anyone with his face and neck swathed in bandages should want to go skating—I would have to go back through the lobby and use a door behind the reception desk, but to go for a walk I should pass through a gate next to where the garages were located, just below the first floor of the west wing.

The gate was small, of solid wood, with a heavy iron handle above an intricate lock. Beyond it the woods started almost immediately. According to the size of the trees and the thickness of their stems, the firs could not have been more than thirty years old. A narrow path snaked between them, downhill, into a grove of leafless trees. I couldn't tell if they were beeches, oak or linden. I could see a sprinkling of birches, white, their bark peeling black, and below them a small meadow, winter brown. On a pole a block of pinkish salt looked like a gigantic piece of chewing gum. Below the meadow, the path became narrower, the trees denser, then they opened up again onto a clearing on which stood a haystack, like a giant molehill. From here, through an opening, I could see far below me and I recognized the terraced vineyards above the wide gray river. The path wound on, steeply now, again between trees, and opened onto another clearing, this time with a crib-stand filled with hay. The third clearing. I hadn't expected to see deer at this time of day, but realized that I had definitely expected to see Rudi.

There was no Rudi. Disappointment made me swallow, almost like a child trying to stifle a sob. I hadn't been aware

107

to what extent I'd been looking forward to talking to him. I glanced at my watch. Twenty to three. Immediately I felt better. I was too early.

I sat down on the hay crib which seemed rather solidly packed. Droppings on the damp ground, the marks of small hooves, bits of hay assured me this was the place he had indicated. Above me some ravens were making the unpleasant cawing sounds of hungry birds. It was when I looked around me that I saw the fence. Several strings of wire were spun between the trees and in the still air I could hear a gentle humming sound, betraying the fact that they were loaded. On touching them the first shock would be gentle, the second, if you cared to try the amount of electricity running through them, harder, and the third would really hurt. At least that had been my experience on farms where the cattle were kept from straying by such a device. On farms, though, the wires were strung high enough above the ground to enable you to crawl under the lowest one and the top wire was usually at a height a man could vault over. But these wires left barely six inches free above the ground, and the top one was higher than any average man's height. If deer were being kept for the amusement of the Lindwurm guests, it would be natural to fence them in, and since the path ran on beyond the fence, there should be a gate where the electricity could be interrupted. But there was no gate. I walked over to the fence but didn't touch it because of the barbs which were unusually long and astonishingly close together. They made me think of fenced-in prison compounds, and I turned away, feeling uneasy, and again depressed.

By now it was three, and still no sign of Rudi. I began to wonder from which direction he'd come, from below the castle, where two nights ago the ambulance had parked, or from above, the way I had taken? I looked up the winding path, but could see only part of it. Beyond the clearing it disappeared between trees and underbrush. I decided that if he came, it would be from below, to avoid being seen. Also it was the shorter way. He could drive to the point where the ambulance had let out its men, and turn left and up the footpath. He would certainly know where there was an opening in the fence.

I sat down on the crib. It was very quiet. Except for the cawing of the ravens and the faint humming in the wires, there was no sound; and those were so monotonous that after a short while I was no longer conscious of them. Above me the wide expanse of sky was pulled into focus by the turrets of the Lindwurm, around me the naked trees formed an almost complete circle, and though I knew I was only thirty or forty minutes walk away from people, I felt like a shipwrecked man on a desert island. The pain in my rib cage, to which, in anticipation of talking to Rudi, I had paid no attention, began to assert itself again. I tried to put it out of my mind by straining harder than ever to hear the fall of approaching steps, but it didn't work.

It began to rain, a gentle drizzle. I looked at my watch. Three thirty. Had Rudi been delayed? Had it been wishful thinking on my part, when I had interpreted Hugo's suggestion as an indication that Rudi would be here today when actually he had made the date for the previous afternoon? Hugo might just have been prattling. A dismal thought. I decided to wait another hour and walk back before dusk. I closed my eyes. It wasn't a good idea. My aching ribs and painful face dragged my mind back to the accident I'd been in. Why couldn't I remember it? Did people suffering from amnesia remember only in part or nothing at all? I had no idea, nor did I know how they were pulled out of it. But not to remember such a vital experience was like having part of my body cut off, a leg or an arm, without which one has to relearn the laws of balance.

Accident.

"There have been too many accidents." Bettina asking me almost pleadingly to confirm the fact that the professor's death had been suicide, not an accident. Our conversation at the Guërzenich came back to me. "Always people I'm fond of." And now the car I had been driving . . . I too could have been killed when it overturned. But why should anyone want to kill me? I wasn't close to Bettina. Or did someone think I was?

I reined in my thoughts which were galloping through my mind like frightened horses. I was alive. I had been saved before the car exploded. Nobody would have dragged me out of the car if I had been marked for death. As it was, I'd got away with a few cuts on my face and a bruised rib cage. Accidents did happen, just as I had assured Bettina, even if I couldn't remember mine.

The rain was coming down harder. Before it had fallen in thin silent drops, now it made a noise when it hit the bare branches of the trees. I tugged at the hay, to form a kind of shelter for myself. As a boy, on my grandparents's farm, I had sometimes taken refuge from a thunderstorm in a haystack. Since then I had often marveled at the different ways haystacks were built in different countries. Some quite intricate structures allowed the air to sift through for faster drying; others, with the help of poles, were made into teepees, with sufficient room to crouch inside them, or they were stacked primitively upright. I had seen a few erected into high round towers, so tall, one had to use ladders to fork off the top layers.

By now I had pulled up enough hay on either side of me, but not enough at my back. I reached deeper into the crib, and my hand struck something solid. Something solid yet soft. I withdrew my hand. I looked at it. Blood was dripping from my finger tips. I got off the crib. I walked around it. I lifted the hay. Below it lay the body of a man.

He had been put in face-down, his legs forced awkwardly into the wooden structure. He had on a brown uniform. His cap had come off; his blond hair was in disarray. He had been shot. The bullet had struck the jugular vein. It was still bleeding. Rigor mortis had not yet set in. I turned him around. His eyes were still open, staring at me through the film of death. Rudi.

I closed his eyes. In spite of the fact that I knew he was dead, I laid my head on his chest to make sure his heart had stopped beating. His spectacle case, with his goggles in them, stuck out of his breast pocket. I took it. One letter was stamped on it, the letter R. I stuffed it into my pocket. For a moment then, I hesitated. What to do? I looked about me. But still no one was to be seen. No sound but the croaking of the ravens and the hum in the wires. I covered him again with the hay I had pulled away, as if the ravens had been vultures. I had always been drawn somehow to the tradition of carrying one's dead within reach of these birds before burying the clean bones inside the home, but I didn't want anyone, human or animal, to disturb Rudi's body. It had to be preserved exactly as I had found it.

I crossed the clearing. I walked back up the path, and with every step I took, it seemed steeper. Halfway up I thought I'd never make it. I made it, of course, although I had to rest twice, leaning against a tree, my hands pressed against my ribs, which seemed to have been transformed into sharp knives. I went straight to the reception desk at the far end of the lobby. This time Richter was in his place. His mouth fell open when he saw me. "My God, sir, what happened? You're bleeding."

"Nonsense."

"But look. Look for yourself."

He pointed to one of the mirrors on the wall, between the armored knights. I must have touched the bandages on my face with my bloodied fingers. It looked as if the stitches behind them had broken open and bled. But I gave no explanation. "Where's Dr. Klausen?" I asked instead.

"He's been inquiring for you for the last hour."

"Well, tell him I want to see him."

"If you'll go to his office . . . he's there now."

I didn't want to be caught in the hospital wing. "Tell him to come up to my room."

Klausen came while I was still washing my hands. "I'll be out in a minute."

I could hear him moving impatiently around in my room, with his soft effeminate steps. A moment later he looked in the half-open door of my bathroom. "Where in the world have you been? Nobody could find you. You should . . ." he stopped abruptly when I turned to face him. "What the devil . . ." He pointed at my face.

"It's nothing. Forget it."

I walked past him to the desk on which stood the tray. I poured myself a drink and gulped it down before I even thought of offering him one. He shook his head. "Did you fall? Let me see."

"Sit down. No, I didn't fall. I went for a walk in the woods."

"For a walk in the woods? When I told you to take it easy? You're in no condition . . . man, don't you know that an anesthesia is a shock to the entire system?"

I took off my shoes and leaned back in the chair. I was trembling, but determined not to let him see it.

"Where does the blood come from?" he demanded with sudden angry authority.

"It's not my blood."

"Not your blood? Then who's is it?"

"One of your chauffeurs, the Lindwurm chauffeurs, I mean."

"One of the Lindwurm chauffeurs? What are you talking about?"

"On the third meadow, where the fence runs and the deer feed, in the crib . . . somebody shot him and buried him in the hay. I sat on him. If it hadn't rained, if I hadn't tried to make a shelter of the hay, I might never have discovered the body."

He looked at me as if I had gone mad. "Again."

I repeated the whole story, this time more slowly and coherently. "Good Lord!" He reached for the bottle of Scotch and a glass, drank fast, and asked, "How do you know it's one of our drivers?"

"The uniform is the same chocolate brown as the others. Besides, the letter L is embroidered on both sides of the collar." I took a chance. I said, "I think his name is Rudi."

"Rudi? Not Rudi Becker, the fellow who helps out when we're short? How do you know his name?"

"I heard you address him as Rudi when he drove us back from the fish restaurant, remember? You didn't want to drive your car back and phoned him."

"That's right. But why should anybody shoot Rudi?"

"You tell me."

Klausen tapped the top of his desk with his middle finger as if he expected a medium's voice to give him the answer. "It could only have happened by accident."

"Accident?"

"A poacher. You know what people are like these days. No respect for anything. Laws don't exist for them. Last year it was so bad, we had to post guards. You say he was wearing a brown uniform?"

"His brown uniform and cap, yes. But how could anyone mistake a human being for a deer?"

"A shot could have gone wild."

"He was shot in the neck. With a rifle. I put everything back just the way I found it."

"I'll have to notify the police."

He lifted the receiver from my telephone. His voice sounded heavy as he told Richter to call Inspector Ginster and ask him to come over right away. "And see if you can reach the manager." Then he turned to me. "You'd better come along. I'm sure Ginster will want to see you. Do you feel up to it?"

I nodded. I rose. I had stopped shaking. To my relief, Klausen's office wasn't situated in the hospital wing but directly outside it. In spite of its ultra-modern furniture, it was a quiet room, with books lining three of its walls. A fire was burning, and I walked over to it, holding out my palms against its warmth. He opened a door to a small consultation room. "Now let's see your face." He motioned me to sit down. The blood on my fingers had penetrated only to the second layer of the bandage, so he simply removed what was stained and replaced it. He had barely finished when, simultaneously with a knock on the door, Ginster came in.

He seemed a different man from the one I had watched on the evening of the professor's death. Interested and alert.

There was nothing sloppy about his uniform or the way he carried himself; only his tone hadn't changed. He spoke in the same jovial, offhand manner as the last time. Possibly, I thought, a mannerism to calm others, or a kind of self-defense in the face of trouble.

"What now? Nothing serious, I hope." He pointed to me. "Are you the fellow who got all botched up when your car overturned? Well, you're in good hands. The best," and he grinned encouragingly.

Somehow the fact that he knew about it had a soothing effect on me, though it made the accident more real and my inability to remember it an even greater calamity. "Well?" Ginster turned to Klausen. "Let's have it."

"If Mr. Waldron will be good enough to tell you . . ." Klausen walked around his desk and sat down. Leaning against the mantel I repeated what I had just told Klausen. The inspector didn't interrupt me. Although he held a pad and pencil in his hands, he took no notes. He listened with his eyes closed, puffing at a cigar which, when I came to the end of my report, he had let go out.

"Thank you," he said, nodding slightly in my direction. "I'm sorry it had to be you who found him. Coming across a body unexpectedly isn't exactly pleasant, to say the least, and in your present condition . . ." He shook his head in commiseration.

I thought I was dismissed and rose, but sat down again when he addressed Klausen. "What do you make of it, Doctor?"

"What do I make of it?" Klausen sounded angry. "What can I say? I have no idea. All I know is that Rudi was well-liked by everyone around here. He was a pleasant and efficient young man. I couldn't tell you anything about his private life. It's one of my principles never to take more than a polite interest in the affairs of any of the Lindwurm staff. Maybe he was having an affair with a married woman; maybe there was a girl he got into trouble—how do I know?"

"Had you met him before, Mr. Waldron?" Ginster asked. He had a perfectly round face with a rather flat nose. Now, with his eyes half-closed, it looked like a ball that could be picked up from his shoulders.

"Of course. That's how I recognized him. He drove me a couple of times."

"You hadn't made a date with him?"

"I've hardly ever talked to him."

His eyes sprang open. "If I may ask . . . why did you go for a walk? Such a long walk for someone in your condition?"

This question I had foreseen. I shrugged. "I felt terribly pent up. I like to walk. I often walk for hours. I thought the fresh air might clear my head. But it tired me more than I had expected, so I sat down."

"And you didn't see or hear anything?"

"No."

"How long would you say you rested?"

"About an hour."

"In the rain?"

"It started to rain only after I got there. Just a drizzle. I hardly noticed it. When the rain really began to come down . . ."

"You tried to protect yourself by covering yourself with some hay from the crib. That's how you found him. Right? But why did you stay there in the first place? Wouldn't it have been wiser to make for home at once?"

"Certainly. But I was too tired. And I thought the rain might stop any moment."

"You weren't by any chance waiting for someone to meet you there?"

I told myself that he couldn't possibly know about Rudi. "I don't know anybody here. I'm in Germany for the first time, and except for Professor Florian . . ."

"Ah yes. Professor Florian. Poor devil." Inspector Ginster considered the wet stump of his cigar, then dropped it into an ashtray and took a fresh one out of his breast pocket. I watched him light it. His eyes seemed intent only on the flame. "Tell me," he said, "while you sat there, or walked around a bit, did you happen to notice any footprints on the ground?"

"Only the marks of hooves, some broken wisps of hay, a few droppings."

"If you noticed the marks of hooves, then the ground couldn't have been so dry that his shoes, or the shoes of whoever shot him and hid his body, wouldn't have also left an imprint. Did you see any?"

I must have seen them, I told myself, and not paid attention to them. "I understand that guests often watch the deer feeding, so I took for granted that . . ."

"Quite. But by now the footprints may have been washed away." He nodded in the direction of the curtained window behind which you could hear the rain falling, hard and steady. He sighed. "What makes you assume his death was caused by a rifle?"

"Its entry. The wound is small, and the bullet came out on the other side. It's the kind of wound a thirty-thirty steel jacket would make. There's no pistol—not so far as I know —that fires a thirty-thirty."

"I see." Ginster leaned back in his chair. He looked as if he was thinking up some more questions. Instead he said abruptly, "That will do. If you don't mind, Doctor, I'd like to interview the manager, and the staff, as a matter of fact, I want to speak to everyone here, your patients included."

Klausen frowned sharply. "That seems unnecessary."

"I can't rule out the possibility that one of your crackpots suddenly got trigger happy."

"How could they possibly get hold of a gun? Really, Ginster. Besides, their every move is checked. Nobody leaves the hospital wing or enters it without it being reported to me." Klausen's voice was cold, authoritative. You could tell what an effort he was making to keep his temper.

"I quite understand," Ginster replied, just as coldly, "that you want to protect your patients and your reputation. But I'm here to see that innocent people can live in peace. Unlike the professor's suicide, this is not a clear-cut case. This may be murder." He nodded at me. "I don't think I'll need you any longer. You may go if you want to. But keep yourself available. And thanks again."

I returned to my room. While I was gone, it had been tidied. The dirty glasses had been cleared away, fresh towels put in the bathroom and the bed had been straightened. I fell on it just as I was, fully dressed. I lit a cigarette, took a few drags but stubbed it out when I discovered that the taste of tobacco made me feel sick. I must have fallen asleep, because when I opened my eyes, I didn't know where I was. The room seemed just as unfamiliar as the room in the hospital where I had awakened this morning. My head felt empty, heavy and empty at the same time. A few minutes slipped by before I could recall the events of the last few days. But even then, everything that had happened since my arrival in Cologne seemed far removed, like something experienced years ago.

Nothing appeared real, myself included, and my surroundings. Only one man stood out clearly—Professor Florian. The night in Rome at Emilio's Bar. The flight of steep steps that led from the street to the cellar. Perched on the high bar-stool like a monkey on the branch of a jungle tree, he had attracted my attention at once. And I had seen him before. Walking along the Ponte dei Angeli, stopping to look at some of the impressive sculptures, gazing at them with delight and admiration. I had noticed him again at the moonlit Forum when, in the shadow of the magnificent Titus Arch I had kissed a girl I had met that afternoon. "Let's go home," she had whispered. "There are too many people. Besides, it's cold."

A week before that he had been sitting in the same restaurant as I was, an outdoor café. Because of the season, it had been glassed in. Small stoves had stood between the tables for warmth. His companion had been an abominably healthy-looking young man with all the characteristics of a German tourist, very much like the man who had sat next to me on the plane from Madrid. The professor had nodded at me, the way two strangers in a foreign country will acknowledge having run into each other several times before. But he hadn't spoken to me. Not then. He had spoken to me for the first time at Emilio's, almost the moment I had sat down. "Here we are again. Will you have a drink with me?" And we had started talking, at first about life in general, then about traveling, and the cities we'd lived in, and why they appealed to us. Eventually he had mentioned Cologne. "When you think that ninety per cent of the city was destroyed, you have to admire the indomitable spirit of its population. In less than twenty-five years they have not only managed to rebuild most of it . . ." And his enthusiasm had infected me. Gratified over the fact that he had persuaded me to visit Cologne, he had slapped me on the shoulder and then, only a few days later, had pretended he'd never met me. His odd behavior could be explained by a brain no longer functioning properly; certainly his shifting attitude toward my presence—at one moment advising me to leave, the next resigned, even pleased that I was staying —was proof of a disturbed mind. Still, something about him bothered me. But again I was too tired to concentrate on it. I switched on my radio. News. Nothing unusual. Millions were dying of hunger; in various parts of the world rebellions, strikes; in Cologne, however, it was the last Sunday of the carnival, with its stupendous parades. But instead of sitting at a window or on a balcony, watching the floats, I was flat on my back with my face bandaged and my ribs hurting to such an extent that the thought of dancing literally made me wince. In spite of myself, though, I felt hungry.

I got up and brushed my hair and was already at the door before I remembered that the sight of me might make others feel uncomfortable. I rang for a waiter and, as I must have hoped secretly, Hugo arrived. As soon as he had closed the door, I asked him point blank, "When you brought my lunch, were you trying to tell me something?"

He looked me straight in the eye, a professional smile splitting his mouth slightly, his eyes staring dumbly, "Tell you something, sir?"

"Well, it was you who put the idea of a walk in my head. And at a certain hour. After lunch, you said, when most of the guests were resting. Remember?"

"I didn't mean to be forward. I just thought that some fresh air might do you good."

He held out the oversized menu. I opened it. "And you're sure no one gave you a message for me?"

"Quite sure. Nobody gave me a message for you. And I'm sorry now that I ever mentioned the woods. It must have been a shock to find . . . the body. But they've got him, sir. They got him about an hour ago."

"Got whom?"

"The man who shot Rudi. It was on the air."

I don't know why, but somehow I hadn't expected the murderer to be found, certainly not so quickly. "Fast work."

"Yes, isn't it? But then, Inspector Ginster is a very capable man."

"Who was it? I mean, who killed him?"

"A man by the name of Mascher. Emil Mascher. A poacher. They arrested him last year but then had to let him go because they couldn't prove that he'd killed the two does that were missing."

A poacher. So Dr. Klausen had guessed correctly. To me it had sounded unbelievable. "Did a shot go wild?"

Hugo rubbed the palm of his left hand along his leg. "I can't vouch for it, but he's supposed to have confessed to killing him on purpose. He'd been after a deer, he said, and just taken aim, when Rudi came down the path, whistling. The noise made the buck take off, and Mascher got so mad, he killed Rudi instead."

It could have happened anywhere. Why should there be

less violence, less senseless anger and pent-up hatred in a German than in an American?

"Now he claims he went crazy. He says he didn't know what he was doing, that there was a red cloud all around him and the shot went off . . . that all he'd meant to do was frighten Rudi. These days they all claim insanity. Makes you wonder. Anyway, they're going to have a psychiatrist see him."

I gave back the menu. "I don't feel hungry right now. Just bring me a sandwich and a bottle of beer."

Concern showed in his eyes. "But you didn't eat very much for lunch. Shouldn't you have a proper meal?"

"I can always have a bite later."

"Will you be going to Cologne tomorrow to see the parades? Rose Monday is the best day."

"I'd like to, but I'm not supposed to do anything strenuous."

"You think it would be too much for you?"

"I'm sure my doctor would think so. He was pretty annoyed about my little excursion into the woods. Besides, the way I look . . ."

Hugo grinned. "Buy a mask, and you can pass for one of our clowns."

No doubt about it, I could. Then I grew alert to what he had just said. "You're not suggesting anything now, are you, Hugo?"

"Well, yes, if you don't mind, sir, but I thought it would be a nice gesture on your part to see Mrs. Becker. After all, you were the one who found Rudi. She might like to talk to you about it." He stopped abruptly, his head cocked slightly, then went on without changing the tone of his voice. "The *petite marmite* is a favorite with our guests, but if you prefer the *Kraftbrühe*, a strong boullion . . ." He nodded when, seconds later, someone knocked on my door. He had heard the steps long before me.

Dr. Klausen didn't wait for me to say "Come in," he entered my room as if it were his own. "I just wanted to see how you are and to bring you some news you'll be interested in. They've caught Becker's killer." He repeated what Hugo had already told me. I pretended to be surprised and asked a few questions to make him feel he was the first to tell me, while Hugo, his face hidden by the menu, remained standing at attention. "I see you're intending to eat up here," Klausen said finally. "I approve of that. Have something soft, so you don't have to chew. Tripe, if I may suggest. Broiled. And no coffee, please. I want you to rest as much as possible." He pulled a small oblong envelope from his pocket. "Take these. One before dinner, another about an hour later. I don't think you'll need the third, but if you wake early, don't hesitate to take it. Right now sleep is the best medicine for you. We want your face to heal as quickly as possible, and you've already had far too many upsets. Normal blood circulation, that's what we're after. In case you want me or the head nurse, dial one-two, one-two." He shook three small red capsules into my hand. "Take one right now."

I put two of the capsules on my bedside table and dropped the third into my mouth. Having made sure it was securely lodged between my left cheek and gum, I swallowed hard, grateful for my bandages, which made it impossible to detect that I had secreted the medication. He reached for my pulse, counted silently, and smiled. "No temperature. Not that I expected you to run a fever. Now I just hope you don't come down with a cold. It was very foolish of you to sit there in the rain."

"*Kraftbrühe*, broiled tripe and some fruit, is that it, sir?"

said Hugo, writing down the order. He left. Klausen, without asking, poured himself a drink, grew aware of what he was doing and asked, "Do you mind?"

"Not if you pour me one too."

He shook his head. "You've had one already, and that's one too much. I advise you to stay away from alcohol if you don't want swollen scars. Our dueling students used to drink to make their scars more conspicuous. Idiots!"

This was a blow, but I'd face its consequences later. Right now there were more pressing things on my mind. "How did the others react to Ginster's interrogation?"

"I managed to keep him away from my patients. As it turned out, it would have been superfluous. The staff was shocked, but not for long. It makes too good a story. They'll live on it for a while. And he only got around to questioning a few of the guests because his right-hand man, Detective Schramm, went straight to Mascher's hut, on a hunch, and found him sitting there, stoned, jabbering to himself. Schramm has a gift for making people say just the thing they want to withhold. He pulled Mascher in and phoned Ginster at once."

"You had the same hunch."

"Because I couldn't think of any other explanation."

He took another swallow. I watched him jealously. "Why did Professor Florian think of himself as Regin?"

The question must have been at the top of my mind for some time, for I was just as surprised as Klausen at the suddenness with which I worded it. "Regin?"

Obviously he had no idea what I was talking about. "According to legend, Sigurd was told by Regin, the dwarf, how to slay the dragon. Sagas were Florian's hobby. I know. I don't think he was particularly interested in them historically, but any heroic tale seemed to satisfy some infantile need within him for escape."

I thought of the drawings and photographs on the walls of the professor's room. "But he must have made quite a study of the Nibelung legend. He knew so precisely . . ."

"Dr. Leise thinks he used whatever knowledge he acquired as an excuse for his crazy notions about reincarnation. Sometimes they bordered on hallucinations."

"I see. But that still doesn't answer my question why he identified himself with Regin, certainly a despicable character, with nothing heroic about him. The dragon was his brother, wasn't he? Fafnir, who was transformed into a dragon after he and Regin murdered their father. Do you suppose the professor had a brother he might have wanted to kill, I mean subconsciously, of course."

"To answer that I'd have to ask Leise." Klausen shook his head. I was just wondering if I should tell him about the professor's odd remarks, when he got up. "I'm giving a small party," he said. "My guests may arrive any minute. If you were well enough, I'd be delighted to have you join us, but . . . sleep well and remember to call one-two, one-two if you need me. Good night."

He almost collided with Hugo, who just managed to save the tray he was carrying from crashing to the ground, but nevertheless apologized profusely. Neither he nor I spoke while we could still hear Klausen's steps in the corridor. Only after he had taken the small tureen out of a square upright warmer did he say, "If you want anything else later, I may not be able to serve you, sir. I'm going off duty in an hour."

"In an hour?"

"At nine thirty, yes."

I had never seen any of the Lindwurm's employees using the front entrance, nor the bridge, when coming or leaving. "How do you get in and out of this place?" I asked.

"By the service elevator." He was ladling out the boullion without looking up. "On the second floor, right next to the Stübl. A small white door leads into it. Do use the straws, sir. They'll make it easier for you."

They did. "And where does it stop?"

"At the bottom of the ravine, a little over three hundred yards left of the drawbridge. At street level. It's quite a walk from the service quarters to the gate in the rock, and very narrow. We punch the machine at the gate, then we have another walk, an even narrower one, to another iron gate. I guess that at some time or other the passage must have served as an escape route." For a moment, eating my tripe, I could see the Lindwurm as it had been once, in the ninth century, when the Normans had destroyed Cologne, or three hundred years later, during the battle of Worringen, which had driven the archbishops out of the city. More of the professor's lore, this time factual. I took a deep breath to test the pain in my ribs. It was still there, in violent affirmation of the bruises on my chest. Still, I'd stood worse pain in some of my landings as a paratrooper.

"Where can I find Mrs. Becker?"

"Rudi gave you his card, didn't he? They lived together."

Suddenly I didn't care any more whether it would embarrass him or not, and asked him bluntly if he wasn't the man who, imprisoned in his heavy armor, had told me on that first night that he was "Rudi's friend." "Yes," he said simply, "I was."

After he had left, I took one of the red capsules. I was going to get some sleep, just as Klausen had advised. I ran a tub and lay in it for quite some time until I could feel myself relaxing. The medication was evidently doing its stuff. I got out of the tub, dried myself, got into bed and turned out the light. But now, when I wanted to sleep, I couldn't. I sat up and lit a cigarette. It simply isn't true, what some people say, that smoking by oneself in the dark isn't enjoyable. I enjoyed very much puffing away and watching the glow at the end of my cigarette eat deeper and deeper into the tobacco. I started to think of Bettina again. By now she had certainly reached Brazil, was perhaps at this very moment telling her uncle that she didn't love him enough to marry him but too much to hurt him. Foolish girl. At her age she should have learned enough about life to know that whatever we do is bound to hurt someone. The important thing is—who is to be hurt, the other person or yourself? And is the hurt justified? Yet there were people who simply couldn't inflict pain on someone else, who preferred to sacrifice themselves, never realizing that every sacrifice has its price. Not only you, but in the end through you, others have to pay. And those who thought so little of their own importance didn't seem to realize that eventually they would be judged by the same small measure. In my mind I followed her through the old house she had described so well. I walked with her from room to room, lecturing her on the dangers inherent in any exaggerated feeling of obliga-tion. The old man never left us alone. He was here, there and everywhere, watching us, and Gevern was watching him. I tried to push her from my mind as if she had been some object lying on a table, but her voice haunted me, a voice defiant even in its despair. "Then it wasn't an accident, but suicide." Again the word "accident" stuck, and suddenly I had a vision of myself sitting at the wheel, driving up the hill, realizing that the curve was badly banked, stepping on the brake and coming to a complete stop when I saw the man. He was standing in the middle of the road, his face protected by one hand against the glare of my headlights, waving with the other, his thumb sticking out in the eternal plea of the hitchhiker. The moment I stopped, he came running. "Would you mind taking me to the Lindwurm?" He had opened the door before I had actually told him to get in.

Just like a screen going unexpectedly dark, the picture was gone. For a moment I waited patiently, expecting it to come on again, but it didn't. I could feel the sweat wetting my cheeks under the bandage. Perhaps my voice could recall the incident.

"There was a man on the road," I said aloud, into the silence of the room, "trying to hitch a ride up the hill. When I pulled up, he got in. Fast. I never saw his face."

I reached for my memorizer. I talked into it. "There was a man on the road; in the middle of the road, so I had to stop whether I wanted to or not. He was trying to hitch a ride. He asked if I'd mind letting him drive up to the Lindwurm with me. Before I could say yes, he had opened the door and got in. I never saw his face . . ."

It didn't help. On the contrary, the sound of my voice served rather to disconnect me from the reality that had swept across my mind a moment ago. I tried again. "There was a man on the road, a man whose face I couldn't see because he had one hand up over it. With the other he was signaling to me. He got into the car when I had barely stopped. Before I had time to say okay. Then . . ."

What had happened then? I couldn't remember. Had I blacked out? Had I started to drive again and the wheel had come off with him sitting beside me? I switched on the light. I looked at my hands. I couldn't envision an unattached steering wheel between them. I could recall only the man.

My height, but more agile. Yes, I could remember the man.

"There was a man in the middle of the road . . ."

"Go on." Klausen's voice. "What kind of man?"

He was sitting beside my bed, smiling affably. He was wearing a formal dinner jacket which gave him an air of aloofness.

"What are you doing here? I didn't call for you."

"You must have been shouting. The floor maid heard you. You didn't answer her knock and your door was locked. She didn't dare to use her passkey, so she phoned the hospital and they called me."

I looked at the bedside table. A small hypodermic with a whitish fluid in it was lying on a piece of gauze. "How long have you been here?"

"A couple of minutes. You were asleep when I came. You woke up when I tried to cover you. Your covers were on the floor and the window was open."

"I didn't open it."

"It may have blown open. But go on with what you were trying to tell, about the man on the road. What road? What man?"

"On the night of my accident. Before it happened. I had already slowed down, when I saw him standing in the middle of the road, signaling to me. I stopped and he opened the door and jumped in."

"Yes?"

"That's all. That's all I can recall."

"What did he look like?"

"I never saw his face."

"You must have been dreaming. If there had been anyone with you when your car overturned, he would still have been there when you were pulled out."

"Couldn't he have got out somehow?"

Klausen shook his head. "Impossible. The doors had jammed and the windows were half-closed. They had to be smashed to get at you."

"How do you know?"

"From the reports of witnesses."

"Who were they?"

"Two guests of the hotel."

"I'd like to talk to them."

"Any time."

"But there was a man on the road."

"There may have been quite a few people on the road." Dr. Klausen spoke softly, evenly, and he was smiling at me as if I were a child who could be calmed by the steady smile of a parent. "Employees coming or leaving at that time. Guests taking a stroll. There's no footpath along that particular stretch of road, and a man, perhaps even one of your rescuers, may have moved into the middle of the road or even been walking facing the oncoming cars. It's supposed to be safer."

"I didn't see anyone else. Just that one man. He waved. He wanted to hitch a ride."

"I don't say that's impossible. Maybe someone did. The last part of the road is quite steep. But what does it matter? The point is that there was no man in your car, because if there had been, he couldn't have got out or away. As I just mentioned, the doors were jammed and the windows only half-open." He sighed. "Anyway, the police took pictures, and I'm certain the management must have copies, to satisfy the insurance. I'll see if I can get hold of them for you."

For that I had no answer. I turned over on my left side but found lying that way too painful. I turned back again. The pacifying smile still lingered in the corners of his wide, narrow-lipped mouth. "I simply can't believe I dreamed it up. Why, I can describe his movements, I still see them so clearly. He was so lightfooted, so quick."

"Hasn't it happened to you before that in a dream you notice details that escape your observation when awake?"

Indeed it had, especially when trying to describe a character in a piece of writing. Subconsciously I had perceived trenchant peculiarities which, consciously at work, I could never have imagined. But I didn't feel like admitting it at this point. "But the man opened the door and got into the car."

"That's what you dreamed, Waldron. I assure you there was no man in your car. And tomorrow, if the illusion persists, we'll prove it to you."

"Why should I dream up a thing like that?"

"Really!" For the first time impatience colored his voice. "For a whole day and half a night you've been trying to pierce the blackout surrounding your accident. I know how frustrating it is not to be able to remember. It's only natural that you should substitute something fictitious, anything, to fill the gap." He reached for the needle. "Let me give you a sedative. I don't want you lying awake, torturing yourself." He pushed the sleeve of my pajama jacket above my elbow and had already wetted a piece of cotton with some disinfectant or other, before I could object. "Don't! I'd rather take the third sleeping pill."

"If you prefer."

But he didn't leave the room. He sat back in the chair, resignation in his eyes. They were strange eyes, very light, a rather faded blue. He kept touching the open palm of his left hand with the finger tips of his right. It made a small but steady noise. It may have been a nervous gesture but gradually it had a soothing effect on me. I closed my eyes. I forgot his presence. I was still intent on seeing the man's face. Why

131

hadn't I seen it when he had been sitting next to me? After a while I heard Klausen tiptoe across the room, switch off the light and close the door gently. I lay awake for another half hour or so. The man who had got into my car remained faceless.

R ose Monday. The last important day of the carnival. The sun that morning shone brilliantly. I opened the windows to let it in. Although it was still early, the courtyard was filled with cars. Two chocolate-brown Volkswagen buses stood ready for guests who preferred the Lindwurm's transportation to driving themselves. Most of the private cars were Mercedeses, and were chauffeured. Laughter hung in the air, rushing into my room, and seemed to echo back from the round walls, encircling me with gaiety. My mind was empty, peacefully empty; my face felt less taut, the pain in my chest was bearable. The uneasiness, fear and shock of yesterday had been subdued by a long, restful sleep. Gradually they came back, but I was able to keep them at bay. I dressed quickly, indifferent suddenly to what people might think of my bandages.

I had no intention of waiting for room service. I went down to the Stübl, where I had breakfasted the first day. On my way to the lobby, I stopped at the first floor and opened the white door Hugo had said led directly into an elevator. It did. A sign said "Employees Only." For the moment it was all I wanted to know. Then I went downstairs and told Richter that I would like to see Klausen. The doctor was at his desk. "I just wanted you to know I'm going to Cologne."

He made no objection. He felt my pulse perfunctorily. "I'm glad you're feeling better, but take it easy, please. Avoid dense crowds. I don't want you to get bumped or jostled."

I showed him the tickets Feldman had secured for Bettina. "All I'm going to do is watch the parades from a window seat in a private house on the Ring."

"Good. But let me know when you get back. I'd like to check on a few things."

One of the omnibuses was just returning from its shuttle service to Cologne. As soon as it had pulled up in the courtyard and let off its passengers, I got in, but was told by the driver that every seat was reserved. But then, after a second look at me, he changed his mind and let me stay. When we had passed the curve where I had lost control of my car, I made a show of looking for my wallet and asked the driver to stop. "I've forgotten my wallet. I'm sorry, but I'll have to go back." One of the passengers shouted that he had been told to get to Cologne well ahead of time or he'd lose his seat on the tribune, and I calmed him down by explaining that I didn't expect the driver to turn around, but just to let me off. I waited until the bus was out of sight before starting slowly up the steep hill.

Just as Klausen had said, no footpath ran along the highway. Whoever had walked on it that evening would have had to walk on the asphalt. Coming around the curve, it would have been quite possible to think a man had been standing in the middle of the road rather than on the side. Possible, yes, but possibilities didn't satisfy me.

Toward the middle of the curve, the deep tracks of tires showed in the stone-spattered winter-brown grass at the side of the road, the right rut deeper than the left. They ran for about forty feet, a sign that I couldn't have been driving as slowly as I should have been. They zigzagged, then came to an abrupt stop about a yard away from a stand of trees. To avoid them I must have braked hard enough to cause the car to overturn. And it had caught fire. A wide semicircle still showed black where burning gasoline had singed the ground and licked at the low dense underbrush. Klausen was right—if someone had been sitting next to me he would hardly have had a chance to get away, in fact none. Since he would have been sitting on my right, I would have fallen on top of him when the car turned over. My face had probably been cut by the half-open window.

I turned back to the road and stood there, ready to signal the next car to stop. I waited for more than ten minutes, but no car came by. Apparently everyone going to enjoy the fun had already left. I had no choice but to walk. I walked for half an hour without getting tired and came finally to a house I hadn't noticed before, a small inn with a few rooms to rent and an outdoor café out front. I ordered lemonade and asked the waitress, who stared at my bandaged face but said nothing, if she would please call a taxi for me. The taxi arrived a short while later from a neighboring town at the foot of the hill, which could be bypassed if you were headed for the Autobahn. I asked him where the police station was; he said in the town he'd just come from, and I told him to drive me there and wait. But Inspector Ginster wasn't in, nor was Detective Schramm, so I asked the officer in charge if I could get permission to see the poacher who had shot Rudolf Becker. He wanted to know if we were related, and the reason for my request. After he had written down my answers he shook his head. Emil Mascher, he said, was in the prison hospital and not allowed to see anyone while under observation, except his lawyer. When I came out, I asked my driver about the poacher, but he wasn't interested in Rudi Becker's death. Emil Mascher, he said, had it coming to him, and Inspector Ginster was a man one did well to steer clear of. What he did want to know though was what had happened to my face.

"I had too much to drink," I told him, "and slipped in the tub."

"Never wash when you're drunk," he said, as we started off again. "Sleep it off dirty. Cleanliness is for sober people."

My next stop was at the equivalent of a Five-and-Ten where I bought a mask. Then my driver insisted on detouring to show me the veterans' cemetery, two thousand graves, Arlington in the Siebengebirge, and he explained, rather touchingly, how two of his sons were buried there. I then suggested crossing the Rhine and taking the Autobahn on the other side to Cologne, but he said not if I wanted to get there the same day, so we took the way I had driven already. My driver, I discovered, was a talkative man; he never stopped chattering all the way to Cologne. He had a grudge against almost everyone in the government—Bonn, on the opposite bank of the river brought that on—held de Gaulle in high esteem, and hated Americans for all the right reasons. He was terribly proud however, and justly so, of the refineries outside Cologne, which could be seen but not smelled from our route, and were impressive. We crossed the Rhine on the Autobahn Bridge; again the cathedral dwarfed the entire city panorama, and I didn't mind suddenly that my stay in these parts was to be prolonged. It would give me time to really "do" the city, not only the cathedral, but the old Romanesque churches, what was left of them, and those that had been rebuilt in a style that had influenced modern church architecture the world over. But all that would have to wait until the streets were cleared of carousers.

When we started inching along the jammed streets, I told my man to let me out. He agreed that I'd do better on foot and seemed to be happy with the tip I gave him.

I found I wasn't too far from the house in which I had a window seat on the third floor. I was shown into what I imagined was normally the dining room but which gave the impression of an overfilled railway station at rush hour. The living room was no better and in the bedroom, into which a lot of furniture had been shoved, you couldn't move at all. Somebody was yelling through a makeshift megaphone to *please* let everyone have a turn at the window. I left. Anyhow, I hadn't come to Cologne that morning to watch a parade.

I made my way behind the grandstands, so loaded they seemed on the verge of caving in, below balconies in no less danger of collapsing, with people, children in their arms, packing them to capacity. Colored streamers floated from them, at times so thick I had to push them aside like a curtain. Music, applause, laughter, the cries of street vendors. I never even caught a glimpse of the famous floats over which different clubs, societies, lodges and guilds had worked for months. Horns tooted, balloons popped, the noise was deafening. I was swept into an alley beyond which buses, diverted from their normal route, were rolling along, almost empty, in deserted streets. I took one to the wide Hansa Ring, which was an oasis of peace. I looked at Rudi's card. Below his office address it gave his home address in smaller print.

I took off my mask, which in the crowded streets had been just as effective as Hugo had said. Nobody had paid any attention to me. I pressed the bell and could hear steps approaching the door. A tall woman, dressed in black, stood before me. Her resemblance to Rudi was so striking, she was obviously his mother. She looked at me, startled, and drew back. "I'm sorry, I thought it was somebody else. I'm not seeing strangers today." She almost closed the door in my face, but I managed to push a foot in before it banged shut. This apparently frightened her, for her mouth began to tremble slightly. Still she said firmly, "Please go away. I told you I didn't want to be disturbed."

"Mrs. Becker, I have to talk to you. About Rudi."

"Who are you?"

"Andrew Waldron. I came to offer my condolences and any help you might need."

"Waldron," she said. "Yes, he mentioned you."

She walked ahead of me into a bright, sunlit room which overlooked the quiet tree-lined street. She sat down in a rocking chair near the window and folded her hands in her lap. She didn't ask me what I wanted to talk about nor did she look at me. It was hard to begin.

"Perhaps you know . . . I was the one who found him." I gave her Rudi's glasses. She took them from me without looking at them, without thanking me. "Yes," she said, her voice cold, monotonous. "Inspector Ginster told me when the police released the body."

"I met him first last Thursday," I said, "when he drove Bettina von Alten and me to the Lindwurm. He gave me his card and told me to call him any time I might need him. He didn't specify any particular need, so I naturally thought that if ever I should want a car . . . now, in retrospect, I wonder what he really meant."

"I wouldn't know."

"He told me quite a few things about Bettina. He seemed worried about her, or perhaps I should say—perplexed.

Especially about her automobile accident. He thought I might be able to find out a little more about it."

"And did you?"

"Yes. It happened on purpose."

"Did you tell him that?"

"I never had a chance. The second time I saw him it was just for a moment, at the Guërzenich. Bettina hadn't yet told me anything. He seemed upset that I had driven to Cologne with Dr. Klausen instead of calling him."

"Dr. Klausen is a reckless driver."

"That's what Rudi said. Later that night he drove our party back to the Lindwurm. That was Friday night. When I got out of the car he asked me to meet him next day, after lunch, at three o'clock, at the third clearing where the deer feed."

"You didn't come."

"I seem to have forgotten all about it. I had lost my passport. Bettina upset me. I hadn't expected her to leave so suddenly. And frankly, I wasn't exactly sober when Rudi suggested our meeting. I seem to have gone to Cologne by myself the following day, and I awakened Sunday morning in the hospital wing of the Lindwurm. I was told I had been in an accident."

"You *were* in an accident," she said, intoning each word sharply.

"How do you know?"

"Rudi tried to call you and a nurse told him."

"What was his reaction?"

"He was glad, naturally, that you hadn't been seriously hurt."

I looked at the flowerpot on the window sill. An extraordinary miniature linden tree, a German version of the Japanese dwarf tree, although this was not an evergreen but a leaf tree. It threw a green shimmer on Mrs. Becker's face. She looked much older than I would have expected; her hair was completely white. She was still holding her hands folded in her lap, and except for the one sharply pronounced statement about my accident, she had given no sign of interest; on the contrary, she had answered all my questions without actually telling me anything at all. Perhaps she was still in a state of shock. I made another attempt to sound her out. "Yesterday the waiter serving my lunch suggested a walk in the woods. After lunch, when most of the guests are resting. His name is Hugo. He suggested that I come to see you."

"Did he?"

"Did Rudi give you a message for me?"

"No."

"But perhaps you know why Rudi wanted to see me."

"I do not."

"You don't? But he mentioned my name. He told you about my accident."

"He told me, yes, but I never asked why you were of any interest to him."

Then why had she let me in? Why had Hugo wanted me to see her? Her face looked closed, impenetrable.

"I can't help feeling that in some way or other I played a part in his death."

"You believe that?"

"Yes."

I was getting nowhere. I should have left, but I did nothing of the sort. I had come, I realized suddenly, not only because Hugo had suggested it, but in the hope also of opening up that segment of my memory which seemed to have got lost in my accident, and without which I didn't feel quite sane. I said cruelly, "I believe Rudi was murdered because he had to be prevented from telling me something."

She said, "I am a widow. I have lost the last of my three sons. You are not very considerate. It is easier for me to believe in a senseless tragedy than in murder."

"But why did he want to see me? Why, if he had nothing to fear, did he behave so secretively? Why didn't he just ask me to have a drink with him somewhere, instead of a clandestine meeting in the woods?"

"He had his own way of doing things."

"Perhaps he was afraid for me."

She answered quickly, too quickly, "Not in the slightest," and tried to take it back, make it sound less positive. "Can *you* tell me any reason why he should have been concerned about you? A complete stranger he had only just met?"

Of course this was a question I couldn't answer. Why, indeed, should he have been afraid for me? I was, as Mrs. Becker had just pointed out, a stranger, and an unimportant one at that.

"You see," she said when I didn't reply, a slight ring of triumph coloring her voice. Her eyes too had changed. In her apparent relief they had come to life.

A timid knock distracted me from continuing this trend of thought. A very young maid slipped into the room. She was holding two wreaths in either hand. "These just came."

Mrs. Becker, without glancing at the cards, nodded, and the girl disappeared into the adjoining room. She came back almost at once, empty-handed.

Mrs. Becker rose. She held out her hand. Now that she had apparently achieved her purpose, my visit was over. "Good-by," she said, then added, as if it was all she had to offer, "You may pay your last respects to him if you wish."

I followed her through the door the maid had opened and closed so gently.

I wasn't accustomed to the tradition of having a coffin in one's home. It stood on a low dais which had been covered with a white sheet. Banked around it was a profusion of flowers, mostly white—lilies, roses, carnations. In the airless room their scent was overpowering. The floor around the dais was carpeted with branches of evergreens, arborvitae, in some parts of Germany considered a cemetery tree. The greens crunched under our feet. Lighted candles were burning, two at the head, two at the feet. The coffin itself was of an expensive black wood with ornate copper handles. In it, on a white satin sheet, lay Rudolf Becker. A small oblong pillow had been placed under his head, his hands were folded on his breast. No beauty parlor mortician had messed with his face. His cheeks hadn't been stuffed with cotton balls nor had they been rouged. His lips were as bloodless as when I had discovered him. Only his hair had been brushed. Suddenly I realized what a handsome young man he had been. Tall, slender, with almost Roman features, a well-rounded forehead, a strong aristocratic nose, a rather voluptuous mouth and a willful chin which, with age, would have grown squarer and heavier.

"Oh, the little fool!" Mrs. Becker moved suddenly to remove a cross from between Rudi's hands. "I told Magda not to. He didn't believe in religion."

Angrily she took away the small cross with an ivory figure of Christ. In her haste the cuff of Rudi's right sleeve fell back, revealing a narrow bracelet, the kind soldiers wear with their dog tags. I said stupidly, "But he was too young to have been in the war."

"He wore it as a memento. I had the number removed after we were liberated, because I didn't want to have his arm marked. I wanted him to forget, not to be reminded daily by the number."

"What number?"

"Every prisoner in a concentration camp had his number branded on the lower part of his arm."

"Concentration camp?"

"Theresienstadt."

The name was familiar, like something out of a history book.

"He was born in Theresienstadt."

I gave her a quick look. She shook her head. "They didn't take only Jews. They took everybody who opposed them openly. And my husband wouldn't leave. He regarded it as his duty to stay and fight them. If every decent German had had his courage, they wouldn't have succeeded."

"I come from German stock. For a long time my grand-parents refused to believe . . ."

"Naturally," said Mrs. Becker. "Who could believe that a civilized people . . . my husband didn't. And when they came for him he thought they were taking him to a labor camp. Or to a punitive battalion at the front. But they took all of us, me, the children, even my old father. I was eight months pregnant, and when Rudi came I had to do it all by myself, with them standing around watching me. In the open. The ground was frozen. But in spite of the fact that I was near starvation, Rudi weighed twelve and a half pounds. That's why they allowed me to keep him, and kept us alive."

"How long was it before you were liberated?"

"In forty-five," she said. "And during those five and a half years my two older sons died. My husband was shot. But it wasn't that . . ."

I didn't dare to break the silence. Finally she spoke again, in a continuation of her last words. "What made it impossible for Rudi to forget was the way his grandfather died. At the end of the war, when they were in a hurry. They had dug a ditch and were piling in the corpses from the gas chambers. Among a new load of dead a girl still showed signs of life. My father took her off the pile. They grabbed him and threw both of them back in. Then they set fire to the bodies."

She leaned forward and rearranged the cuff above Rudi's wrist. "For years he would wake up in the night screaming, and rush through the room in search of water to quench the fire, or flail with his arms at something he imagined to be flames." Suddenly she pushed back his sleeve again and unfastened the bracelet. She held it in the palm of her hand, away from her, as if it were an object she had been offered for appraisal, then she put it around her arm.

We went back into the living room. Unasked I sat down in the chair I had occupied before. She glanced at me, pursed her lips, but didn't object. She sat down in her place at the window. For a while neither of us spoke. The only sound was the slight slur the rocker made on the shiny floor. I could think of nothing but that its runners must have been lined with felt or rubber, since they didn't leave any marks on the parquet flooring. When all at once she addressed me by name it came as a surprise.

"Mr. Waldron," she said, "I have been thinking. I want you to promise me something."

"What?"

"I don't want you to voice your doubts, I mean now your doubts concerning my son's death. Whatever you may think, don't try to find out the truth."

"Then you're not convinced that . . ."

"Mr. Waldron. I just asked you . . ."

"But if it was murder, how can you possibly not take steps to get to the bottom of it?"

"It wouldn't suit Rudi's purpose."

"And what was his purpose?"

She turned to face me. Her large dark eyes were wells of unshed tears. "I had hoped to persuade you by my attitude that there was nothing more to it than one man's insane violence. I didn't succeed. You didn't leave when it was time for you to go. You sat down. You waited, waited for me to say something. If I keep silent, you'll go to others and ask them the questions I wouldn't answer. I see now that it is better for me to tell you than to have you running around making matters worse."

She reached across the table for a small etui. I wouldn't have thought that she smoked. I lit her cigarette before taking one of my own.

"I told you," she said, "that Rudi could never forget the way his grandfather was killed. I doubt if he forgot anything else he witnessed, but we never discussed any of it. Although I tried. I didn't think it was good for him to keep it all to himself. When he was fifteen, he implored me to leave Germany, to go anywhere—America, Australia, New Zealand. He said he didn't want to grow up among Germans, that he couldn't regard Germany as his fatherland. I felt differently. Like my husband, I didn't think it was right to run away and with new citizenship have done with the past. On the contrary, I felt it was our duty to stay and prove, if not to others then at least to ourselves, that we hadn't been totally corrupted."

She paused, as if listening to the echo of her own words, then looked down at Rudi's bracelet which was too wide for her small wrist. "How often I have wished since then that I had done what he asked me to do. He stayed, of course. I think he would have gone into politics if he'd had the chance. It was the only thing that interested him once we had decided to stay. He was outraged to find so many former Nazis in high positions or back at their old jobs. In Austria, in Vienna, there lives a man who has dedicated his life to tracking down Nazi war criminals. Rudi got in touch with him, worked for him, getting information . . ." she sighed, "until a certain group began to absorb all his interest. They were the nucleus of what is today a party to fear —the NPD."

At eighteen, a student at UCLA, there had hardly been a night when I hadn't been involved in political bull sessions, but after I had dropped out of college, politics had interested me less and less. Probably a mistake. I was chagrined to have to admit that I knew few names, and had dismissed them all as a handful of fanatic neo-Nazis who didn't have a chance in a West German Republic that seemed to be pretty solidly entrenched. Besides, the mind balked at the very idea that anything like Hitler could possibly happen again.

"Hasn't the NPD changed its original manifesto and overhauled the entire party?"

Mrs. Becker's face registered impatience and contempt. "What idiocy to believe anything of the sort! And it's just what Rudi was afraid of—people lulled into a lack of awareness until again it would be too late. He never gave up. In the end his tenacity led him to the Lindwurm."

Yes, I thought, a hotel like the Lindwurm would make an ideal setting for underground activities. Under the mask of patients, anyone could hide in the hospital wing; as ordinary guests they could be assured of a privacy rarely available at other hotels. And if any one among them should be threatened by arrest, the extraordinary location provided ample opportunities for warning. At carnival time, masked . . . I stopped myself from being carried away by my suddenly sparked imagination.

"Rudi saw several men who at one time or other had been party members, but then how few were not? Yet it seemed to him, as more and more of their friends arrived, that they hadn't come for just a few days or weeks of rest and fun but for different reasons."

I looked at her questioningly. She went on.

"He felt certain that they were holding meetings at the Lindwurm, because on several occasions, shortly after their get-togethers, there would be demonstrations against Americans, or against the government in Bonn, or vandalism in Jewish cemeteries. Hakenkreuz signs appeared on walls, unexplained fires broke out, frequently in synagogues, and there would be strikes at vital factories. Nothing outstanding, yet summed up they seemed to be organized, and they left their mark. For years he was convinced that the group at the Lindwurm wasn't acting on its own initiative but was being given orders by someone. He made it his task to find out by whom."

"And you think he was murdered because he finally found out who it was?"

She said dryly, "It looks that way to me."

"But if he had found out, why did he want to talk to me?"

"I can only imagine that in some way or another he needed your help."

"*My* help?"

Here I had been wondering if for some mysterious reason my life was in danger. The professor's warning, which later he had dropped, and Rudi's whispered messages had made me feel uneasy. Now it became clear that they had been concerned about me because they intended to involve me in whatever they were up to. "*My* help?" I asked again.

"I know Rudi thought of you as someone he might use if

it became necessary. You were a stranger, uncommitted . . ."

I lit a cigarette and smoked for a few minutes in silence,
trying to straighten the thing out in my mind. Then I said,
"He must have had friends working with him at the Lindwurm. I presume Hugo is one of them. Who else?"

"I am not at liberty to reveal their names."

"But he didn't want to endanger them."

"You might have been able to do something without any
danger to yourself, whereas they . . ."

To be involved in anything emotionally was bad enough,
but to get mixed up politically was to my way of thinking a
deadly trap. I had seen enough to know that the individual
had no chance whatsoever to shape history, unless desire for
power and influence was backed by money, or fanaticism
went beyond all logic. When three idealistic young men,
peace workers, had been slain in Alabama, I had felt compassion for them, yet at the same time seen their idealism as
a utopian dream. One didn't tangle with elements more
forceful than oneself if one wanted to stay alive. Yet here I
was, to be used without my knowledge in some political
shenanigans, and I rebelled, rebelled against the whole
thing.

"Don't you think I should have something to say about it
if I'm going to be . . . shall we say 'used?' "

"Perhaps that is what Rudi was about to do."

"Who is the man he was after?"

"You haven't met him."

Her answer eliminated with one stroke any of the persons
I knew—Klausen, Inspector Ginster, Richter, Gevern.

"The night I arrived," I said, and told her about the men
dressed as eagles who had had their grotesque bit of fun
with me.

147

"Rudi knew them," she said. "Conservatives of the far right with minimal functions in the NPD, but of no great importance. There are millions of malcontents, anti-intellectuals, anti-liberals, quite a few of them in government positions."

"You said I haven't met him. Shall I?"

"I can't tell you."

"Look, you've told me so much, can't I know his name?"

"Mr. Waldron," she said, "if I talked to you on a day like this, I did it out of necessity. You had to be stopped from speculating in public on Rudi's death—was it or wasn't it murder? You have to realize that at this point no one may risk a word too much. Under no circumstances must they be warned by anyone that we don't believe it was the poacher who shot him. Please accept it as fact and let it go at that."

I watched her rise quickly, almost briskly. As she stood there in frail dignity, very straight but obviously tired, Rudi's bracelet dangling from her small wrist, I had the feeling that I would never see her again. "But you," I said, "are you safe? If Rudi was killed because he knew too much, couldn't you . . ."

A faint smile lifted the corners of her mouth. "Death has never frightened me," she said. "You are perfectly right. After all, it would be understandable that a widow who has lost her last son would commit suicide. But I have learned not to be afraid."

"But you were when I pushed my foot in the door."

"Not for myself—for you. I regretted that you had come. Just in case this house is being watched, someone might wonder why you considered it necessary to see me. Why should Rudi or his mother mean anything to you unless . . ."

In my search for the missing link in my memory, I had

failed to consider how my actions might look to others. I had found Rudi, I had sounded the alarm, I had roused Klausen, I had stopped at the police station to ask if I could see the killer and finally gone to Rudi's private address . . . yet as far as I knew, I had not been watched.

"If you should be asked," Mrs. Becker said, "you will say that you found me bowed down with grief, unable to talk, and that you came because, having been the one to find Rudi's body, you felt impelled to offer your condolences."

She sounded as if she wanted to add something to these last words, but she said nothing more. Then came three rings, two short, one long. "It's all right," she called out, to stop the maid from answering the bell, and walked into the hall to open the door. I couldn't hear her greet anybody. She came back followed by a girl. Bettina.

She was wearing something black and very short. It looked more like the jacket of a military uniform than a dress. A cape of the same material had slipped askew across her shoulders, and her long hair hung straight, almost like a curtain hiding her face. She didn't seem aware of a third person in the room. She went straight to Mrs. Becker, throwing off her cape and gloves as she moved, and knelt down in front of her. She buried her face in the old woman's lap and began to sob. I had a sudden picture of the two as they might have looked years ago, a little girl crying for some childish heartbreak, and Mrs. Becker comforting her. But Mrs. Becker did nothing of the sort now. It was quite a while before she spoke and then her voice was steely. "Please control yourself, Bettina."

Bettina lifted her tear-stained face. She looked as unattractive as anyone who has cried for a long time without caring what it did to their eyes, nose and mouth. "How can you be so hard?"

"I asked you not to come."

"But I had to. Don't you see, I had to. When I phoned you last night and . . . oh, Pauline . . ." and she began to sob again. "I loved Rudi. You know I did. And I never stopped loving him. Pauline, remember all the times we were happy together, when with you was home."

"I can't afford memories."

"Then at least let me share your grief. Let me stay with you for a while and be of some use. Let me help you through this."

"You can't be of any possible use to me now. I didn't want to see you. I don't want to see you ever again."

Her hands moved suddenly and with such impatience that Bettina drew back as if she had been struck. Her eyes narrowed as they searched Mrs. Becker's face in disbelief. "But you hate me," she said, in a small horrified voice. "I never thought you'd hate me."

"I don't," said Mrs. Becker, "if only for the reason that I have no feelings left."

I felt like someone who had come too late for the first act of a play and was therefore forced to figure out what had gone before. They were like two actors, so intent on their parts that they had forgotten their audience. But I was wrong, for Mrs. Becker suddenly addressed me. In spite of the hard expression in her eyes, there was something almost pleading in their glance. She was, I realized, at the end of her strength. "Mr. Waldron," she said, "would you please take her away."

Bettina turned to face me. I couldn't tell what startled her more—that I should be there, or that Mrs. Becker had asked me to take her away, or perhaps it was just my strange appearance. Her lips parted, but for the moment she said nothing. Gradually then her mouth set. For the first time I saw the hardly perceptible lines running from her nostrils to the corners of her lips which one day would mar the still childlike roundness of her cheeks. She scrambled to her feet. "All right then, let's go."

Quite possibly no further word would have been exchanged between the three of us if Mrs. Becker hadn't said, when we were halfway across the room, "You forgot your gloves." But she didn't hold them out to Bettina, she merely pointed at the long black suede gloves lying in front of the rocker at her feet. The gesture of contempt broke down Bettina's last efforts at self-control. Grief, humiliation and pride, or whatever she may have been feeling, made her say suddenly, vehemently, "Don't treat me as if I had murdered Rudi."

"He might still be alive if you had acted differently."

Obviously this was a reply Bettina had not expected. She began to tremble visibly, and I held out a hand to steady her. She didn't notice it. "Oh God, is that what you are thinking?"

Mrs. Becker's silence was answer enough. Desperate now, Bettina cried, "But you can't, you can't really think that!"

"If you didn't feel guilty you wouldn't have accused me of the thought."

Bettina stiffened. She was very pale but once more in control of herself. "No. I don't feel guilty. Do you think I would have come if I had known that you . . ."

Mrs. Becker said nothing.

"Rudi understood. I thought you did too."

Again she ran into a wall of silence, and although I didn't want to interfere, my curiosity was stronger than my instinct to stay out of any situation so fraught with emotion. I asked, "Rudi understood what?"

"That I simply couldn't do it."

"What couldn't you do?"

"Spy on my uncle."

Mrs. Becker rose, and her chair went on rocking for quite a while after being released from her weight. I watched it, thinking what a good shot it would make in a movie, the empty chair, rocking symbolically, forward onto the rug now, as if it had a life of its own. Then I realized that my idea was outdated. It had been done already.

"Until then," Bettina was saying.

"Don't." Mrs. Becker interrupted her sharply. She was standing in front of us now, more erect than ever, as if the mere closeness of her physical presence could stop Bettina from continuing. But Bettina was no longer desperate or frightened. "Until a couple of years ago," she went on, "I thought you and Rudi were the most wonderful people in the world. But on the day you suggested that Hannes might be a war criminal . . . Of course I refused. What else did you expect me to do? I thought it was immoral of you to ask me to spy on him. It seemed just as horrible as what the Nazis did when they asked children to report on their parents, employees on their employers, janitors on tenants, friends on friends." She was trembling again, but she managed to pull a cigarette from a pack of Gauloises and wave away the match I struck for her. But now she turned to me.

"You see, I didn't know anything really about the whole Hitler business. I mean, what child growing up in Brazil did? And by the time I came here, it was all over. Rudi was the first one to tell me about the terror of it. He made me read books about it; he showed me illustrations. Still I couldn't believe it. Probably I didn't want to. When I went back to Pôrto Alegre I asked Hannes what he knew about it. He said some dreadful things may have happened but he had never seen them happen. He believed for the most part they were enemy propaganda, or had been done by the Russians, or even by the Americans when they had overrun Germany. But I had seen Pauline's number branded on her arm, and I fought him on it. That's why he didn't want me to have the Beckers for friends and took me out of school."

Her words were so rushed, it was hard to keep track of what she was saying, still I could imagine her at fourteen, incredulous yet curious to discover the truth about a country which she had been taught to esteem. I could also picture her uncle, disturbed to see a young girl burdened by such knowledge and denying it, perhaps because he didn't want her to feel guilty or ashamed of her ancestry. Or he may really not have known better at the time. I could recall other Germans who hadn't, who had believed honestly that facts were being distorted. In a way my grandparents had had the same attitude.

Bettina was still talking. "But I couldn't see why that was any reason to spy on him. I couldn't make myself sneak into his room, open his desk, look through his private papers, eavesdrop on him and his friends or take photos secretly."

"Stop being dramatic," said Mrs. Becker. "We never asked you to do any of those things."

"But what else does spying mean?"

"More important things were at stake than your scruples," Mrs. Becker said quietly. "And you seemed so eager to have a share in what we were trying to achieve. I think you would have forgotten your ethics if it had been anyone but your uncle."

Fleetingly I wondered what I would have done in her situation, what would have been more important to me—

the truth or illusion, politics or private life, a possible new threat to humanity or a person to whom I was bound by love and gratitude.

"You refused for one reason only," Mrs. Becker went on, "because you loved him."

"And you made me love him even more by suspecting him and his friends. Just because he chose to leave Germany and start a new life in Brazil, he was a villain. Well he isn't. And he never was. And now that Rudi is dead, you behave as if I were to blame. How could I have protected Rudi if he was to be killed? Even if one of Hannes's friends is the man you are looking for, you can't be so naïve as to assume I would be told."

"Perhaps you told them."

"Told them what?"

"That Rudi believed the man he was after was staying at the Lindwurm."

"You must be mad."

"Am I?" asked Mrs. Becker.

"It's years since Rudi and I talked about any of these things. You know that as well as anyone." Now Bettina's voice was gentle, almost as though she were talking to someone sick. "We hardly ever saw each other any more."

"Then why did you meet three nights ago? You left the Guërzenich separately and went to his office."

"I was shocked by Florian's death. I wanted someone to talk to about it, someone who understood me, who knew how much he meant to me."

So that was why I hadn't been able to find Rudi in the crowd and for quite some time hadn't seen her anywhere.

"You could have come here for that," Mrs. Becker told her.

"His office was closer."

"Bettina," said Mrs. Becker, "there was a safe in his office, a small safe, under his desk, under the floor. Until that night nobody knew about it, nobody knew where the mechanism was hidden that lifted the floorboards—except me. But on that night, Rudi opened the safe, to show you something."

"Yes."

"I went to his office as soon as Inspector Ginster had called me. The safe was empty."

"You can't be thinking that I . . ."

"Not you personally. But I have to think that you told someone about it."

"If I refused to betray Hannes's trust in me, how can you possibly think that I would betray you?"

"Your uncle may have brought pressure to bear . . ."

"Never!"

"But you began to be afraid . . ."

"No."

"Then why did you think it was odd that the warning sign disappeared from the bridge just a few minutes before your friends drove across it?"

"They were your friends too." Bettina spoke deliberately, slowly, stressing every word like someone memorizing a lesson in pronunciation. "And it was you who hinted that Hannes or one of his friends might be to blame for their death, because they had spent some time in Brazil and might have found out something incriminating." She paused, then went on in the same slow calm voice, so incongruous for anyone her age in her present situation. "If there was any pressure, it came from you, to destroy my faith in Hannes and make me do what you wanted."

"You found it hard to believe Lisa died of a ruptured appendix."

"Because of your insinuations. What do you think it does to you when people you love and respect keep hammering at some theoretical possibilities? That's why I began to feel uneasy at the Lindwurm."

"But you went back, again and again."

"Only when Florian was there, to work with him."

"And he died too. In an accident."

"It was suicide," I said, "I was there," and felt like an idiot because neither Mrs. Becker nor Bettina as much as glanced at me. They went on talking as if I were non-existent.

"The fact remains," said Mrs. Becker, "that my son was murdered. Very few people knew what he was doing. Only two people knew about the safe in which he kept his files on those he suspected. He was shot not quite three days after those files were stolen."

"The man will be tried. The trial will . . ."

Mrs. Becker shook her head. "He hanged himself. He was found dead a few hours ago, although he was supposed to be guarded at all times against just such an eventuality. We shall never know who paid him to kill Rudi."

Actually I wasn't astonished, nor did Bettina seem surprised. And Mrs. Becker behaved as if she had rather expected that Emil Mascher would never have to stand trial. Our tacit resignation to such circumvention of the law could have been called callous, but all of us had lived through too many similar situations to be shocked by them.

"My only hope now," said Mrs. Becker, "is that, with Rudi gone, you will finally . . ."

"No," said Bettina.

She went into the next room and stayed there for quite a while. We didn't talk during her absence. When she came back, she went up to Mrs. Becker and kissed her, then she nodded to me. I bowed to the silent woman in her rocking chair. She didn't respond. We waited for a few seconds before we left, then we took the elevator. We didn't speak until we reached the street, and then only after we had walked a block or two. I asked her how she had heard of Rudi's death.

"I called him and Pauline answered."

"You called him?"

"Yes. From Paris."

"Whatever for?"

"Never mind." She changed the subject. For the first time she mentioned my appearance. "Pauline told me about it. What a horrible thing to happen," and for a few blocks I had to assure her that my injuries were minor, however ghastly I might look at the moment. She looked away, straight ahead, "Another accident."

I wanted to distract her. We passed a movie house, a newsreeler. I suggested we go in. It was almost empty. And cold. The proprietor, not expecting a full house, had turned down the heat. Bettina pulled her legs up under her to warm them. The news was boring, the animated shorts were stupid, so stupid we laughed in sheer desperation. After a while she said, "It all began for Rudi when they desecrated the synagogue, about ten years ago. On Christmas Eve. He said it started a wave of anti-Semitic barbarism all through Germany. A year before he'd seen the swastika again, and for the first time, slogans scribbled on walls. When he saw the sign "Yankee Go Home," he felt the time had come to act. He became an agent. He took a job with the Internal Security people, the Federal Office for the Protection of the Constitution, or whatever it's called."

"I found him, you know."

"Yes. I know." And after a pause, "Pauline told me. She

said the man Rudi was after might be at the Lindwurm. But if he is, how could it be Hannes, who is in Pôrto Alegre?"

"She didn't actually say it was he, but that it might be one of his friends."

"I didn't see any of his friends or acquaintances there."

"Did you go with Rudi to his office?"

"Yes. Please don't let's talk about it any more."

We left. The streets were still fairly empty. A sharp wind had sprung up. It made Bettina shiver. I said, "I need a drink."

She didn't object. We went into the next restaurant. The bar was crowded but there were some empty booths at the back. She ordered a grog—red wine, a lot of sugar and a cinnamon stick stuck through a piece of lemon peel like a thin Swiss cigar. Remembering Klausen's advice, I asked for the same. "How did you manage to break away from Gevern? He was like a watchdog when you left on Saturday."

"I told him I had something to attend to that was none of his business, and after that I was returning to Paris."

"And are you?"

"Yes."

"Does Gevern know about Rudi?"

"Of course not."

"And he didn't object to your not returning to Brazil with him?"

"He did, but there wasn't anything he could do about it."

"But what about your uncle? Didn't you feel you should be there?"

"The operation has been postponed."

When you want to ask a lot, you sometimes say nothing at all. To have to find the right approach, to phrase your words carefully, tactfully, kills all spontaneity. At least it does with me. I watched her sipping her drink and wondered why she had let me kiss her in the car when she had hardly known me. I had appealed to her and she had responded without the slightest hesitation. She was fingering the lapel of her jacket to see her watch, which was stuck like a yellow daisy in the top buttonhole. "Twenty past four already. I forget what time exactly my train leaves. And I've got to collect my luggage from the Dom."

"Today?"

"Hm."

I called for the check and we went out with a wave of raucous laughter following us into the dusk. I took her hand. "Let's go somewhere, anywhere we can find a room."

She hesitated, then she said, "Why not? I can always take a plane."

It wasn't easy to find a place. The Dom and all of the better hotels were crowded; to take her up to the Lindwurm was impossible under the circumstances. We shopped around for a bit, then I realized that if I didn't make up my mind pretty soon, she'd prefer to go to the station instead, and I became less choosy. We landed at a dump, a house with signs in the window, "Rooms for rent, weekly, daily, by the hour." A beaded curtain, a room with a false fireplace, an assortment of plaster madonnas, several toys, the kind you win at fairs, and an old-fashioned roll-top desk. A woman with curlers in her hair sat in front of it, her fat varicose-veined legs stuck in a pail of steaming water. "What a crowd! My feet are falling off. They'll never hold up for the dancing tonight."

Bettina pulled some bills out of her bag. "Here, let me pay. I want to get rid of my German money." It annoyed me. We climbed up two flights of steep steps and walked along a narrow corridor to Number 14. The room was small but clean, with just a bed and two chairs beside a dresser. It smelled strongly of disinfectant. A man in shirt-sleeves came in on our heels. "Champagne?" he asked, and when we said no, he went to the window to draw the curtains. "Well, you looked like champagne." He folded the bedspread deftly into a square. "Bathroom two doors to the right. If you take a shower it's extra. Here are your slippers."

He handed us two pairs made of paper, with a tiny bell on each tip. I locked the door after him and watched Bettina undress and crawl under the covers. She folded her arms behind her neck and stared up at the ceiling. I took off my things while she wasn't looking, and stopped short. I had forgotten about my face.

"Anything wrong?"

"Not really. It's just that my ribs are acting up."

"Lie flat and keep still."

There are many ways of making love but none of them worked. We tried, by God we did, and bit back the anger of frustration and lay quiet for a while, hoping that two bodies that knew each other so intimately might find some comfort in a mutual warmth and need. Instead our closeness made us nervous. The mattress was lumpy, the heavy covers kept slipping down, her shoulder on my rib cage weighed a ton, my bandage scratched the soft skin of her back and my face was itching unbearably. Finally Bettina got up.

"It's all my fault," I said.

"Don't be an idiot."

"It was a bad idea and I suggested it."

"I could have said no but I wanted it."

"It or me?"

"Anything that could make me forget, for a while at least."

She lit a cigarette. "I thought you didn't smoke."

"I'm smoking now."

She gave me the Gauloise and it made me cough and that hurt. Excrutiatingly. I crushed it and she said suddenly, crossly, "That wasn't very polite."

"I'm sorry."

She put on the jacket of her suit, which barely covered her small muscular behind, and went to the door. The bells on her slippers actually tinkled and reminded me of my grandmother's cat, an overfed beast to which I had been allergic. "Where are you going?"

"Where else but to wash?"

While she was gone I got dressed. It had never happened before that I couldn't make a woman come. Or for that matter myself. It made me feel old and depressed and slightly ashamed. Bettina came back, smelling of cheap soap. "I took a shower after all." She glanced at me. "What's the matter with you?"

"I'm sorry I let you down."

"You've had too many sedatives, that's all. Come on, sport."

It was an expression I hated. She must have picked it up from some American crowd in Florence or Paris. And why not go to Paris with her? Then I remembered my passport. It was too late now to call the police. "Listen," I said, "I'm stuck here. Can't you stay? Stay with me for a few days."

"It wouldn't do any good."

"I didn't have just sex in mind."

"It wouldn't do any good," she repeated. "Don't you see? I'm terribly upset. I need to be by myself."

"I understand," I said. "But just in case I want to reach you . . ." She gave me her address and telephone number, automatically, as if I were someone who might call her on business.

I saw her to the station, pure modern magnificence, one

side all glass with the Gothic filigree work of the cathedral glittering through, arched low in concrete, with its own hotel, shops and movie. Already they were taking down the grandstands around the cathedral. She sent a porter to the hotel to get her luggage from Feldman. We had a bite in a sort of super hamburger joint. Neither of us felt hungry. After that there was still a half-hour before her train was due to leave. "Don't wait around," she said. "I'm too tired to talk and prolonged good-bys are a bore."

I felt exactly like her, and left.

Ash Wednesday.

The air was damp and raw. You felt it in every bone. My depression hadn't worn off. The day before I had taken the car ferry across the Rhine to Bad Godesberg, where the American embassy and consulate were located. "It's much prettier than Washington," my driver had told me with obvious pride on our five minute leisurely float across the river. "You may have the cherry blossoms but we have the most modern swimming pool, and our parks have trees which are a sight to behold. And we have just as many embassies, and people running around in their native dress. And as far as landscape is concerned, you must admit that the Potomac can't compare with the Rhine. Now just look back at that range of hills we're leaving, and the old castles." I had looked dutifully. "There's the Löwenburg, that's the highest one. Restaurant halfway up and a nice old ruin on top. And that's the Wolkenburg, the lowest one. You've been up the Drachenfels, of course. You haven't?" This had seemed beyond belief. "There's a cable-car runs up it. But you can drink the famous Dragonblood, that's the wine that comes from there, right here in Bad Godesberg. And Washington has no vineyards and no therapeutic springs."

There had been no stopping him, and I had had quite a time persuading him that I hadn't come to Bad Godesberg for sightseeing, but to get to the American consulate before it closed. When we had finally reached the Mehlemer Aue and the American embassy and consulate, housed in concrete blocks on piles, a stern girl had looked at me impatiently and advised me, like Richter, to wait a couple of days until the carnival was over because my passport might still be turned in. But I had no intention of waiting. Bettina in Paris made it imperative that I be free to travel out of Germany if I wanted to. The girl had then proceeded to lecture me on my carelessness and said it would take several weeks to get another passport issued, and that I'd better pull some strings if I was in a hurry. "Anyway," she had concluded, "you'll need photos, and with your face all bandaged up . . ."

"I always carry some extras," I had told her, and given them to her. She had studied them, refraining with barely disguised curiosity from asking me what had happened to my face, muttering under her breath, "Well, I guess I'll have to take your word for it that it's you," as she had handed me an application form which I filled out while she powdered her nose. As she checked it—number of my missing passport, date of issue—she had shaken her head, "How can you remember all that if you lost your passport?"

"I make a note of such things," I had told her, "and I didn't lose my passport, I was robbed."

A knock at the door. Hugo with my breakfast. A gray spot of ash sat like a third eye in the middle of his forehead. I hadn't thought he was religious.

"As of tomorrow I won't be able to serve you any longer, sir. I enjoyed waiting on you, if I may say so."

I gave him a tip which he pocketed with a grin. "Have you been fired?"

He shook his head. "No. I'll be around. But in the dead season I work as a waiter only when they have a convention and need extra help, or an extra chauffeur."

"Taking Rudi's place?"

"If you want to call it that."

He gave me his telephone number and address. "And of course you can always reach me through Pauline Becker."

Later in the day it began to rain softly, and I thought of the third clearing in the woods and Rudi's corpse under the hay. To distract myself I went to the window and watched car after car taking off. None of the guests were using the Volkswagen buses. I thought of what Mrs. Becker had said, that the man Rudi was after might be at the Lindwurm, and wondered if he could possibly be among those leaving. All day long the noise of motors, horns, and the rumble of cars crossing the bridge drifted up to my room. By the time dusk fell, most of the Lindwurm's clientele had gone, and the sudden silence had an oppressive quality. I asked for a connection with Paris, and it came so unexpectedly soon, I had no time to figure out what I wanted to say, which proved to be no calamity, since there was no answer. A little while later my phone rang, but it was only the German operator, asking me if I wanted to place the call again. I said no. Then Dr. Klausen called, as he had done yesterday, to ask if I felt like having dinner with him. We agreed on eight o'clock.

When I went down to meet him, the deserted hotel struck me again with melancholy. In the lobby, the young man who took Richter's place around this time, sprawled in his chair without getting up or even looking at me as I passed him. The mirrors seemed less bright and the armor along the walls blacker in the diminished lights of the chandeliers. I could understand the owner's decision to use part of the Lindwurm as a sanatorium to make the thing pay. Dr. Klausen met me in front of his quarters. "Feeling better?"

"On the contrary. Lousy."

He smiled understandingly, then said he wanted wine with his meal, and since I seemed to need cheering up, I could have a glass too. I took it for granted that he'd choose what he wanted from a list, but he insisted that I come with him to the cellars, which I would have preferred to avoid. The professor's death was still too fresh in my memory. The wine cellars, though, were magnificent, and well worth a visit. Rows upon rows of dusty bottles. Large wine casks cut to table height had been placed in the low-vaulted rooms with comfortable chairs for anyone who might like to sit down and sample the wines. On each one stood a fat candle of dark beeswax in an iron holder, several long-stemmed glasses and small round silver tasters, the kind that dangle from wine stewards' chains.

Choosing the wine turned into a lesson given by a connoisseur to a layman. Tiptoeing in front of the rows, Dr. Klausen read aloud names I'd never heard of, "Deidesheimer Herrgottsacker, Ruppertsberger Kreuz, Jesuitengarten, Niersteiner Heiligenbaum, Nackenheimer Engelsberg, Bodenheimer Kapelle," so many of them names with a religious connotation because the vineyards had belonged to monasteries. To show I wasn't entirely unfamiliar with wines, I suggested a Liebfraumilch but was told that it was no longer grown on desirable terraces. There were still quite a few good vineyards around the Liebfrauenkirche in Worms, which had given this famous wine its name, but a landslide had done away with the best of them. Since then vintners far away from the original site had been given permission to name their wine after the milk of "our dear lady," and it had become second-rate. The best "Rhine" wine, Klausen assured me, came from Hochheim, level with Mainz, and not on the Rhine at all. He preferred the Mosel wines, in green bottles, to differentiate them from the brown bottles of the Rhine wines. But Johannisberger, Markobrunn and Rauenthal, from the district between Bingen and Mainz, had their excellent years too. He finally opened a Rauenthal, because it was the fruitiest. The way he manipulated the corkscrew was as deft as if he were performing a delicate operation.

"When will the bandages come off?"

He smelled the cork. "Friday, the day after tomorrow—" he said, "or latest on Saturday." He rang a bell. A waitress appeared and served us a fondue in a chafing dish over a flame, and a basketful of small pieces of white bread to dunk in the bubbling cheese.

"It's the way they taste the new young wines in Switzerland," he said. "I hope you don't mind sitting here for a while. We can go upstairs later for something more solid to eat."

He dimmed the light and lit a candle. I didn't mind at all except for the fact that it made me think of Bettina and her preference for wine, and I wondered if she had ever sat here and learned about grapes, and the soil they grew on, their specific taste and bottling, from Klausen. I almost asked him but then thought better of it, for I felt very much in the mood to talk and might quite easily have been indiscreet.

The wine went to my head more quickly than I would have believed possible, and perhaps because of the flickering light of the candle, I could suddenly see Rudi, lying in his coffin with his hands folded on his chest. My surroundings changed into the airless flower-bedecked room in which Rudi was lying in his coffin, but his eyes were wide open, staring straight ahead with such intensity that he seemed alive.

"What is it?" Klausen asked. "What made you sigh? Are you in pain?"

I hadn't been aware of sighing and shook my head. "It's nothing, just that I can't get Rudi out of my head."

"He was buried today. A small ceremony. He was cremated, according to his wishes."

"I went to pay my respects to Mrs. Becker on Monday."

"That was nice of you. Poor woman. But she must have expected it."

Suddenly I was sober. "Expected her son's death? Why? I thought you considered the shooting unpremeditated. Wasn't it an accident?"

He shrugged. "What's the use of going into it when there's nothing to be gained? No, to us who are in sympathy with Rudi's views, it was murder. Unfortunately we have no proof. Didn't Mrs. Becker tell you?"

"No," I said. "Why should she talk to me about anything like that? After all, I'm a perfect stranger."

"And how much easier it is to talk to a stranger, sometimes, than to some friends." He poured another glass of wine and sipped it slowly. Apparently he wasn't going to say any more. I waited for a while, then I said, "I'm a stranger to you. Why don't you tell me?"

He put down his glass and regarded me thoughtfully. "I don't know how much you know about German politics."

"I've heard about the new Nazis, if that's what you mean."

He nodded. "Well then you must agree that a look at the roster of the NPD makes you shudder. It seems incredible that two-thirds of their thirty-member executive committee were important Nazi functionaries, and six of them SS men."

The figures shocked me. I looked disbelievingly at Klausen who didn't seem interested in my reaction but was biting off the end of a cigar, holding it up to his ear to make sure it wasn't too dry, then lighting it carefully before he went on. "But they are prominent and therefore easy to keep an eye on. Rudi was after those who have disappeared from the public eye. And they're all over. Everywhere. Among the refugees from those parts of Germany that had to be given up, among the old soldiers, in other right-wing parties, in Bonn itself, among the thousands of readers of right-wing papers—malcontents, anti-Semites, anti-democrats. Racists. Rudi and his group were fighting them. I don't know where he made a mistake, but that among his enemies someone should feel so menaced as to . . ."

Without his noticing it, I poured myself another glass. "Somehow I hadn't put you down as interested in politics."

"Primarily it's my work that counts, but I'd hate to think that . . ."

"I admire a man like Rudi, but I don't have that kind of idealism or dedication. I can understand it though. What I can't understand is the attitude you're taking. If you believe that Rudi was murdered, why do you keep quiet about it instead of . . ." I stopped. I was contradicting myself. Anyone trying to find Rudi's killer might well put his own life in jeopardy.

"Most of us are physical cowards," said Klausen, rising

to get another bottle. "I know I am. So was Florian, but not his brother, it seems. You know, curiosity got the better of me after you asked me why Florian identified himself with Regin, and I talked to Leise about it."

"Well, did he have a brother?"

"He did. Apparently he never mentioned it except in analysis. Then he talked about him a great deal, sometimes with admiration for his good looks, his charm and courage, at other times he would complain bitterly about his coldness, even cruelty, but above all about his feeling of superiority. He suffered under it as a boy. He had the misfortune to be the older one, but everybody took him for the younger. You know what he looked like. And it seems that as he grew up, he had to surrender all his rights of the firstborn. Leise says he never got over it. He was called 'Dwarf,' his brother's nickname for him, and of course he hated it."

I could see the two boys—the one tall, charming, courageous, the other ridiculously small and ugly.

"Poor fellow." Klausen opened the fresh bottle and poured the wine. "He did everything conceivable to stretch his body, even after he was full-grown. Ridiculous efforts. He'd hang for hours on rings and go through all sorts of painful exercises. He also tried to rid himself of fear. It seems that the younger one—undoubtedly Florian's ideal image—liked to create situations to test his older brother's courage, and Florian knocked himself out trying to make his younger brother proud of him. He could think up quite a few crazy tests on his own. I remember once he implored me to stitch a shirt to his skin and tear it off again, just as Signy had done to her sons, in one of our gruesome Teutonic legends, to see if they could stand pain without flinching. He was riddled with guilt, mainly over his cowardice.

On top of that he wasn't very smart. The brother, it seems, was quite brilliant. So Florian tried to make up in the arts what he lacked in physical strength and attractiveness. No doubt about it, there was a strange ambivalence in their relationship, a dichotomy of . . . shall we say the soul? Anyway, a state of chronic torment. Maybe he's lucky that it's all over. After all, death . . ."

Steps along the passage. Klausen surprised me by cocking his head just as Hugo had done when he had heard steps approaching my room. But while the expression in Hugo's eyes had been cautious, Klausen's unmistakably showed fear. Stark animal fear. The steps passed our room. His expression eased. "The watchman. Or the wine steward."

Trying to sound as natural as I could—I didn't want him to know that I'd noticed his fear—I asked, "Death, you said . . . what about it?"

He answered almost violently. "Let's not talk about death. We've had quite enough of it. We should be able to find something pleasanter to talk about; if you're going to do something wrong, at least enjoy it." He raised his glass. "To a happy future."

Even though I hadn't had much to drink, not being used to wine, I had a hangover next morning. Though the room had at last stopped going around and around with me inside it, everything still looked somehow askew. At one point I found myself trying to straighten out a print which, I finally discovered, had been hanging perfectly straight, and I spent quite some time finding the nail in the wall from which I had removed it. A cold shower didn't help. On the contrary. Having to keep my head out of the stream of water so that the bandages wouldn't get wet, I lost my balance and came down hard on the tiled floor of the stall. I asked for a thermos of coffee and felt a little better after two cups, yet my eyes still refused to focus correctly. The small type of my portable made me feel nauseous and I gave up the idea of working. I didn't know what to do with myself. All the things I had wanted to see in Cologne had lost their attraction. Vaguely I considered a walk, but couldn't face the idea of the silent woods. For a while I wandered idly around the vast premises of the Lindwurm. The movie had been closed, so had the bowling alley, but the billiard room was still open. I chose a cue that lay comfortably in the palm of my hand and pushed a few balls around without managing a single decent shot. I took the elevator to the solarium and found the iron-grilled outer door to the parapet locked and chained. I tried to push the professor out of my mind, but he and Rudi had become squatters there and refused eviction. I grew more and more disgusted with myself and with Germany. If only I had had my passport back, I would have hopped the next train or plane, not caring if it meant another doctor would have to finish the treatment of my face injuries.

I didn't feel better the following day. Again I couldn't settle down to work nor muster the energy or inclination to go sightseeing. The only thing I could decide was that the best wines in the world weren't good for me. From now on I'd stick to hard liquor.

On Friday Dr. Klausen called and told me to come down in an hour sharp. The pit of my stomach felt hollow as I went into the hospital wing. Schlau, the male nurse, greeted me as if he were meeting a long-lost friend. He guided me to Klausen's office at the end of the long corridor. Walking behind him I was struck again by the agility with which he moved his massive body, with the grace of a boxer in complete control of every muscle. It seemed incredible that the professor should have been able to escape him. I felt in no mood, though, to linger on that subject.

I had to wait in a small verandah-like room in which papers and magazines hung from pegs on something that looked like a clothes stand, the kind you find in coffee houses where people go to read rather than for food, and linger for hours over a cup of coffee or a glass of beer. I leafed through a New York *Herald Tribune,* European edition, glancing first at the headlines, then at the obituaries. Nobody of any significance had died. I turned to the theatrical and movie news. From inside Klausen's office I could hear animated voices, and gradually he ushered out four women with their faces lightly bandaged. "Americans," he explained to me, after they had fluttered off. "From Bad Godesberg. Officers' wives. They're used to playing bridge every afternoon, so they decided to have their faces lifted at the same time in order not to miss their daily game." He giggled. As always, his laugh, with its high-pitched effeminate tone, startled me. "I have quite a few additional patients since Bad Godesberg has become such an international community." I said it spoke for his reputation. He giggled again and said, with what I thought was disarming modesty, "I think it's more a question of money. I'm less expensive than your plastic surgeons."

I followed him into the consultation room. He made me sit down on a chair, a tubular one of stainless steel. He didn't call for a nurse but himself put out a tray with some cotton and bottles. "You don't like Sister Elly," he said, "and all the others are occupied. The hospital is always busiest in the dead season, when everybody not laid up may wander around without embarrassment. We're filled to capacity. All forty beds taken."

He began to unwind my bandages and I stared unbelievingly at the yards of gauze he threw into a slop pail beside my chair. He turned the light higher and put a black plastic ribbon around his head, with a magnifying glass attached to it, such as eye doctors and dentists use. He was trembling, very slightly, and I thought how dedicated he was to his work, that seeing the results for the first time should still, after so many years at it, fill him with such excitement. He washed his hands again before he probed my face with his thin forefinger. "Formidable," he said at last, "the way your skin heals. Better than I expected."

"I'd like to have a look."

"Certainly. But you won't be able to tell much, not for a few more weeks. That is, of course, if you continue to heal this way. Now don't expect to fall in love with yourself."

He reached for a hand mirror and held it up to me. My face was a mess. Red and swollen, and in a few places puffy, with tufts of short beard here and there. Unrecognizable. "My God!" I exclaimed. "I didn't think I'd look that wounded."

"You'll be looking that way for the next three weeks."

"Three weeks?"

"At least. If you don't want to get depressed about it, I would advise you to stay away from mirrors. And you absolutely must not shave until I tell you to."

"When will you take the stitches out?"

"In about four days."

"And that won't make any difference?"

"Not much."

"Well then, how long until I'll look myself again?"

"Six to eight weeks, six, I'd say, with you."

"I look as if the eagles had gotten their talons into me."

He glanced at me uncomprehendingly. "The eagles?"

"I was kidnaped by them the evening I arrived, or let's

say I fell into their nest. I must have pressed the wrong elevator button."

"Oh, those old men."

"But what a ludicrous get-up."

"Does the Ku Klux Klan dress less ludicrously?" He smiled. "At least the eagles are harmless."

I handed back the mirror. "Are you sure I'm going to be all right?"

"I guarantee it."

He took a bottle with a nozzle from the tray, told me to close my eyes, no, not tightly, just naturally, and sprayed my face. "There you are."

"I'd rather have the bandages again," I told him. "I'll frighten myself."

He smiled. "The air has to get at it. You'll get used to it."

I knew I would do nothing of the sort, but I didn't say so. There was something more important on my mind. "Tell me, I've had quite a lot of drugs, haven't I? I mean, is the stuff you've given me very powerful?"

"Quite."

Heaven knows why men dislike to mention anything affecting their sexual prowess. Anyhow, I did. "Powerful enough to make a man . . . well, I had difficulties. The other day . . ."

"Normal," said Klausen, "absolutely normal. Painkillers tend to influence the sexual organs. And since you're apparently not even used to sleeping pills, your reaction would be stronger than normal."

"May I leave off them now?"

"If you can sleep without them."

I reached for the mirror again. "Weeks, you said. Damn it all!" I got out of the chair, nearly upsetting it. He shook

174

his head. "I'm sorry, but there's nothing you or I can do about it. With each day it will be a little better, a little less red, a little less swollen, but it will take time. Resign yourself, Waldron. Actors have to, and gladly suffer a short period of ugliness and discomfort for their careers."

"I'm not an actor. I could have done without this."

"No. You're more fortunate. You write. Use these weeks. Try to work. And get your body back into shape. You're flabby. We have a good gymnasium here. Use it. Have a massage every day, visit the sauna. Work out a program for yourself and live by it. In the end you'll be grateful that this forced you to do something for your general health."

Good advice, undoubtedly, but how dismal it sounded. Bristling, I told him that he was treating me like an elderly patient. He shrugged and said something to the effect that the sooner I learned to make the best of conditions, the better for me. This being my own theory, and left with not much choice, I finally did what seemed best under the circumstances. I refused to think about my face—I never looked at it. Every morning before breakfast, I exercised for an hour. I wrote until lunch, ate sparingly, rested, worked for four more hours, went down to the saunas, sweated for twenty minutes, enjoyed a rubdown, slept for a while, dined and went to bed after the eleven o'clock news. Routine has a magic power. I could feel that my beard was growing; but so was the pile of typewritten pages. *Bachelor in Madrid, Bachelor in Paris, Bachelor in Rome,* in Copenhagen, Oslo, London, Tokyo, began to take shape without my having to resort to the various cartridges of my recorder. I found I could write better and more easily unhampered by notes. Satisfaction made me smug; the physical discipline I had imposed on myself—especially in regard to drinking—made me feel stronger. Klausen had been right. After ten days I was definitely in better shape than I had been for quite some time. Only one thing rankled—my performance with Bettina, yet I felt no inclination to call her up. Maybe it was all for the best that my passport hadn't come through yet. Certainly I didn't want her to see me the way I probably still looked. And then, one morning, as I shook open my napkin, monogrammed with the Lindwurm insignia, a large L with a dragon underneath it, something fluttered to the floor. A piece of paper with Roman numerals scribbled on it. I had to search my memory before I could decipher them. The only person I could think of who could possibly have sent me the note was Hugo. It seemed odd that he shouldn't have come to my room if he was working at the Lindwurm, or called me from Cologne, so I took the precaution of phoning him from the booth in the solarium. He was very short. "Yes," he said, "she expects to hear from you. Early tomorrow. In Paris. And she doesn't want anybody to know about it."

That Friday I was up earlier than usual, but instead of going to the gym, I walked down the winding road to the little inn where I had stopped to order a taxi after inspecting the location of my accident. It had just opened for business and I had a cup of coffee while waiting for the connection which this time took quite a while. She came on sleepy as a woodchuck, but her voice changed the moment she recognized mine. There was a lilt in it even though all she said was, "Drew!" Then, for a few moments, neither of us quite sure, both still cautious, we asked each other how we were and how our respective work was progressing, yet the stupid, polite phrases were like tentative caresses which grew in intensity the longer we talked to each other.

"You know," she said, "I can't get over Rudi. All day

long I manage not to think of him, but the nights are awful. I wake up and see him lying in his coffin with that horrible, surprised expression on his face."

"I haven't gotten over it myself," I told her, stretching the truth a little. For the last six days I hadn't actually given Rudi Becker or his mother a thought. Writing usually did that for me, occupying me to such an extent that there wasn't room for anything else. But I hadn't been able to forget Bettina.

"There are a lot of things I want to talk to you about."

"So do I."

"I miss you," she said, with the frankness which had first attracted me. "I miss you very much."

"Good," I said, and then I couldn't be smug about it. "I didn't expect you to."

"You didn't? Don't you know me at all?"

"When you want something very much, you never dare believe the other feels the same way."

There was a moment's silence, then she asked me if I would come to Paris. "It's still a bit raw, but my studio has two extra heaters. And a modern bathroom!" She laughed. "Will you come?"

"Tomorrow," I said, "and we won't need the heaters."

Suddenly both of us were laughing like children who have lived in terror of separation and discover to their relief that their fears have been unfounded. "Tomorrow," she repeated. "That seems an endless time to wait."

"I'll see if I can catch a plane today," I said, then stopped abruptly, cursing.

"What is it? Anything wrong?"

"My passport. Damn it all, I still don't have it. It should be here any day now, but in the meantime I'm stuck."

Her sigh was like a kiss. She didn't complain, she just

said, "All right, then I'll come to you. Meet me . . . meet me . . ."

"What about the Dom?"

She thought it over for a moment. I could almost see her shake her head. "I'd rather not. No, not the Dom."

"I still look pretty awful," I said, giving her time to decide and at the same time warning her. She ignored that end of it and suggested a small inn, not far from Cologne, on the Rhine—the St. Nicholas. "Today?" I asked, and could hear her low laughter, a little catch in it as she said, "No, Drew. Tuesday."

"I'll make the reservation."

Oddly enough she said, "No. I will. I'll be there around twelve. So long," and she hung up before I could say anything more.

That day I worked better than ever. I missed lunch and my afternoon nap. To hell with routine and regimen. On Monday morning, without much hope, I went to the American consulate in Bad Godesberg. Behold, my passport had arrived! But when the girl saw my face, she opened it, looked from the photo to me and shook her head. "I must say, you don't look much like your picture."

I grinned cheerfully. "Don't worry, I will, in due course."

After a moment's hesitation, she handed it to me. I hadn't realized how uncomfortable I'd felt without it until I held the small booklet in my hand. Once more I was free to move wherever I wanted to. I debated whether to call Bettina to tell her I could come to Paris after all. It might be a good thing to change my surroundings completely and meet her somewhere where neither of us would be reminded of Rudi and the professor. In a different atmosphere it might be easier to restore the casualness with which we had first met. On second thought I dropped the idea. She might be all ready to leave, and I didn't want to upset her in any way or spoil the mood she had been in . . . both of us had been in, on the phone. But I certainly wasn't going to let her go back to Paris alone.

I thanked the stern girl at the consular office for the trouble she'd taken, and told her I wouldn't be bothering her again because I was leaving Germany in a couple of days.

Next I went to a flower shop and picked out a bunch of long-stemmed red roses to be sent to the inn next day, then changed the order to violets. They seemed less compromising. Still I had trouble phrasing what I wanted to say on the card. Finally I wrote what I had written so often, "I wish what you might wish if you were wishing that I wish it," tore it up and simply wrote my name, "Drew." Then I went into an elegant men's shop and bought myself a suit, dark gray flannel, which fitted as if custom-made, three white shirts, half a dozen socks, a few ties, a pair of black shoes, a dark red silk robe and two pairs of pajamas. In the end I also had to buy a piece of luggage, which my new acquisitions made necessary, this time something less conservative and more distinguishable. On an impulse I called Hugo to tell him I was leaving. Like Rudi, upon my arrival in Cologne, he asked me if he could drive me anywhere. I said no. I didn't want anyone to know where I was going or that I was meeting Bettina. He offered again to pick me up any time, drive me anywhere, before accepting my refusal. "Well, I'm glad you feel well enough to travel. All the best."

Now that I was leaving, I felt sorry that I hadn't seen more of Cologne, Bonn, even Godesberg. About the latter I could still do something, and I spent the next hour strolling through the spa. The district around the consulate, which faced the Rhine, transplanted me briefly into an American atmosphere—broad American voices all around me, shop windows displaying American goods—all of which changed when I came to the old quarter. There the ancient Godesberg tower sticks up like a thumb on a hill high above that section of town, ringed by houses which had survived the war. Again, attached to the ruin, a modern wing, glass, steel and concrete. Wherever you went, this extraordinary coupling of the old and the new, not always happily in my opinion. But I found I was too restless to concentrate on architecture. By the time I got back to the Lindwurm it was only three o'clock, which gave me until night to wind up a chapter on how to attract girls in Madrid without bringing the wrath of their escorts down on your head. But by eight I hadn't finished half of what I'd planned, and decided not to interrupt with dinner. I had some cold cuts sent upstairs and worked through until midnight. Then I packed the few things I'd brought with me—I hadn't bothered to unpack my new finery—and fell asleep. My dreams were happy. St. Nicholas, patron of the Rhine boatsmen, after whom the inn was named, blessed us as we lay in bed and told us to stay there.

I got up at six thirty—so as not to miss the gadgets reserved for me at the gym—partly out of habit, partly because it would be a long time, if ever, before I would again submit myself to such punishment at such an unearthly hour. I breakfasted, dressed, and at nine o'clock went as usual to see Klausen. He had insisted on checking my face daily and once or twice taken photos for his files. Otherwise we hadn't seen each other. After that night of drinking in the cellar—to which he had never referred—he had explained that he didn't want to disturb my work, but I had the feeling that he was uneasy, as if he'd said more than he wanted to that evening and was avoiding any opportunity for further political talk.

He rose, politely as always, "You're looking better every day."

"But older."

"Older?"

"I noticed it a couple of days ago and was quite depressed about it."

"Don't be." He smiled, the encouraging, artificial smile doctors use when they want to ease their patients' minds. "It will all settle back into eternal youthfulness. With your face not yet in shape and some of the scars still red and swollen, it's quite natural that you should feel depressed. Avoid looking at yourself for a while. You've lost some weight, haven't you?"

"Twelve pounds." I was rather proud of it.

"Don't put them on again."

"I don't intend to."

"No, I don't think you will. And don't worry too much about your looks. For the time being there's nothing we can do about that, but if it should prove necessary—which I don't expect—we would have to wait five to seven weeks anyway before we could do a corrective operation."

"Well," I said, rising, "then I want to say thanks very much and good-by."

"Good-by? Are you thinking of leaving us?"

I nodded. "An hour from now."

"You are? Quite a sudden decision, isn't it?"

"Not really. If I'd gotten my passport back before, I'd have left the moment you told me I was all right."

He took a cigar out of his leather etui which held three, and lit it without the usual little ceremony of smelling it and holding it up to his ear. "What a pity."

"Why?"

"Well, as a doctor I'm disappointed. Naturally I'd prefer you to stay at least a couple of weeks more. Sheer selfishness on my part, but I'd have liked to see the results more clearly."

"I understand. Sorry that I can't accommodate you."

"But you can do me a favor." He was seeing me to the door. "Have some photos taken. In four or five weeks, let's say, and send them to me. I'd like to find out if I've accomplished what I set out to do. And I'd like to have you in my files."

"I'll do that," I promised. "But if I may ask a question— at the time of the accident you said the Lindwurm wouldn't charge me for . . ."

"That's right," he said. "There won't be a bill. It's the least the management can do after all the discomfort you've suffered."

"I certainly appreciate it."

"And where are you going?"

"To Paris."

"Lucky you. I can't tell you how I long sometimes to get out of the rut I'm in, but whenever I take time off, it's to attend medical conventions." He accompanied me to the door. "And by the way, when you think back of Germany, remember that there are a lot of decent people here who wish for a truly working democracy. Well, here's luck to you. Take care, and don't forget about the photos."

I took the elevator to its last stop and ran up the ten steps to my room. I checked, I always checked upon leaving anywhere, by pulling out every drawer and looking into closets and the bathroom. Typewriter, pocket radio, memorizer, camera. My old black suitcase stood packed but still open. It was when I took my manuscript from the desk to put it on top of everything that I heard a sudden sound. It wasn't much of a noise, but it stopped me short. It came from my door. I went to the door. I moved the handle. It didn't give. The door was locked. No, I thought, jammed. Doors jam when it's very cold or hot. Wood expands and retracts. I tried again. The door didn't budge. I picked up the phone. The line was dead. I touched the fork once, twice, then quickly again and again. There was no response. I went back to the door and hammered on it. The sound of my fists reverberated through the room. That was all. There was no bell to summon a servant because all orders went through the phone. I went to the window and looked down into the courtyard. I opened it as wide as I could. Below me I recognized Hugo. He was talking to one of the men at the entrance door.

I had never been so glad to see anyone. He had come, in spite of the fact that I had refused his services. He had known . . .

I couldn't lean out because of the iron grillwork I had once thought so decorative. I couldn't stick my head through any of the ornately cut spaces, they were too narrow. All I could do was yell, "Hugo!"

He didn't look up. He didn't hear me. The distance was too great and too deep below for my voice to reach him. If I could have leaned out . . . Still I tried again. "Hugo! Hugo!" I saw him turn and yelled as loud as I could, my lungs at bursting point, "Hugo! Up here! Up here!" But he didn't look up. He went over to a car, a chocolate-brown car, the kind all the chauffeurs at the Lindwurm drove. He climbed into the seat. He drove across the courtyard, across the drawbridge, and out of sight.

Although I have often denied it, even to myself, I have known quite a few moments of fear. The first when I was a child. I had stolen a few dimes from my grandmother's old milk pot in the kitchen, and after the spanking, had been locked into one of those vast closets which don't exist any longer. Some old coats were stored in it. At first they remained what they were—discarded coats, smelling familiarly of mothballs, but in the dark they soon became ghosts, touching me unexpectedly whenever I moved. Yelling like crazy, hammering against the heavy oak door until my knuckles bled and finally threatening to hang myself on my belt from the rod above, I frightened my grandmother sufficiently to let me out. Now I knew I could shout as much as I wanted, nobody would respond. I could kick the door with all the strength I could muster, it wouldn't give. Years ago, after having parachuted into enemy territory, I'd found myself, upon landing, entangled in the cords. I felt like that now. Caught. Helpless. I hadn't been afraid of death then. Of death I had been afraid for the first time in Spain, in a small village where I had stopped to watch some boys and men wrestling with the young bulls that were being driven through the narrow cobblestoned streets to the football field. Man and beast measuring their strength and cunning on an equal basis. It was far more exciting than the formality of a bullfight in an arena, where the animal was doomed from the start. I accepted the challenge of a youngster to take part in their sport. I'd never faced a bull before. He came at me with a black speed no onlooker could possibly judge. I jumped, tumbled, fell, and would surely have been gored if one of the boys hadn't had the courage to leap on top of me to provide a new target. The bull was coming at me now.

After a while I forced myself to get up and went over to the door. I examined the lock. Maybe I could spring it. But I had no wire or tape. I went back to the open window, with its grillwork, which suddenly looked like bars, making a prison cell of my room. The distance to the courtyard below seemed to have doubled. Yelling would certainly do no good. Nobody would hear me. Hugo hadn't. If the Lindwurm had still been filled up, there might have been a chance of my voice carrying to one of the rooms below, but they were empty now. I had been given a tower room on the highest floor which couldn't even be reached by elevator, and I had liked it for its isolation, its view, its perfect, unaccustomed roundness. In it I had felt as sheltered as a pit in an apple. Now its privacy sent shivers through me; its cornerless walls were a cage in which, like a squirrel, I would have to step on a treadmill to keep moving, and its height above the ground suddenly gave me vertigo. The professor. Perhaps he had had no intention of committing suicide, but on looking down, hadn't been able to resist the temptation to throw himself into space. The sky above me, its vastness broken only by the one tower I could see, changed into the surface of a stormy ocean, deep blue, with the clouds like crests of waves which, as I watched, increased steadily and became denser, until their angry gray had subdued all former color.

I lay down on my bed. I lit a cigarette, I watched the smoke curl up and fade in the direction of the window as if nothing else concerned me. I told myself it was all a mistake. A nightmare. I was imagining the whole thing. I went back to the door. It remained locked. I tried the telephone again. As before, the line was dead. I sat down. Any comfort the chair had once given me was gone. Now it was an ordinary chair with a footrest, a rather ugly footrest, something you kept in the attic and got down only when everything else was worn out. I said to Bettina, "Don't be impatient, my love. I'll get there. In a little while. Don't get in a huff and leave. I can't help being late. Just wait. I'll come. You know I will, don't you?" And in my mind she answered, "I know, darling. Don't worry."

I took a lukewarm bath. They always tell you to take a lukewarm bath to calm your nerves. I set up my typewriter and realized at once that this was ridiculous. Work was out of the question. Nothing would come to me but the thought that I had to get out of the Lindwurm, that I had to get a taxi, catch a bus, a local train, and somehow, anyhow, get to Bettina at an inn on the Rhine called St. Nicholas. But as the time went by and the minutes ticked on into hours, I stopped imagining Bettina in the room or rooms she had reserved for us, unpacking, waiting. Waiting. There was nothing on my mind but to get out.

At lunchtime there were steps outside my door. A key was inserted in the lock. Schlau came in. The sight of him threw me. I had forgotten what a solid piece of muscle his body was. I rose. I crossed the room. I stopped in front of him and looked straight into his face, into his yellow beady eyes. He was the black bull. And he stood there like a bull, motionless, his feet spread, his neck lowered; then as if to improve his stance and accelerate his speed should I attack, he moved back slightly to block the door. I thought of the professor again, how Schlau had grabbed him and held him high in his strong arms. Anger, frustration and fear made me break out in a clammy sweat. Nevertheless I said, "I'd like to get out of here."

He knew I didn't have a chance against him, an answer therefore wasn't necessary. Without as much as glancing at me he opened the large menu. "If you'd be so good as to tell me what you'd like to eat . . ."

I kept my voice under control. "Get Dr. Klausen up here."

"Dr. Klausen?" he repeated. "I'm sorry, sir, but Dr. Klausen left an hour ago. For a short vacation. I think it was your talk about leaving that made him suddenly decide to take a holiday himself."

I hadn't credited Schlau with a sense of irony. My stomach knotted up. With Klausen gone, a last faint hope vanished. The psychiatrist's name jumped into my memory, although I'd never met him in person. "Then call Dr. Leise."

"Dr. Leise has no knowledge of your presence here. I doubt if he ever will have."

"Then call . . . who is the manager here?"

"Mr. Werner has gone skiing in the Eiffel, this being the dead season right now."

That strange voice of his, so even, pitched high, with no guttural undertones. A eunuch's voice. An emasculated voice. I hated having to humiliate myself but there was no avoiding it. "What's all this about?" I asked.

He pretended not to understand me. A sleeping child couldn't have looked more innocent.

"Why have I been locked up in my room? Why are you blocking the door?"

"Orders," he said.

"Whose orders?"

"I don't know, sir."

"You don't know? Stop talking such rot. Who told you to lock me up."

"I am only an employee, sir, and am not authorized to pass on information."

Nothing is more infuriating than impudence coupled with servility. I almost made the mistake of rushing him and risking having my bones broken. He sensed it and held out a menu. "What would you like to eat, sir?"

Apparently his orders included a warning to avoid a fight if it could be prevented. "Get me a shaker of martinis," I said. "Very dry. And olives. A lot of them. And some cheese. Edam. Crackers too."

"Sorry, sir, but you're not supposed to drink."

"As long as I'm locked up in this room, I'll do as I damn please, and you'll get me that drink."

Schlau left, turning the key in the lock again.

My only chance was to take him by surprise. The door of my room swung inward. If I stood flat against the wall and let him enter, I might be able to jump him from behind. There was a door-stop in the floor. It gave me the exact width to which the door would open. I stood against the wall, listening for his steps, my heart pounding.

I heard him long before I'd expected to. He opened the door just wide enough to survey the room, then slid in sideways with the agility of a cat, foiling any opportunity to clutch his legs. He had sensed what I was up to. He slammed the door. "Now, Mr. Waldron," he said, in perfect imitation of Sister Elly, "we don't want to upset a perfectly good drink, do we?" He put down the tray unhurriedly and pointed to a full container of ice which he had added to my order. "And we don't like our martinis watered down, right?" By God, he'd brought me what I'd asked for.

"We also should have something more solid to eat," he went on, still speaking in that hateful plural which made me one with him and debased me to the level of a ten-year-old. "An empty stomach tends to make us restless." He pointed to the menu which he had put down on the desk.

I chose to ignore it. "There's a slight difficulty in placing an order," I told him. "The telephone isn't working."

"I'll be outside your door," said Schlau, "at your beck and call. All you have to do is knock."

After he'd gone, I poured a martini from the decanter and gulped it down. It felt marvelous. It warmed my insides and I drank a second, which made me slightly dizzy. Breakfast hadn't been much, my unexpected imprisonment had harrowed my nervous system, and abstinence seemed to have lowered my tolerance. Still, my brain started to function slowly. Soothed by the alcohol, my panic abating, I asked myself—calmly now—the question I had just asked Schlau. The first thing that came to my mind was Bettina. Bettina hadn't wanted anyone to know she had called. She had used Hugo to give me her message. Had anyone, had Gevern suspected she would contact me when she had suddenly refused to go on with him to Brazil? Or had I been watched? Had the waitress in the little inn down the road gossiped about the guest who had preferred a long walk to the easily available convenience of the telephones at the Lindwurm? I had had to ask her for change, quite a bit of change, to make the call, and a stupid operator might have rung back to assure herself that the connection with Paris had been terminated. And had Gevern decided to make our meeting impossible? As matters stood now it must look to her as if I'd changed my mind and stood her up. Bettina, though, wouldn't be satisfied with any such explanation. She would wait for a while, then call Hugo. Hugo would say that all he knew was that I'd left. She would then throw all caution aside and call the Lindwurm and be told the same thing. After that she might inquire at the American consulate as to when they had last heard from me, and probably be insistent enough to finally reach the girl who had given me my passport. Pressed, she might tell Bettina that I had intended to leave Germany in a few days. This might upset her for a moment and make her wonder if, with passport in hand, I hadn't perhaps changed my plans. But not for long. She was fully aware now of what she meant to me, or our whole telephone conversation could never have taken place. With her fear of accidents . . . *"And they always happen to people I'm fond of . . ."* she would . . . Accident. I had had an accident. But she wouldn't think of what was past, she would be afraid that something had happened to me on my way to her. Where was I? I had lost track of something that had been unfolding in my mind.

I poured a third martini. My hands were trembling. I mustn't spill a drop, I told myself, though I had no idea why that should be so important. I took a sip and started again. Why am I locked up? All right, let's say to prevent my meeting Bettina. But they didn't have to lock me up for that. They could have let me go and found a way to stop me from reaching Bettina. How? How could they have stopped me? Of course they could have created some kind of accident. Accident? What about my accident? Let's see if I can work it out differently. Suppose my whole assumption is wrong. Let's say being locked up here has nothing whatsoever to do with Bettina. Then why . . . ? No. Let's start with the facts. I'm locked up at the Lindwurm. Why? To what purpose? If they don't want me to leave the Lindwurm, they must have a reason for keeping me here. What reason? Forget that for a moment. Go back to the assumption that they want me at the Lindwurm, no matter why. I told them I was going to stay a few days only, the most important days of the carnival, and probably leave on Ash Wednesday. That turned out to be impossible because of the accident. The accident and the missing passport. Two reasons why I couldn't leave as planned. Was my passport stolen on purpose? Now hold it. Don't have another drink. You're doing beautifully. Am I? And what about the accident? Even without a passport I could have moved to another hotel. Cut that. You're forgetting something important. Remember they offered to pay for everything, Klausen's operation, your staying on, indefinitely. Because they felt responsible. But this is the sort of establishment that would do that in any case. Yes, have another drink, but water it down with some ice. Jesus, it's slippery, the ice, I mean. Like little pieces of eel that keep moving even after you've cut the fish into pieces. Do they really keep moving? Or do you have to put salt on them to make them jump and slide? There now. That'll do. Two little icebergs. So . . . where were you? That comes from drinking too much. It's difficult to find your way back. You can never find your way back. No hunter returns. That's a beautiful title. For a book. Unfortunately used already. Come on now, concentrate. My passport was stolen and I had an accident. But an accident that didn't kill me. If anybody had wanted to kill me, I wouldn't be sitting here now, sipping martinis, with Schlau at my beck and call outside my locked door. So they didn't want to kill me but they wanted me to stay. Why? Never mind. Go on. What have I got? Where was I? They didn't want to kill me but they wanted me to stay. That's got rhythm, that line has. And the passport alone wouldn't have assured them of that. I could still have traveled wherever I liked in Germany. So there had to be an accident. The accident wasn't serious enough to prevent me from leaving the Lindwurm. According to Klausen, on the morning after the operation, I could be moderately active. So, theoretically, I could have left, but when he told me I was welcome to stay on without having to pay for a thing—medical care, food, board, all in delightful surroundings, I naturally chose the pleasantest way . . . I'm rushing things again. Stop. Stop at the accident. You were coming from Cologne; Bettina had left with Gevern. She was on her way to Brazil to marry an old guy just because she was grateful to him. Maybe. My God, if I'd taken every girl seriously just because she'd been good to me . . . Now Waldron, that's neither here nor there. You're drunk. So what. And my passport hadn't been turned in at the police, nor at the consulate. You'd had quite a bit to drink and screwed a girl . . . was it the girl in the plastic bottle? After we'd smashed it, of course. Anyway, she stank. It was dark. Yes. I knew about the badly banked curve. How? I hadn't driven a car in this neighborhood, nor anywhere else in Germany. And there was a man on the road. Even Klausen agreed there might have been a man on the road because the last stretch up to the Lindwurm is so steep . . . Bettina, I've slept with a lot of girls . . . let's not say a lot . . . a number of girls . . . sounds better . . . pleasant ones, unpleasant ones. I mean unpleasant in the way they pounce on a man, making an object of him, if you know what I mean. But no, you wouldn't. You were never a pouncer. Let's say I've slept indiscriminately. That's the word for it. You'd better know. But you do anyway, don't you? If you don't, that's just too bad. What was I going to say? That most women are greedy but you were not. *Are* not! Why did I say "were?" Though I thought you were when you let your gown slip and stood there naked. I almost told you to go away. I was tired from the trip, from too much food, from too much drink, I'm drinking too much now. And then you were there, with your feet curled up under your naked body, drinking to me, and so quiet when you came into my arms. So quiet. And giving. Not taking. I guess you know what that means to a man. For once not to have to be the stud. Relaxing. Gathering strength.

"Drew, darling," said Bettina. "I know all that. Go back to the accident or it's hard to follow."

"I woke up at the hospital wing of this cussed castle. Nice alliteration. Cussed castle . . ."

"You woke up in the hospital wing and were told you'd had an accident. That your steering wheel . . ."

"There was a man trying to hitch a ride."

"Klausen said there couldn't have been. Because if there had . . ."

"I never saw his face. I stopped and he got into the car . . ."

"All right. There was a man and he got into the car. And then?"

"Then he hit me."

"He hit you?"

"He certainly did. Under the chin."

"And you passed out."

"Passed out? Why do you say that? Yes, I guess I passed out. It all happened so fast."

"Try to remember."

Suddenly I was sober. Suddenly I could remember. I could remember who had got into my car with an agility I'd never seen in any person before. A solid muscular body, with legs like the trunks of trees, and oversized arms, like a gorilla? With one hand he had reached for the wheel and with the other he had knocked me out. Schlau.

"Schlau?"

"Yes," I said. "Schlau."

Claustrophobia now became the bull with which I wrestled during the day and most of the night. I wrote to Bettina every morning and sometimes before going to bed, letters that would quite possibly never reach her. Therapy, to preserve my sanity.

"I don't know," I wrote, "which are worse—the days or the nights. During the day I try to work, but more often than not, I can't. Then I sit at the window and look out at the sky and imagine a helicopter cutting through it. It lands in the courtyard. You get out. You enter the Lindwurm. I can hear your steps on the stairs. You walk beautifully. That's what I noticed first. Your walk. As if you were striding across a trampoline, so sure of every move, so balanced. You don't bounce like so many women do when they're in a hurry. And you always seem to be in a hurry, except when you're in bed. And then I watch the courtyard. There's very little traffic now, but the drawbridge is down most of the time. You stop your car on the other side. You hesitate, but you don't look down into the ravine. You wave because you've spotted me at the window. Where are you, Bettina? Why don't you come? Why do you keep me waiting? During the night I can't see you. I'm sleepy but I can't sleep. I don't dare to take any pills. Some inner voice commands me to stay awake. I mustn't let myself be taken by surprise, not at any time. Taken by surprise I mightn't be able to put up a fight. I know I can't win, but I refuse to surrender without at least an attempt at defense. So I catnap."

I wrote other things. "You never told me about Rudi, but you loved him, didn't you? I saw your eyes when you came from the room where they had laid him out. Something had gone out of your face. He was the first, I'm sure. And he was gentle. Everything he did, he did gently. The way he handled the wheel, as if it were made of delicate material. And when he poured your beer, just an inch of foam and none of it ran over. I'm glad he was gentle. I knew a girl once who became a lesbian because she'd been hurt so badly the first time. Did Gevern hurt you? I still can't understand it. Any of it. With how many men have you slept beside those two? Not that it matters. I'd just like to know, because I want to know as much as I can about you. Relationships are important. They form a person, especially his likes and dislikes. In a way you seem quite whole, yet in another, not at all. You know what I think? I think that beside Rudi and Gevern you never slept with anyone. There was just too much bravado in your behavior. Unhooking your dress with nothing underneath it. And every night I see you next to me."

Schlau came into the room. He came in six times a day—in the morning to serve my breakfast, which was always the same. Though I forced myself to eat, I never finished all of it. Later to clean my room. At lunchtime he asked what I'd like to eat, and I made a show of choosing carefully. At teatime he brought a beverage with cookies, at six thirty the dinner menu. I asked arbitrarily for dishes that weren't listed, and got them. Oh yes, the sixth time, around nine, to take away the tray, open my bed for the night, and put a fresh container of ice next to the bottle of Scotch on my desk. Oh yes, I had ordered and got that bottle, but I didn't drink. Except for my orders, we never talked. On the third night, though, he said, "If you're bored, sir, I'm pretty good at gin rummy." The idea of sitting down with him to play cards gave me the creeps. I almost told him I'd prefer to get stoned, but restrained myself, shook my head and said I hated cards, which wasn't true. A good game has always relaxed me. "What about chess?" he asked. "Too pedestrian," I said. "Where I come from, children play chess at five and the retarded ones keep it up and get into tournaments with the Russians." He didn't get it.

When I was too tired to type, I dictated into my memorizer. "One can get used to being confined to one room. Claustrophobia, unless it drives you mad, wears off after a while. And at least this room is pleasant. It has a view. But I often wonder how people can stand a cell such as I saw once—a six-by-four with no conveniences. No running water, no toilet. The smell of excrement. To have to wait for the guard to take out the pail. I try to console myself by thinking back in history. The idea of a dungeon fills me with horror. Dark, damp, vermin-ridden, chained to a wall, fixed in one position, your muscles atrophying, your body racked with pain, with no hope of release. How could men endure it? How could men endure concentration camps? The hunger. Having to do hard labor, faint with malnutrition, knowing that if they fell behind in their work they would lose the right to survive. Having to undress for death, queuing up in freezing temperatures, robbed of all individuality. And the knowledge constantly that they might be tortured whenever one of their tormenters felt it would be amusing to watch someone trying to preserve his dignity under enforced pain. "I'm well-off," I told the machine. "I'm fed well, I have a soft bed to sleep on. Within my confines I can do as I please, sleep when I want to, bathe, pace up and down, work, listen to the radio . . ."

"But," I wrote to Bettina, on the Lindwurm's expensive stationery, "I doubt if I'll ever get used to this fear of the unknown. It's the one thing I don't seem able to cope with. So my work is poor and my letters to you are repetitious. You see, the fright of going into battle or on a dangerous mission is something different. You know your luck may desert you, still you have a certain amount of faith in it. I guess that's why kids volunteer. They're so confident, and too young to know how a body can hurt. Pain still comes as a surprise to them. That their flesh can let them down astonishes more than it frightens them. In my situation I have no way of gauging what will happen next. Okay. I've already been taken prisoner, I may yet be tortured, I may be taken out and shot, and there are moments—they get more frequent all the time—when I'd prefer death to this may-or-may-not-happen. Usually at dawn, when I can hardly bring myself to face another day on which I am not my own master. Until now a new day meant . . . well, what keeps people going in the face of this kind of uncertainty? In a group you're perhaps helped by the fact that everyone's in the same boat, and it becomes bearable. Alone . . .

"They say fear is the first enemy. I'd say imagination runs a close second. And at night my imaginings . . . I don't dare to put them on paper. It would make them even more real. Now you may answer—and rightly so—that life in itself is a gamble, that we don't know from one moment to the next what's going to happen to us. But we've been raised to accept that and take it so much for granted that we usually don't give it a thought. My present situation might also be called fate, but I see it as a carefully designed one—not by God, or whatever or whomever you turn to—but by men, and no man should have the right to decide another's future. Now, when some people speak of reinstating the death penalty, I for one shall be against it."

I paced my room by the hour. Fate? How did I get to be here? How did I ever get to Germany, a country I had always consciously or subconsciously avoided? To the Lindwurm? Had I started myself on this road to imprisonment, despair and fear? Was it a coincidence that the little apartment I had rented outside Rome had become suddenly unavailable? If I hadn't been at loose ends, unwilling to settle down to work only to have to change place and atmosphere again a few weeks later, could the professor have persuaded me that rebuilt Cologne and the nonsensical fun of a carnival were what I wanted?

"I never quite got it," I wrote to Bettina, "why he was so eager for me to come to Cologne and then just as eager to have me leave. Klausen said he had played along with the Nazis, and you confirmed that. Even had an excuse for him. Or am I wrong?"

One day I did speak to Schlau, but only to ask him if Klausen had returned. He shook his head. Why had Klausen left a couple of hours after the door had closed on me? Had he known I was going to be locked up? And was he really absent? The day before, in the afternoon, I thought I had seen his slim elegant figure in the courtyard. Was I beginning to imagine things?

"Bettina," I wrote. "What do you know about Klausen? He seemed to share Rudi's views, and he gave me the impression, one night in the wine cellar, that he was afraid. Why has he disappeared? Is he in the same spot I'm in? I

like him. At least right now I like him. I didn't at first, not
when he stopped Florian from joining us, but later he spoke
of him with sympathy and understanding. I can't make him
out."

"There's something bothering me," I told her, in one of
my sleepless nights. "What made you decide to come back
to Cologne instead of going on to Brazil as you'd said you
would? Wouldn't your telephone call—considering your
estrangement—have sufficed for offering condolences? And
why did you call Rudi anyway? You were so concerned
about your uncle's health, you had to leave right away, you
couldn't wait a day longer. Why could you, suddenly? Why
did you come back? Why did you go back to your job in
Paris and not to Pôrto Alegre? You said, 'Never mind,' and
changed the subject. And why haven't you come here?
Can't you come? And why can't Hugo get a message
through to me? He managed to before. Just so I'd know that
you know."

Then came the day I went to the bathroom . . . it was
early morning. With no saunas or massage, I had forced
myself to continue with exercises that would keep my body
trim and my mind balanced, more or less. I had a shower. I
went to the washbasin, as usual, to brush my teeth. As there
was no mirror above the basin, just a small cabinet for
toothpaste and so forth, it hadn't been difficult to obey the
doctor's order not to scrutinize my face daily. Since I
couldn't shave anyhow, I had not looked into the shaving
mirror that jutted out from the tiled wall on a flexible alum-
inum rod and could be turned any way you wanted. But now
I felt I could expect a less repulsive image. I therefore took
a good look. And drew back. I couldn't believe what I saw.
I turned on the lights—it changed nothing. My face was

not my own, not the face I had known all my life. It was the face of an old man.

I can't remember how long it was after the initial shock that I went back to lie on my bed. The scream I had been trying to swallow was still stuck in my throat, and I kept my teeth clenched so that it wouldn't escape and bring Schlau into my room. It wasn't that I cared about giving him the satisfaction he must have been waiting for all these days, I simply had to be alone.

Since I didn't have a pocket mirror, I had to go back to the bathroom to make sure I wasn't having hallucinations. I was not. My face was still partly swollen and slightly red, but unmistakably it had been changed into the face of a man at least thirty years older than I. There were lines in my forehead, three more than there had been before; there were lines of age around my eyes, or would be once the netlike structure of crowsfeet had healed completely. There were deep shadows underneath them. Of course they could be caused by my beard. My beard. If I shaved . . . Klausen had told me not to shave until he felt it was safe, but he wasn't there to tell me anything and I wouldn't have consulted him at this point if he had been. I plugged in my electric shaver, but in spots my beard had grown so thick, I had to use scissors. My hands were shaking. I waited. I couldn't afford to have them tremble when I used the shaver. It revealed deep lines running from my nostrils to the corners of my mouth, and hollow cheeks, their flesh loose. Between them my nose looked pinched. Even the lobes of my ears didn't look quite the same with the proportions of my face changed, and when I turned my head there was some loose skin on both sides, below my chin. And on the left lower cheek, three bluish marks that wouldn't come off. Birthmarks that I hadn't had at birth.

Something went dead inside me. For the first time in my life I wanted to weep, but I had no tears. For the first time in my life I felt the possibility of going crazy. I thought of taking one of the sedatives Klausen had provided, which I had scarcely touched since Bettina and I had tried so unsuccessfully to make love in that dreary little room.

Bettina. What would her reaction be? And then I saw her, not as she had been with me, but with Gevern. The way she had left my arms to dance with him when he had come up to us in the Isabellensaal to say it was time to change partners. I'd wondered why she hadn't objected, wondered even more after she'd told me all about him. My mind began to spin around the man. Could Gevern possibly have persuaded Klausen to perform an operation on me which would make it impossible for Bettina to love me?

Ridiculous. Ridiculous also from Klausen's point of view. No respectable doctor, no man with his reputation . . . I *was* going mad.

Then suddenly I was calm, with a calmness that came close to a paralysis of mind. I surprised myself by finding I was standing at the window one moment and sitting in a chair the next. My brain had planned neither. Schlau came in with my breakfast. "My," he exclaimed, "but we're looking distinguished today."

"I'd like to go to the library," I told him. "You can stand guard over me there."

"I'm afraid that won't be possible. But if there's any book you want specially, let me know and I'll be glad to get it for you."

I didn't want him to know that all I was interested in was a medical encyclopedia. "Let it go," I said.

I drank three cups of coffee but couldn't eat a thing and emptied more than half of the food on my plates into the can so that Schlau wouldn't notice how off balance I was. Childishly unnecessary, but pride had become a point with me. Then I put a clean sheet of paper into my typewriter and began to write to Bettina. I had never believed in the supernatural, but since my incarceration, thinking of her and speaking her name had worked rather like spiritualism. She appeared and talked to me. And now, after a while, I could hear her voice, her laugh, rather, which had enchanted me when we had first met.

"Don't laugh," I told her. "I woke up this morning and discovered that I no longer look like myself. Klausen has altered my face. I look like a man in his sixties."

For a long time she remained silent, then in her customary practical way she said, "Don't be so desperate, darling. You can have another operation, I mean a corrective one."

Klausen had used the word "corrective." When? In my confused state I needed a few minutes to find my way back in time to the morning I'd come to his office to say good-by. He had mentioned that if I required a corrective operation, I would have to wait for at least another five to seven weeks. Why had he said that? I *had* to get hold of him.

I knocked on my door just as Schlau had told me to do if ever I should need him. He answered almost immediately. "What can I do for you, sir?"

"I'm suddenly in great pain."

"Pain? Where?"

"My insides. Appendix, maybe. Or my kidney. I've had stones before. I need a doctor."

Into his glance, which he usually kept expressionless, there crept a shimmer of concern. "If you'd kindly undress . . ."

Stumped, all I could say was, "But you're not a doctor."

"I'm studying to be one," he told me. "I know enough to tell if it's serious or not. If necessary, we'll take some x-rays."

There was nothing I could do but take off my robe and lie down on my bed. His sausage-like fingers were deft and knowledgeable. Now, in such close proximity, I could smell that he and Klausen used the same perfume. Chanel No. 5. And I had a sudden vision of the two men in each other's arms.

"I can't find anything," he said. "You may dress again."

"I'd feel safer if someone else would have a look at me."

He didn't answer, he didn't even smile at my unsuccessful ruse, he just left.

I said to Bettina, "I think Gevern did this. Maybe you said a word too much, maybe you were not quite as careful as you thought, or we may have betrayed with a glance how we felt for each other."

Bettina made no reply.

I didn't feel like wasting any more time speculating on Gevern's insane jealousy which years ago had made him almost kill the girl he loved, but I had to get into his perverted mind to find out how it may have worked in my case, ridiculous or not.

Step one: stage the car accident so that I could be operated on without becoming suspicious.

Step two: persuade Klausen to use his medical know-how and famous plastic surgery for such an unethical act.

Step three: arrange for my imprisonment at the Lindwurm so that I couldn't bring them to trial and have them jailed.

Yet, I thought, how could he avoid my eventually getting to the police, unless he planned to keep me locked up for the rest of my life?

For life? That was impossible. No man could be locked away for any length of time without someone eventually finding out.

Then what could he do?

Kill me, of course.

"No," I said aloud. "Stop right there. Something doesn't make sense."

What didn't make sense was that if Gevern wanted me dead, Schlau could have seen to it that I died in the faked accident, or Klausen could have given me a fatal injection any time. But I was alive. Then what *was* the point? Again I was lost in a quagmire of confusion. This time my brain was clouded without alcohol or sedation. I struggled for logic, and the more I struggled, the more entangled my thoughts became. Alive and at the Lindwurm. With a face that wasn't mine. *Why?*

Days went by, days and nights in which I learned to despise myself for waking up with fear pinning me to my bed so that I could barely move. The black bull. He was standing over me with his head lowered, his horns almost touching my belly, his hot breath coming at me in great violent gasps, his smell so overpowering, I wanted to throw up but swallowed the vomit in my throat, afraid that one careless move on my part would cause a move on his. After the first night of this sort of terror, I kept the lights on. Like Bettina, I had grown afraid of the dark. It didn't help much. Whenever I closed my eyes, there he was again, ready to attack. Scotch and sedatives stood on my night table. I didn't dare to take them. I didn't dare to knock myself out. To remain conscious at all times was the only clear determination in my mind.

The days were no better. Already at dawn I would stand in front of the mirror in my bathroom, inspecting my face. If it hadn't been mine, I might have been fascinated to watch the almost imperceptible changes, every day now, as the puffiness continued to go down and the redness grew less. It was not a bad face, and in time might even look, as Schlau had said, distinguished. But it was not my face. It was a face I had been forced to wear. Sometimes it was the question why mine had been taken from me that made me shudder, sometimes the fact that I looked so old. When I shuddered for the latter reason, I could at least turn on myself. Vanity be damned. What was wrong with looking twice your age? Think of people who have had a leg or arm amputated, I told myself, men whose faces were grotesquely marred by war. Think of napalm, think of sickness, of any disease that has the power to age and cripple at the same time. Your health is fine, as a matter of fact it couldn't be better. Shit on your vanity. But when the question of "why" took over, and more often than not it did, there was no way of reasoning with myself. It invariably threw me into a deathlike stupor and while that lasted, all hope was gone. I would switch off the radio. A world in which I could have no part might as well be dead too.

And I could no longer summon Bettina. I wrote to her more than ever, but it didn't work. I could say her name over and over again, yet was unable to recall her smile, the sound of her voice, the way she walked, the fragrance of her body or what touching her had meant to me.

The following Sunday, exactly six weeks to the day that I had awakened in the hospital wing, Schlau entered the room. It was shortly after breakfast, not a time when he usually appeared. "If you would kindly follow me, sir."

"Where to?"

"To the library, if you please. You did want to visit the library, didn't you?"

I was unable to answer, rather, I was afraid my voice would betray the terror that filled me. He held the door open and motioned me to go ahead. With him always a step behind me, I walked down the stairs as men must have walked to the guillotine, knowing that in a few minutes all would be over, and praying, if not to God, then that the executioner would be experienced and the blade sharp enough to sever head from body at one stroke.

Schlau directed me to the elevator. The door stood open, I guessed in order to prevent anyone else from using it until

I was out of the way. In a few minutes it stopped at the second floor where the library was located. A sign outside gave the hours it could be used. Eleven to one and three to six. I looked at my watch. It was nine forty.

A book-lined room has always quieted me with its atmosphere of a wealth of knowledge, but I could see no books. The shelves were hidden by darkness, only in the center there was light. It came from four powerful reflectors, all focused on a small dais on which stood a stool. It had a back. Schlau guided me to it. "Sit down, please."

There were three rungs to the seat which I had failed to notice. I wished there had been a railing, something, anything to hold on to, but managed them with surprising ease when I sensed that I was being watched. Schlau manipulated a screw so that the stool swiveled up to its full height, strapped me to the back and stepped down from the dais to disappear in the direction of the door. A second later I could hear it fall shut after him.

Because of the way the lights had been arranged, I could discern nothing, only hear the breathing of people I couldn't see, a slight rustle of papers being handed out, the clearing of throats, a whisper from one corner, "Ready," and a light jumped up in front of me and cast its strong ray just above my head. "I shall now turn his face to face you."

Klausen's voice.

Hope has a life all its own. For a second all I could think was—he has returned. Now I'll be able to question him and at last find out why my face . . . He came forward, out of the shadows into the circle of light, dressed in his three-quarter length white coat. He was holding a bamboo stick, the kind teachers use. He turned my face to the right and pointed. As if his gesture had been a signal, a motor started humming. At first I assumed it was a moving picture camera that would now take the photos of me Klausen had wanted to have, then I realized, by a sudden faint light that came from behind me and shimmered eerily on the ceiling, that the thing with the eye was a projector, casting a picture on a screen that I couldn't see because it was behind me. I tried quite automatically to turn my head but was stopped immediately by a sharp command. "Don't turn or Schlau will hold you in the required position. I thought he had been given a sedative. Well, never mind. Proceed."

The voice was vaguely familiar, but hard as I tried, I couldn't place it. By the way the light from behind me grew suddenly dimmer, I could tell that the square of the screen was darkened by a picture. Apparently it wasn't the right one, for Klausen said, "No. That's not number one."

A moment of utter silence, then a sound of satisfaction from in front of me, and Klausen lifted his stick again. It hung in the air for a moment, then moved, trembling a little, to my forehead. "Please notice the sagittal front lines," moved on to my eyes, first my right then my left. "Here we have the temporal lines," along my nose, "the nasolabial lines," and down to the corners of my mouth, "the angular oral lines."

Not once while he spoke did his eyes meet mine, and his voice was as impersonal as that of a professor addressing his students. "Klausen," I said under by breath, "for God's sake, what's the meaning of this?"

He gave no sign of having heard. The sweat poured down my face as I began to realize that for him I was a dummy in a medical arena on which he was demonstrating an operation he had performed. "Klausen."

A voice I couldn't place asked for absolute quiet. I

208

wanted to scream, but my vocal cords refused to function. "Slide number five," said Klausen, and again his stick moved across my face. "I would have preferred to have the time," he said to the men I couldn't see, "to do the job in two operations, so that the tissues . . . but we were lucky. He healed extraordinarily well. And fast. As you can see, here I had to remove the buccal fat, and here the orbital lines had to be put in. Slide six, please." The stick probed my cheek. "The subocular pigmentation might not have been absolutely necessary, but since it is quite clearly visible on the left profile of the subject . . ." the stick left my cheek and pointed to the slide being projected behind me, "I felt it should be included. I hope my job pleases you, gentlemen."

A wave of applause. Someone offered congratulations, another said, "Excellent," a third, pleasure making his voice almost gay, "A perfect double!" The light behind me went out, the light focusing on my face was turned off and the ceiling lights went on. They shone on a row of chairs occupied by four men dressed in ordinary business suits, but all three wore the skullcaps of surgeons on their heads, and surgeons's masks hid the lower part of their faces. Their eyes were unrecognizable behind large tinted glasses. And I thought of the first few hours I had spent at the Lindwurm and how, coming up from the saunas, I had found myself trapped in what had looked to me like an eagle's eyrie, and been interrogated by men dressed up as eagles. What had been explained to me as a carnival joke had been anything but that. I knew those voices.

I looked away from the four men, at a fifth, dressed like the others, the man who had operated the projector. He was putting the slides back into their box. Nobody was paying any attention to me now. If I could get hold of those slides . . . But I was strapped to the stool, immobilized, and had to sit there, helplessly watching the man put the box with the slides into his pocket. Schlau came in to open the door for him and he left the room while the others were still talking to Klausen.

"Two weeks, you said?"

"Two weeks, yes. Better three. Three should certainly do it."

"You have our thanks," said the tallest of the four. He motioned to Schlau. "Take him away."

Thinking that Schlau was coming for me, I stiffened, but Schlau passed me by and stopped in front of Klausen. With all the respect due to a superior, he said in his high-pitched voice, "Will you please follow me, Herr Doktor?"

Klausen didn't move.

Schlau held out his hand and repeated what he had just said. Still Klausen didn't move, but he spoke. The very words I had spoken a little while ago. "For God's sake, what's the meaning of this?"

His question was met, as mine had been, with silence. I watched him plant his feet a little further apart in a stance a fighter takes for better defense. "Have you gone mad, all of you?"

The tall man replied, "Not at all. On the contrary."

Klausen began to shake. He shook so hard, his voice was almost inaudible. "Haven't I done everything you wanted? Haven't you yourselves just said how grateful you were for the excellent job I did?"

"We are grateful to you, and you have done an excellent job, but you must understand . . ."

"Understand what?" Now Klausen was screaming. "Understand what? What is there to understand?"

"You know too much," the tall man said softly, "for someone who did a fine job with not quite the right enthusiasm. We are sorry."

Klausen swung around. Of all people he faced me. I hadn't been mistaken that night when he had listened to the steps in the passage of the wine cellar. Fear was in his eyes, the fear of a cornered animal. Suddenly I knew that the stick he had used to point at my face hadn't trembled on its own, but that the hand holding it had shaken. And he hadn't been able to look at me, even if he might have wanted to, because he was too intent on fighting his own battle for survival.

Someone called Schlau's name. And Schlau moved. A scene began to repeat itself, the scene in the courtyard when he had grabbed the professor on Klausen's orders. Like Florian, Klausen resisted. With surprising strength he managed to push Schlau away. "Tell him to leave me alone," he said. "I'll go by myself."

Schlau, who had stepped up to him again, drew back slightly, waiting for the tall man's decision. The tall man nodded, and Klausen pulled himself up to his full, slender height. With enormous dignity he walked slowly across the library, his right hand in his pocket, his left swinging gently at his side. Schlau was following him, a long arm's length behind him, and almost collided with him as Klausen stopped abruptly in front of the heavy oak door. I saw him turn around to face the four men once more. He pulled his right hand out of his pocket and lifted it in the Nazi salute, then clamped it over his mouth as if to stifle a last plea or scream. As Schlau passed him to open the door, Klausen, only a moment ago perfectly upright, fell to the floor.

I was back in my room, one thought chasing the other without taking on clarity or coherence. The various scenes I had witnessed since I had arrived at the Lindwurm were like pictures in a kaleidoscope, changing with the slightest twist of the tube. Florian, pointing to the print showing Sigurd fighting the dragon; Bettina unfastening the hook of her sea-green dress; Klausen pulling the string on his skullcap to make the tulip on it stand up straight; Gevern accompanying me to the Lost and Found at the Guërzenich to report the theft of my passport and money; Klausen explaining the wines; Rudi's body under the hay; Florian's lying crumpled on the rocks; Rudi in his coffin; the girl in the plastic bottle; Pauline Becker's accusing face; Bettina's paper slippers making a noise like a cat with a bell on its collar; Klausen taking out the stitches . . . Toward one o'clock I heard Schlau at my door. I wished he wouldn't come in, I wished my door had a slot through which food could be passed so that I wouldn't have to see his face. "Suicide or accident?" Bettina had asked when told about the professor's death; now I knew it had been neither. It had been murder. And if Schlau had killed Florian and later staged my car accident, there was little doubt in my mind that he had shot Rudi too.

I went into the bathroom to avoid having to face him, and called out to him that just fruit would do. Night fell. Although I was exhausted, I couldn't sleep. I opened the drawer of my night table. All my pills were gone. To see if

Schlau had possibly moved them into the medicine chest, I went to the bathroom—they weren't there. And my scissors were gone. So they were afraid I might commit suicide. The thought had never entered my mind, but they were certainly taking precautions, for when I looked in my closet, I saw that my belts and ties had been removed.

I went back to my bed and lay awake. Again and again I went over the facts and realized with a clarity which, until then, I had been unable to arrive at, that the professor, Rudi and Klausen had only been pawns in a game, a game that was still being played, and they had died because of me. Each in his own way, in the words of the tall man, had known too much and not qualified as reliable. Klausen had known the man whose face I now was wearing; Rudi couldn't be permitted to take me into his confidence or warn me that my life was in danger, the professor . . . what had he known? Thinking back, it was clear that he had been aware of something or other all along. It explained his strange behavior to a point, but what? And then I had it. In the correct sequence. It took my breath away. I began to write it down.

"Bettina, I see now that I was lured to the Lindwurm. I thought I had come of my own volition, but I was wrong. A travel agent showed me an ad in an Italian paper. It was just what I wanted, a small two-room apartment to let, incredibly cheap. I took the next flight to Rome. I sat beside a young blond man whom I recalled vaguely having seen before, on other flights. When I got to Rome, it turned out that the apartment wasn't available, not for two weeks or so. I couldn't settle down to work as I had planned. I was at loose ends. I bummed around, revisiting places I'd enjoyed before. At almost every one I saw the dwarflike figure of the professor. There seemed nothing unusual about it; tourists tend to frequent the same sights and restaurants. One day I saw him sitting in a café on the Via Veneto with the young man from the plane. It didn't strike me at the time that either of them might be following me. Then came the night at the bar when Florian invited me for a drink and drew me on the back of the wine list, full face and in profile. You know that it was he who suggested Cologne as a city not to be missed, particularly at carnival time. You know how oddly he behaved after that. He wanted me to go back to the station and leave, this after pretending not to recognize me. Later, at the Lindwurm, he warned me of you, then suddenly resigned himself to my presence, in fact seemed quite cheered by it. I can only figure out that he and the young man had finally come across a type with a face which, with skill, could be made to correspond to the face of some other man who wants me to look like him. And he must have guessed or known from the start what was going to happen to me. But after having lured me to Cologne, he evidently regretted the part he had played. What I can't find an explanation for is why he should have changed his mind *again,* and suddenly been content to have me stay.

"So here I am, Bettina, being carefully preserved, with another man's face, the face of the man whose photos were projected on a screen I couldn't see and with which mine was compared down to the minutest detail. And found to be an excellent resemblance. Why?

"Think for a moment—why does a man need a double? A double who, by force and treachery has been made to look like him, a man therefore who can never be called upon to cooperate, a man who—there is no other logical answer—*when it suits them, is to be found dead, for him, as him.* So that he may go on living. Under a different identity."

I was doomed. And although, subconsciously, I had probably feared this all along, the certainty of death now filled me with such rebellion, I smashed the ice container against the wall in a fit of violence. I could not, would not reconcile myself to dying so that another man might live, and to an end that, literally over my dead body, could only be evil. "Bettina," I ended my letter, "I am doomed." Then my eyes lit on a line I had written, the one that read, "Later he warned me of you." All violence left me. Suddenly I was cold and calm.

"Why did he warn me of you, Bettina? Were you a part of it? I don't think I would have gone to the Lindwurm if it hadn't been for you. I think I would have insisted on getting the room I had reserved at the Dom. You came at the right moment. You suggested . . ."

And she came now, and said, "That's not true. I didn't suggest you should come to the Lindwurm. That was Feldman. Don't you remember? You must be mad. Drew, think . . ."

"I wondered already in the car why you let yourself be kissed by a perfect stranger. And later. I didn't pursue you, you pursued me. You came to me. I don't believe in love at first sight."

"You made that quite clear. But people are different. A woman is more intuitive than a man."

"Now I know why you slept with me. You did it to make me feel safe. The professor had died under suspicious circumstances, and I felt like leaving. You couldn't let me leave."

"Drew, stop it! I know you're under a terrible strain, but . . ."

"And Pauline Becker. She was quite right to accuse you. You knew about Rudi, you knew what he was involved in.

You were the only other person who knew about the safe. If he had lived . . ."

Bettina said nothing. I couldn't see her eyes.

"Look at me," I said. "You refused to help them. Don't you know that by refusing you made yourself one with the people who . . ." I stopped myself as the logical consequence of what I was saying revealed itself. "Bettina . . . that second night, didn't you say that Hannes and I were the same type? You did. Don't deny it. I can remember it clearly. You can tell me the truth now because it doesn't matter any longer. Has Hannes . . . is Hannes the man I have been made to resemble?"

Bettina turned away.

I heard her crying all night, and the next night, and the night after that. I took her in my arms. "Here," I said, "put your head on my chest. You don't have to be careful now. My ribs are okay. Stop crying, my love. Of course I don't believe for a moment that you had anything to do with it. If you could say no to the Beckers because it seemed immoral to you to spy on anyone who trusted you, how could you have . . . I'm not myself today. I'm having hallucinations. Stop crying, please. Please."

But Bettina went on crying. I tried to kiss her tears away but couldn't stop their endless flow. "You'll make yourself old and ugly. Come on. Stop it now. I'm sorry. Bettina, say that you forgive me."

"I forgive you," said Bettina. Still she went on crying.

There came the hour one night when I could hear the tall man's voice as clearly as if he had been standing next to my bed. He wasn't talking to me but to Klausen. "Two weeks, you said?" And Klausen's voice, "Two weeks, yes. Better three. Three should certainly do."

They went away as silently as they had come and I could

feel the cold sweat forming in every pore of my body. I hadn't forgotten those words, I had simply failed to accept them as the date set for my death. In two weeks, three at the latest, my scars would have become as good as invisible. In two or three weeks there would no longer be a reason for me to be alive. And of those two or three weeks, ten days were gone.

I lay motionless, and the black bull stood over me, his yellow eyes bloodshot. I held my breath and again could feel him coming at me like hot steam, and suddenly I moved and seized his horns. The element of surprise made it impossible for him to throw me and I was on the floor, wrestling with him. We wrestled for hours. Finally, with dawn breaking, I had worn his neck muscles out. A shudder went through his body, as if he had been touched by a powerful electric wire, and he lay still. I went back to bed and fell asleep immediately. From that night on, I began to feel totally unconcerned about what was to happen to me.

Schlau came in more often than before. He would bring up dishes I hadn't ordered, such as caviar, with all the trimmings—chopped egg white, egg yolk, parsley and lemon. Or game. This made me feel even more like a man who, just before execution, may ask for anything he wants to eat, and every time Schlau presented me with such luxuries, I asked myself if I hadn't been mistaken to think my death was still so-and-so many days away. But I ate everything brought to me. He didn't know that I was dead already. I had died when I had wrestled with the black bull. For a man without fear is dead.

He came for me three days later. He came at one o'clock in the morning, or shortly after one. I had just fallen asleep. The first few hours of sleep are usually heavy, supposedly the most restful ones. I hadn't heard his steps, nor the key being turned in the lock of my door. He had to touch me to waken me. His hand on my shoulder was rough. It took me a few seconds to notice that he was shaking me. Like Klausen, I drew back in revulsion.

"Get dressed," he said, his voice strangely gruff, as if he had a cold. "And hurry."

I was in no hurry to be killed. I got out of bed slowly. He threw my clothes, which I had folded neatly on a chair, over to me. Underpants, shirt, trousers. "Don't you have a sweater?"

Without waiting for an answer he opened the upper drawer of my dresser, then, when he didn't find what he wanted there, opened the lower one. He held out the sweater to me, with my socks. "I need my shoes," I said. He shook his head but picked them up and handed them to me. "Carry them. Come on."

But I didn't move. I wanted a last look at my room, the room in which I had finally come face to face with myself. He put his hands on my shoulders and again like Klausen I said, "Leave me alone. I'll go by myself." Nevertheless, he pushed me to the door. Before he opened it he put his forefinger to his lips in the age-old gesture of silence. I stared at him in bewilderment. Waldron, I told myself now you've gone off the beam. He can't be warning you. He saw

218

the disbelief in my eyes and said, "Don't talk. Be as quiet as you can."

He opened the door and locked it noiselessly. He stood and listened down into the dark, quiet passage below the small flight of stairs. When he was satisfied, he snapped on a flashlight. In the thin ray of light, he motioned me to follow him.

At the bottom of the stairs lay a man I'd never seen. I could only guess he was the guard who relieved Schlau. I wasn't sure if he was dead or merely unconscious.

Schlau walked on ahead of me to where other stairs led to the lower floors. We walked down to the first floor and through the white door next to the Stübl, which Hugo had told me opened into the service elevator. It went down soundlessly and stopped finally on the floor where the kitchens were located. I could tell by the slight odor of coffee coming from it. A moment later I saw a night watchman walking back and forth, a steaming mug in his hand.

Schlau waited until the man was out of earshot before he put his mouth to my ear. "To the left. On your belly."

Suddenly it was war. I'd just been dropped into enemy territory. I was on reconnaissance. Met at the spot by a double agent to guide me. Uncertain if the guy would really do the job or stab me in the back at the slightest sign of danger. After a long while there came the smell of gasoline. Schlau beamed his flashlight. Just for a second I saw a door. He pushed it gently. A narrow staircase led down to the garages. They lay in darkness. He took my hand and guided me past a row of cars to an open window. He picked me up from the floor as if I had been a child, held me up to the window sill, whispered, "It's not much of a jump. Try not to make a noise." I dropped into the darkness outside.

I hurt my left foot and was holding it when he came

sailing out of the oblong square like a black cloud. He landed close to me, an upright cat. Again he gave me his hand and pulled me up and away. Another door, the heavy wooden door in the high wall, which gave out into the woods. Its complicated lock didn't present any difficulties; he had the key. Suddenly I heard sounds and stood still. "It's your radio," he said. "You usually kept it going all night, just as you kept your light on. Lately." I could see the light of my room, a dim beacon high up in the sky. Although the curtains were drawn, the pattern of my grilled window was drawn on the black ground below. Schlau pulled a gun from his pocket and gave it to me. "Try not to use it." Then he stepped away to inspect how far the light from my room lit up the winding path. "We've got to crawl for a while," he said. So we left the shelter of the wall and moved like snakes until once more we were in complete darkness. Then Schlau stood up.

"Where are you taking me?" I asked.

"To Godesberg. I have a boat waiting to get us across."

I was as numb as a man just seated in an electric chair who has been told he may get up. Execution postponed. For a moment it was all I could grasp. We walked on. The woods were full of sounds I couldn't define, but twice we heard something resembling footsteps and threw ourselves away from the path and into the shelter of the trees. Every now and then Schlau would stop to look back and up at the Lindwurm. No powerful lights had gone on in the towers yet. There were a few stars, but no moon.

We hurried on. The third clearing. There was the crib filled with hay under which I had found Rudi's body. I passed it quickly and gave a little groan of pain. Schlau stopped immediately. "What is it?"

"I wrenched my ankle."

"It won't be long now. Sit down and rest."

"Not here. I'd rather go on."

He disappeared into the dark and I followed him as I'd followed him all the way down, not by sight but by straining my ears for the sound of his feet on the fallen needles and moldering leaves, on a twig torn down by a gust of wind. Shortly before the wire fence he bore sharply to the left. We covered about fifty yards, then he jumped a small ditch before he switched on his flashlight. He hadn't miscalculated. In front of us were the two poles from which the wires could be lifted on insulated hooks. He replaced them quickly as soon as we were outside. "We've got to run now," he said. "They have an indicator in the machine shop. Whenever the wires are touched, a light jumps on to show the electricity has been interrupted. If the guard isn't asleep . . . shall I carry you or can you make it on your own?"

"I'll run."

We ran for about half a mile and soon could hear the whirring of cars on the road that ran downhill, between forests and vineyards, to the Rhine. He turned to look at the Lindwurm once more. "Seems we've made it," he said, and suddenly thumped me on the back. We slowed down and soon reached the road, a two-lane, winding ribbon. Schlau pointed to a stand of trees, black against the blue-black night. "Stay here. Don't move until I get back."

I leaned against a tree, becoming one with it. So easy, I thought. So goddam easy, it's ridiculous, and with that fear came back, the fear that now, almost saved, something might happen to endanger my freedom. I was alive again.

A moment later a car, its headlights dark, stopped in front of where I was standing. Schlau leaned out of it. "Get in."

I jumped into the seat next to him. I put on my shoes. He drove off. Then he reached into his pocket and held out a crumpled pack of American cigarettes. "Have one." But he didn't take one himself when I passed it back. He started to whistle, and I sat there next to him, still unable to grasp the fact that the man I had thought of as my executioner had become my rescuer. "I'm certainly no judge of character," I said.

"My looks are against me," he replied, in a voice that was no longer high-pitched but normal, just a little hoarse.

"I owe you an apology." It sounded abysmally trite, but I couldn't find any other words to express the emotions that were flooding me.

"You do not," he said. "If I hadn't been able to fool you I certainly wouldn't have been able to fool the others. I always wanted to be an actor but was told I had no talent. Besides, they'd have had a hell of a casting problem." He started whistling again, a gay little tune I didn't know.

"Before I gave up hope, I thought that if anyone, Hugo would come to help me."

Schlau stopped whistling abruptly. "It didn't work out that way. Hugo was found drowned over a week ago."

It took me a while to take that in. "Another murder?"

"Probably. He was a thorn in their side. A German aristocrat, a patriot to the core, but fighting against them." After a while he said, "Yes, we believe it was murder. But take the professor's death. I struggled to save him. I risked my life on that damn parapet because Rudi was so sure he had the information we were after."

"What information?"

"Rudi had found out that Florian was the brother of the man we wanted. The night he died I thought I could get a look at the bust he had made of him, which he always kept locked up. But he got away and as you know, destroyed everything. No, he lost his balance all right, but to you, of course, it looked like murder."

"It did. Not at the time though. Later."

"In a way it was a lucky thing for me that he fell. I hadn't expected Klausen to come back, and if he'd found me and Florian talking, it would have been the end of me."

"What about Klausen?" I asked.

"That was the most difficult part of my assignment," said Schlau. "I didn't think I could follow through on that, but you find you can do anything if it's important enough to you."

He went on whistling the tune he had interrupted a moment ago, but the gaiety was gone from it. In the light from the dashboard his ugly face looked young and vulnerable. "You know," I told him, "I grew to like him, after a fashion. Again you can see what poor judgment I've got. Even after what he'd done to my face, I couldn't help but feel sympathy with him there in the library, when he was betrayed."

"Ever heard of Ravensbrück?" said Schlau. "It was one of those camps where they used men, women and children as guinea pigs. Unnecessary operations, transplants, freezings. Those ordered to the operating room never knew if they'd come out without their eyesight, or minus a limb or some vital organ. The operations were performed without anesthesia, the patient was given no drugs so that their reactions could be observed. Threshold of pain experiments. Klausen was the doctor in charge. If there's one thing I regret, it's that he took cyanide. I'd been looking forward to strangling him."

"You knew that when you took the job?"

"Yes. Pauline Becker spotted him. After Theresienstadt

223

she was sent to Ravensbrück, and survived. Miraculously. At first she wasn't sure. It was years since she'd seen him, and he was using a different name, of course. Thousands of leading Nazis were issued passports with false data before the end came. That's what makes it so difficult to ferret them out. Klausen got away, to Egypt first, later to South America. When he finally came back, a lot of water had flowed over the dam and most of the people he had tortured had died. The Lindwurm was the ideal place for him." Schlau adjusted the side mirror, glanced at it, nodded, satisfied that no car was following us. "Rudi decided it was more important to watch him than to have him brought to trial. We were after a bigger fish—the man who was behind the whole organization."

"What organization?"

"How do you think those bastards got out? Where do you think the money's coming from for their publications? And the funds to build a new dictatorship?"

"I see. And you think the man you're after now is the head of it."

"We assume he is."

"I thought you were after a war criminal."

"He's that too," said Schlau, "and that's what he'll be tried on. You see, he would never have had to leave Germany if he hadn't gone berserk at the end of the war and signed an order to shoot every Allied prisoner in a camp in Thuringia. But the really terrifying aspect of the man is the fact that he was the brain behind all financial transactions, a master organizer and coordinator. He's the last one we want back here."

"Back here? Is he coming back to Germany?"

"According to my latest information he is."

"So my face has been made over to resemble his."

"We're not sure," said Schlau. "We were never able to lay our hands on any pictures of him, and believe me we tried. But he always kept in the background. Very few people knew what an important part he was playing. He let others take the credit and kept out of the limelight himself."

"What was his name?"

"Johann Muller. Today he travels under the name of Johannes Bolte."

So my struggle to find my way out of chaos had led to more clarity than I would have thought possible. Still there were a few unknown factors. "Perhaps you can explain something to me."

"What?"

"Florian's vacillation." And I told Schlau briefly about the professor's extraordinary instability of attitude toward me.

Schlau scratched his knee. "Evidently he couldn't make up his mind whether he wanted it carried out or not."

I didn't get what he meant and said so, and Schlau, still scratching whatever was bothering him on his leg, said, "It was his idea, the whole thing, to search for someone suitable, a man whose face and body bore a certain similarity to his brother's."

"And whose death would solve the problem of his return."

"Exactly."

Florian's idea. Although I had known from Klausen about Florian's love-hatred for his brother, it came as a shock that the professor should have conceived such a devilish plan to for once and for all demonstrate his superiority of mind and at the same time the depth of his devotion. I could imagine the many years he must have spent looking for the right person and how triumphant he must have felt when he had discovered me; and then, having lured me to the Lindwurm, the torment he must have suffered when he had become aware that he was causing the death of a human being for his own satisfaction. Or perhaps he hadn't felt compassion for me at all; I may have been nothing but the victim of his constantly fluctuating relationship toward his brother.

And had Bettina known that Florian was her uncle? "No," I told myself. She would have told Rudi if not me, and Rudi would have warned me. Bettina had been used all the way.

For a while we drove in silence. We had been winding sharply downhill, and now we could see the river. The lights of Godesberg lay like a colored veil between town and sky. Freedom was still too new to be taken for granted, and I sat there, hugging it in my mind with its many aspects which I had never cherished sufficiently. Nor had I ever felt so deeply grateful. I tried to express my feelings, but it turned out to be impossible. In the end all I could say was, "I don't know how to thank you for rescuing me. You risked your life, didn't you?"

"Naturally," he said. "Don't you realize how important you are to us? It's through your face that we can finally verify our suspicions and get this man tried."

"But if you don't know what he looks like, if you don't have a photo or drawing to compare my face with his, how can I be of any value to you?"

"The girl will know."

"The girl?"

"Bettina."

Until then I hadn't thought of Bettina. I hadn't permitted my mind to become confused by emotion, not consciously anyhow.

"She's made one condition—that we don't notify the police or the American embassy before she's seen you.

226

Which we wouldn't have done anyway. He mustn't be warned before we're ready to act. We won't let him escape again."

For a moment then I let go. "Bettina, my love," I said, as if I were holding her in my arms. "When shall I see her?"

He glanced at the watch on the dashboard. "Soon."

After a few minutes, he cut the headlights and braked. For a while we sat in the dark, watching the road behind us. There were no cars. Presently he drove on, carefully now, and slowly. Then he stopped again. "We'll get out here."

A barn loomed in front of us. "Is this it?"

"No. I'm going to leave the car here. Don't come with me. Stay outside."

When he came out again, he took my hand. A dirt road, a path through the vineyards. My eyes, growing used to the dark, could make out the bare scaffolding of the vines. As we proceeded downhill, we could see the river again, close to us now, flowing sluggishly, like black liquid glass. About fifty yards away there was a boathouse. He motioned me to stop. "The boat is anchored five hundred yards to the left," he said.

Through the night came the hooting of an owl. It startled me. Schlau said, "It's only me." He hooted again. This time his signal was answered by the thin sound of a bell such as scarecrows wear around their necks, such as Bettina had worn on a pair of paper slippers in a dreary hotel room. "Let's go," said Schlau.

I ran for the boathouse. The door opened before I could reach it, and Bettina came out and straight into my arms. We didn't speak. We just stood there in the dark, embracing. Schlau interrupted us. "Sorry," he said, "but we have no time to lose."

"One moment more," Bettina whispered, "just one mo-

227

ment more," and I didn't know if she was pleading for us to remain together or for respite before she would have to see my face. A sudden hardness, caused by the impatience to get it over with, seized me. Almost brutally I separated from her. We stepped inside the shack. It was dark. Then Schlau turned on his flashlight. Sheltered between his huge hands, it lit up the inside of his palms rather than me. In a dim rosy shimmer I could see a bench, tools stacked in a corner, ropes, a boathook, an outboard motor, and Bettina, with her back to us, her face turned to the wall. "Look at him," said Schlau.

As she turned slowly, he shone his flashlight full on my face. Just for a second. In that second Bettina's eyes narrowed, then opened wide in an expression of horror. She put out a hand as if seeking support, then, without a word, slipped to the floor. The odd thing was that neither he nor I moved forward to catch her. We simply let her fall, listening to the slight thud her body made as it hit the floor. We stared at her before we looked at each other.

He was the first to speak. "I guess that's proof enough. Take care of her while I get the boat."

After he'd left, I kneeled down beside Bettina. There was no water to wet her forehead, no brandy to wet her lips. But she was coming to. "Wake up my love," I begged. "I know what you're going through but you've got to face it. We mustn't spoil everything now. I'll make you forget it all. I'll have another operation. You don't have to look at me until I look like myself again. But now pull yourself together, Bettina." Still a few minutes or more went by before she was breathing normally again. I stood her up gently. I opened the door and led her outside. She began to talk. More as if to herself than to me.

"It all started," she said, "that night at the Guërzenich,

228

when I went with Rudi to his office. When I told him I was going to Brazil because Hannes was to have an operation, he said he had heard that Hannes was preparing to come to Europe."

"Later, my love," I said, "later," but she went on talking, as if to hold it in would kill her, and now she was talking to me.

"I didn't believe it. Why should Gevern have lied to me?"

"You're stumbling," I said. "Give me your hand."

She did, and it lay ice cold and trembling in mine. "And then . . ."

"Later," I said again. "When we're safe. Don't talk now."

She ignored me. "I called Pôrto Alegre. Not Hannes, but his doctor. He said Hannes was perfectly well and planning to go on a trip. He didn't know where. I told him not to mention my call, that I'd known about Hannes's plans but had just wanted to find out if they wouldn't be too strenuous for him. Something like that."

Again I tried to hush her, but she tore her hand out of mine, and refused to walk on. "Don't interrupt. Let me tell you. Just let me tell you. I've got to talk about it. Of course I defended Hannes when Pauline . . . I was still too horrified about it all, too afraid that it might be true, but when I heard that they had done something to your face . . ."

She sagged, but this time I caught her and said as sternly as I could, "Now stop it. There must be nothing on our minds but to get out of here. Absolutely nothing. Right now that's all that matters."

She was quiet then; she walked on with me, but after a little while she said, "You know I did it because I love you."

"I know," I said.

We had reached the road which, right here, ran along the

embankment. A few yards below there was a small dock with a dingy moored to it. "Schlau," I called softly. "Schlau."

There was no answer. Bettina reached into her pocket, took out a tiny bell and shook it. It was answered almost immediately by the hooting of an owl. "It's all right," I said, as the figure of a man appeared from the direction of the boat. "I'm sorry we took so long."

The next moment I was on the ground. I heard Bettina scream, and in the sudden powerful headlights of a car on the road behind us I could see Schlau, lying a yard or so away from me. He had been roped. The first noose had caught his legs, the second had broken his neck. His eyes were bulging, his tongue was sticking out. I reached for my revolver, and Gevern's voice said, "Don't be a fool. I've got my gun trained on you."

Another man came from the direction of the car. The young man I'd seen before, on the plane, in the company of the professor. He tied me up and dragged me to the car, careful not to harm my face. Then Gevern came with Bettina, her hands tied behind her back. He sat her down in one corner of the car and me in the other, then he got in between us. The young man drove. None of us spoke. I guessed that shock was making it impossible for Bettina to break the silence; I could say nothing, I was gagged. It was Gevern who, his gun in his hand again, turned to Bettina. "He *does* look like Hannes, doesn't he? It's fantastic." And when she said nothing, "Well, doesn't he? Don't you think so?"

There was a note of anxiety in his voice now, as if he felt responsible for the job done to my face and needed her reassurance. "Turn the inside light on for a moment," he told our driver.

Bettina turned to look at me, then coldly, calmly, she said, "Yes. He looks exactly as Hannes did before he fell from his horse. It certainly will do."

I heard Gevern suck in his breath as the light went out again. "What do you mean—will do?"

"From what I've heard, you planned to make him look like Hannes so that Johann Muller can return to Germany without fear of reprisals."

"I always suspected you knew too much. You should have been eliminated long ago."

"You tried that, didn't you, when you crashed into the truck?"

"No," he said. "My orders were to prevent the man in the truck from getting away. But I could hardly tell you that."

In the darkness I heard her laugh softly. "And I honestly believed you were crazy enough to risk our lives because you wanted me to sleep with you."

"That was Hannes. He wanted it. Did you never suspect that he was impotent? The only way he could enjoy you was through me," and Gevern's laughter rang out like a gong announcing her utter defeat.

"You shouldn't have told me that, Günther," she said softly, and it seemed to me that with these words she had obliterated his triumph.

He lit a cigarette and after a while said, "Does it matter? You won't have much time to reflect on it because by tomorrow it will be all over."

"For all of us," said Bettina. "Thank God."

He didn't grasp the full meaning of her words right away; when he did, he turned and grasped her shoulders. "What did you say?"

"I said it would be over for all of us, thank God. And now stop hurting me."

"Not until you tell me what you meant."

"But Günther," said Bettina, "do you really think I would have been stupid enough not to notify the police once I . . ."

The revolver in his hands turned in her direction and I wanted to cry out, "Don't believe her. She didn't. I know she didn't because she made a condition to see my face first." Yet hard as I tried, I couldn't get rid of the wet gag in my mouth.

"Turn off the highway," Gevern ordered the driver, and once more we climbed a road into the hills.

"Shooting us won't help," said Bettina, when the car stopped somewhere in the dark. "What might help is to let us go. You wouldn't have any dead bodies on your hands and it would give you a chance to warn Hannes. You might both be able to escape."

For a moment it looked as if Gevern were considering the proposal, and there was never any way of knowing what he might have done if in the end Bettina hadn't lost control of her voice. Instead of remaining coldly and effectively superior, she sounded pleading suddenly, when she said, "Let us go, Günther. Please."

With that Gevern pushed her back into her corner of the car and turned to me. He switched on the inside light. He had a pill in his hand. He tore the gag out of my mouth, forced my teeth open, threw the pill back into my throat, and clamped one hand around my mouth and nose until I almost suffocated. I made one last effort not to swallow, but he bent back my head and I felt the pill slip down my throat. I tried to catch Bettina's eye. She was looking straight ahead. Bettina, my love, I thought, bless you. There were a few minutes of silence before I passed out.

When I came to, I couldn't grasp that I was still alive. I hadn't expected to wake up again after the pill Gevern had made me swallow, and for a fleeting moment had been grateful that death, after all, should come so simply. Only then had I lost consciousness.

My eyes felt heavy; I couldn't open them; my lids seemed sewn to my pupils. I tried to lift my hands to them. They were tied together. So were my feet. My throat was as dry as if it had been burned to ashes. I couldn't produce any saliva. And my body was heavy.

I was lying on a bed. Somehow I managed to push the blanket covering me aside and roll over and onto the floor. I moved on my belly. I hit my head against a piece of furniture, then against a wall. Probing it with my forehead, I discovered the wall was round. And by the way chair and desk were arranged, I knew I was back in my room in the tower. I found the entrance to the bathroom, I was able to get into a kneeling position in front of the tub. After several tries, I turned on the faucet. I pushed my head under it and let the water run for a long time. Finally I could open my eyes.

I saw my red robe hanging on the hook as it had hung last night. I had not been mistaken—it was my room. I shuffled over to the basin. Finally I had the water glass between my teeth. It still smelled of the mouthwash I had used yesterday. I let it drop on the floor. It broke into three fragments, leaving the bottom whole, with jagged edges sticking up. I pushed it against the wall and the cord that tied my wrists across it. I was careful not to cut a vein. Slowly the cord began to fray and my hands were free. Pain, as the blood coursed through them again. I exercised them until I was able to work on the cord around my legs. It occurred to me that they might not expect me to wake up yet. Whatever Gevern had forced me to swallow had either not been timed correctly or my particular reaction had let me regain consciousness before the expected time. I wound up the cord that had tied my wrists and picked up the piece at my feet. It might become necessary to retie myself if I was to trick him. Then I went back into my room. With every step, walking became easier.

On the desk stood the ice bucket and the barely touched bottle of Scotch. I took a large swallow from the bottle, and another. Then I hid it under my pillow. It might serve as a weapon, for naturally the gun Schlau had given me had been taken away. Schlau. I could see him lying on the ground in front of the dock, roped like a steer. I couldn't imagine how Gevern could have caught him unawares, he had been so cautious. There had been another man with Gevern, the young man from the plane, the one I'd seen with the professor. What had they done to Bettina?

I looked out of the window. The sun was coming up. It was early morning. I went back to my bed, lay down, and pulled the covers over me. Why hadn't I been killed yet? Why was I still alive? Yet these questions were of no importance now; important was only to figure out a way to overpower Gevern, or whoever entered.

I got up again, and stood in the small space where I would have to hide when the door opened. It seemed years since I had planned to stand behind it and grab Schlau's legs. But like Schlau then, Gevern would use every precaution. Or would he, thinking I was tied and probably still unconscious? Would the moment of surprise on not seeing me in my bed be sufficient for me to attack before he swung around and drew his gun? This gave me another idea.

I took off my jacket and stuffed it until it looked like the upper part of a man's body. I took a pair of shoes and filled a pair of socks with my remaining socks. I tied them together and arranged the bedcovers in a way that left them showing from underneath. I pushed a pillow over the place where my head should be. In boarding school, like every other kid, I'd used this ruse to get out of my dorm.

I discarded the idea of hiding behind the door. It was too obvious. I went back into the bathroom instead. If luck was with me, Gevern would come in, step up to my bed, possibly bend over me, and even if he didn't, the five yards between door and bed should be sufficient to jump him from the back. If he came alone . . .

After that I waited. More than anything, as minute after minute passed by, I wanted a cigarette but didn't dare to light one. The smell of smoke might give me away. Again I thought of Bettina. What would they do to her? Suddenly there was a noise.

I tensed but didn't move. The drawbridge? I was afraid to go to the window and look for fear I might miss the sound of steps. An hour went by. Then, from far away but clearly, there came the hum of a plane. How many days or weeks since I had imagined Bettina landing in a helicopter to save me? From where I stood I could see the 'copter cutting through the sky, heading toward the Lindwurm. I edged up to the window. Several men, whom I couldn't recognize from above, stood in the courtyard. As I had expected, the drawbridge was up. A few minutes later the 'copter set down on the small square, as gently as a butterfly on a calyx. Two men got out, one very tall, the other about my size. Gevern, shouting something I couldn't understand, ran out of the entrance, shook hands, and the three disappeared inside the Lindwurm. Johann Muller, I told myself, had arrived.

Again minute after minute ticked by to make an hour. I counted them in my mind, one by one. I didn't dare to look at my watch. I kept my eyes fastened on the door through which eventually Gevern would come. Or all three men?

It was Gevern who came, and he was alone, I could hear his steps, and only his, on the stairs below my room. He was taking them two at a time. He came through the door, gun drawn, closed the door and headed for the bed. "Waldron. Bolte wants to have a look at you."

I rushed him as the black bull had rushed me, head down, and threw him before he could fire. Falling, he dropped his gun and I kicked it out of reach before I was upon him. We rolled across the floor in the terrible embrace of two men determined to kill each other. He had both hands around my throat and was smashing my head against the wall when I managed to hook my right foot around the leg of the writing desk. It came crashing down on his back. For a second his hands loosened. It gave me a chance to reach for the heavy bronze inkstand which had fallen close to me. With all the strength I had left, I brought it down on his skull. I don't know how often. He lay still, and I couldn't tell if I had killed him or not. When I could get up, I dragged him into the bathroom, locked the door, took his revolver, locked the door to my room and went down the steps.

Below the steps, the door to the first room on my right was open. It was the room Bettina had been given on our arrival. I went into the bathroom and washed off the blood that had run from my nose. I went over to the phone. The line in my room still didn't work, but it might be working here. It was. Imitating Gevern's voice as best I could, I told the operator, "Get Inspector Ginster up here," and banged down the receiver. I took Gevern's pistol. It was a Luger with a silencer. Then I went in search of Bettina.

I went from floor to floor, through deserted passages, without hearing voices. I didn't know where to look. But all at once instinct told me that the most logical place would be a tower room from which no one could hear her. The professor's room.

I took the elevator up, wondering if Ginster knew about the entrance below the ravine, the only way of getting to us with the drawbridge up. Without him and his men, Bettina and I would have no chance. And I wondered suddenly if Ginster was on Bolte's side, if I hadn't perhaps made a mistake when I had called him.

At the bottom of the stairs leading up to the room where Sigurd and the dragon hung on every wall, a man was standing guard. He was staring straight ahead, picking his nose. I crept up on him, clapped my hand over his mouth to stifle any scream, and knocked him out with the butt of my gun. He fell like a bag of flour. I took his gun away and pushed him into the next empty room and locked it. As I walked up the ten steps I could hear voices coming from the professor's room, the voice of a man. And Bettina's. "I am not interested in anything you have to say." Cold, hard, in her refusal to listen.

I hesitated, then I knocked, and the man answered, "Yes, Günther, send him in."

I uncocked the gun, put it in my pocket and kept my right hand on it. Then I staggered into the room as if I had been pushed from outside.

Bettina was leaning against the window. She glanced up, but neither surprise nor relief showed in her eyes, and I had the feeling that for her I had already died. And I realized that it was this acceptance of our inevitable death which enabled her to preserve her dignity, a dignity that was a total detachment. I wanted to shout to her that we still had a chance, but of course I remained silent. Opposite her, in the chair I had sat in while the professor had held forth about the slaying of the dragon, sat the man whose face I was wearing—Johannes Bolte. A man my size, my build, in a dark suit, elegantly tailored. It was like looking into a mirror. Except for the difference in our noses, we had been cast from the same mold.

He was smoking, inhaling deeply. He didn't look at me but went on speaking in a leisurely fashion, giving the impression he probably wanted to give—that time no longer mattered and he could waste it at will. "For your consolation, Bettina," he said, "you were not a fool. Let's just say I was cleverer."

No triumph colored his voice, no malice; it stated the two facts without a trace of emotion. He flicked the stub of his cigarette into an ashtray and lit a new one, still without looking at me. Suddenly I grasped that he was not putting on an act but was trying to prolong a moment for which he had been waiting for a long time. When he finally swung around to face me, it was with an abruptness I hadn't expected, but again it wasn't done for effect. He rose politely. "Mr. Waldron. How do you do?" Then he sat back again and smiled. "I can hardly find words to tell you how much I have been looking forward to meeting you in person."

I listened to the words, which should have filled me with rage, with the cold objectivity of an onlooker who wasn't personally involved. His unaffected graciousness in a situation like ours, ridiculous as it was, gave evidence that he had lost none of the charm Florian had resented. It was all there, not only in his voice and manner but in the way he sat, gracefully yet all male. The dragon, I thought, and Florian's words came to my mind, "Not that I look upon you as Sigurd, you innocent little American without a goal. But to kill the dragon you have to know where he is vulnerable." Where was he vulnerable?

"I see they haven't dyed your hair yet," he said, cocking his head to one side a little. "Otherwise I must say I'm satisfied." His blue eyes narrowed. "But they shouldn't have roughed you up so badly." He pointed to the marks the cords had left around my wrists and the bruises on my throat, caused by Gevern less than half an hour ago. Obviously he thought they had been inflicted last night when I had been ambushed. Again his eyes went over my face and his smiled deepened. "You look exactly as I did before the stallion threw me. Indeed, an excellent job."

Again he spoke neither viciously nor gloatingly, but was simply expressing his pleasure with a task faultlessly executed. He turned back to Bettina to pick up their conversation which had been interrupted by my entrance, if indeed it had been a conversation and not a monologue on his part. "My dear child," he said, "I realize that from your point of view it is hard to understand, but try to see it my way. It was my duty, my destiny, to act as I did. I shall go down in history as Germany's savior."

There was about him the dignity of the fanatic, but Bettina remained unimpressed. She looked down at her hands instead of at him, clearly denying any interest whatsoever in what might have motivated him. Hatred, fear, even shame for ever having loved and trusted him, would still be a link. She had to deny that he had ever existed.

Bolte, perhaps for the first time accepting the fact that he could not breach her withdrawal, shrugged, and addressed me.

"I believe in destiny," he said, "but I also believe that certain men are predestined to shape it to serve their specific calling." He nodded toward a chair, but I preferred to remain standing and silent. He smiled as if he understood that I couldn't want any part of the explanation he was offering. "You, Waldron, had no chance, and for one reason only—you were still floundering at an age when you should have been making up your mind—should have *made* up your mind, as to the part you wanted to play in life. The uncommitted will always be the prey of the committed. But then, too, you were unlucky. If we had spotted you a few years ago as the correct type *and* the person whose circumstances were likely to cause the least trouble, nothing would have happened to you because the time was not yet ripe." He took a cigarette from a gold case but didn't light it. "America," he continued, "was still united; Russia not yet threatened by her vassals or China; Africa still groping for a sense of nationalism; the Jews were no danger; the Middle East was unorganized, and the youth of the world still inarticulate and in bondage to past traditions. Today . . ." He paused, a strange light in his eyes which seemed to spread over his whole face, giving him almost a messianic aura. "Today," he went on, "political developments have combined to give Germany a chance. I can see possibilities of a rapprochement with Russia. You must agree that with such high stakes, the death of a few is irrelevant. If the division of Germany can be brought to an end and her honor be restored . . ." now his smile was almost benign,

240

"after all, your men are dying for a far less justifiable cause."

At any other man I might have laughed. I couldn't laugh at Bolte. Because, incredibly, he sounded neither insane nor pompous. Even in his madness he was completely sincere. He believed in his own charisma. *He had been chosen.* With that he became one of the most formidable enemies of mankind.

At last Bettina spoke, not to him but to me. "I shall never forgive myself," she said, in a low, curiously vibrant voice. "If only I had done what Rudi begged me to do, I might have prevented all this." And I knew that she didn't mean our personal tragedy; like myself she sensed the disaster Bolte could create.

For the first time Bolte seemed irritated, yet at the same time gratified to see her react at last. "Are you so afraid of dying?" he said. "I thought I had raised you to meet death with courage whenever it came."

"I don't care if I live or die," said Bettina, "but to have to die because a madman, a destroyer who thinks he is a savior, can then carry on . . ."

He won't, I told her in my mind, he won't . . . but my silent effort to reach her was drowned out by his voice. It seemed to get louder and louder, although actually he didn't raise it, nor did he pay any further attention to Bettina, but addressed me again in a tone that was almost bored yet at the same time impatient to bring the matter to a conclusion. "Mr. Waldron," he said. "You will be flown to a small place near Frankfurt. There you will be given a choice. A pill will be offered to you that causes immediate, painless death. If you refuse to take it, you will be shot. In either case our men will report that when they discovered your true identity, you preferred suicide to arrest." Again his eyes narrowed as he looked at me. He was probably expecting some kind of reaction on my part. When I didn't speak, he raised his voice. "Günther," he called. "Come in."

You act automatically, because you have planned to do a certain thing, or on an impulse; sometimes without thinking at all and sometimes after reflecting too long. With me everything came together. I wanted to shoot Bolte, yet I didn't want to, because, alive, he could be brought to trial. Yet what a trial would do to Bettina delayed my decision. It would be easier for her if he died before being arrested. I resolved to kill him.

His eyes were fixed on the door through which he expected Günther to enter. He waited only a second beyond the time it would take to open it before he straightened up in his chair. I saw him reach into his pocket. Bettina must have seen it too for she leapt forward and in front of me. Bolte and I fired at the same time. My bullet hit him just above the abdomen, his hit Bettina in the chest. She swayed, blood gushing from the wound. As I reached for her to prevent her from falling, I fired once more at Bolte, but the chair in which he had sat a moment ago was empty. In his effort to rise, he had slumped to the floor. Seeing him lying motionless, I was certain he was dead, or at least unconscious, and I turned to Bettina, who was lying at my feet, as motionless as he. I knelt beside her. She was deathly pale and terribly still. Don't move her, I told myself. I heard a door slam. I looked up. Bolte was gone. He couldn't get far, I thought, finding it almost impossible to concentrate on anything but Bettina. I grabbed a gaily colored plaid from the couch and covered her. Steps. Inspector Ginster came in, gun in hand. He glanced at my face. A gasp of surprise escaped him, but he didn't ask any questions. As though he had been in on everything all along, he said, "He just passed me in the corridor. I wasn't sure who was who."

"You passed Bolte? But I shot him. Don't let him get away."

"Call the hospital wing and have them send somebody at once," Ginster said, and was gone.

A young doctor I had never seen before came and gently cut open Bettina's dress. He took her pulse, he probed the wound, he stuffed gauze into the hole between her breasts. He said, "She's still alive, but she's got to be operated on at once."

I asked him if he couldn't do something, anything. He shook his head. "I'm not a surgeon. I don't dare to touch her."

"We've got to get one. Who's the best you know?"

After a moment's hesitation, he said, "That would be Professor Matthieu." He picked up the phone, but had to wait for the noise of a plane's motor, which drowned out his voice. A helicopter was rising into the sky. When it was quiet again, he spoke. "Matthieu will be here as soon as possible. I'll go down and have emergency prepared. I'll be up with a stretcher."

I went back to Bettina and again knelt beside her. The gauze the young doctor had stuffed into the wound was already soaked through. She moved. I told her, "Lie still. Lie as still as possible, my love. Everything will be all right. Don't let go. Hold on, Bettina. Just a few minutes more. You can't leave me alone, you know."

"I won't," said Bettina. Her voice was scarcely audible. "Don't worry, Drew. I won't die."

But after a little while, she did.

To this day they haven't found Johann Muller.

ABOUT THE AUTHOR

MARTHA ALBRAND has spent much of her life in Europe—
the setting for most of her novels. When Miss Albrand
came to this country as a voluntary exile from Hitler's Germany, she brought with her an already established reputation as a writer. *Rhine Replica* is her eighteenth work of
fiction. In private life Miss Albrand is Mrs. Sydney Lamon,
and divides her time between New York and New Milford,
Connecticut.

Uninvited, an old man sat at the table of Andrew Waldron one night during his vacation in Rome. As the old man sketched a portrait of the young American, he convinced him to go to Cologne for carnival time.

Andrew went to Cologne. From the moment he arrived, small things began to go wrong. Beneath the surface of the gay, colorful city lay an indefinable threat.

Andrew found lodging in the exclusive Lindwurm castle, where a beautiful young woman, Bettina von Alten—whom he had met in Cologne—was also a guest. Bettina, with her cunning and her fears intrigues Andrew, and the more attractive she becomes to him, the more he wonders what her role is in the grotesque nightmare that is engulfing him.